ROGUE: BOOK 1

To all who think life is too short to
seek revenge...it's not.

Bloodline

ROGUE: BOOK 1

BRITTNEY KREIGHBAUM

Playlist

COPYCAT by Billie Eilish

O.D.D. by Hey Violet

Teeth by 5 Seconds of Summer

Too Close by Alex Clare

River by Bishop Briggs

All I Have by NF

my strange addiction by Billie Eilish

Darkside by Neoni

Unstoppable by Sia

Sway by Hey Violet

That Bitch by Bea Miller

Last One Standing by Skylar Grey, Polo G, Mozzy, & Eminem

Contents

THE CORE

LUKE AND I WERE MEETING in an hour. He was a highly-skilled fighter and had been training me for a year now. I was becoming more advanced with each session he had me complete, which was now five days a week. A few months ago, he even began teaching me the different techniques to disarm someone solely using my body as the weapon. That only made me more motivated and determined to work harder. My goal was to become his equal in the sparring ring. To be able to hold my own in a fight against a man twice my size.

The coffee in front of me was empty; I needed another if I was going to continue reading the book in my hands. It was in Italian and there were many words I was struggling with. Determined to learn the languages that I was exposed to most in my line of work was another goal of mine. I was already fluent in English and Russian. Italian was third in frequency, then Spanish. Later, I would have to ask Scarlet about these words I didn't know. I typed them into the notes on my phone so I wouldn't forget before going back to reading.

It wasn't long after I had gotten back into my book when I noticed a guy approach my table out of my peripheral vision. He helped himself to the seat next to me. *Dammit, can't a person just read without being interrupted?*

"Hi," he stated, his voice low and borderline sultry.

He had an accent, Russian for sure. The familiarity of it made a ball of unease tighten in the pit of my stomach. I automatically tensed as I was worried they had found me again. *Pretend you don't care, be nonchalant.*

"Not interested," I responded, not looking up from my book.

Or I'll just be an asshole.

"I like your tattoo...got any more?"

His attempt at being seductive was unsuccessful as I glanced up, my eyes shooting daggers at his. His short blonde hair was combed back neatly. A trimmed goatee encircled his thin lips. His light blue eyes moved down and back up my body to make it obvious that he was checking me out. I closed my book dramatically with a huff. Dropping it into my black backpack beside me. He must have thought I was going to give him the attention he wanted as a smug smile crossed his lips. *He thinks!* Instead, I stood up, slinging my backpack over one shoulder, then the other. When I reached for my coffee, he grabbed my arm, squeezing it enough to stop my movement.

"Let go—your one and only chance," I ordered.

"Do it, dude, she doesn't mess around," the barista warned

from behind the counter, hushing the customers as they began to watch the situation unfold.

The guy laughed, standing up to get closer to me. All right, he was tall and muscular, but I could take him. His hand was still wrapped around my arm.

"Come on beautiful, I just want to talk to you. Why don't you sit back down?"

Without warning I grabbed his wrist with my free hand, pressing on the pressure point on the inside of it just below his wrist bone. The reaction of this particular pressure point causes the grip to weaken. I pulled my arm free of his grasp. *Get him, girl!* He stood there, eyes wide, in shock for only a moment, then his expression turned angry. His jaw twitched as he clenched and unclenched it. Not sure why he'd be angry when he was the one bothering me. I reached again for my coffee. As I did, he attempted to grab me just like he had done the first time.

This time I took ahold of his wrist with one hand, using my other to grab him by the back of the neck. With all my strength I shoved his face down toward the table and twisted his arm behind his back in one smooth motion. He hit the table with a loud thud. One of his legs swung back to keep his balance, knocking over his chair. His eyes filled with anger, and the flaring of his nostrils indicated he was pissed off that I'd just manhandled him in front of the coffee shop customers. The muscles in his body tensed as he struggled under my grip. All the wiggling he had done caused his shoulder to tip over my fresh cup of coffee, spilling its contents across the table. I let out a frustrated growl as I yanked the arm behind his back upwards toward his head causing him more discomfort.

"All right, I get it," he winced as he ceased his attempts to escape my hold.

There was no way he was one of them, he would have fought back harder. I let go of his neck, reaching into his back pocket in search of his wallet.

"What are you doing?" he asked.

Retrieving his wallet, I let it fall open. He only had a twenty. *Welp, sucks to be him today, I guess.* I pinched the bill between my pointer and middle fingers.

"You owe me a new coffee," I explained leaning against my hand, my elbow resting on his back, "when I let you go you have two options. The first one you walk away and never bother me again. If that doesn't sound appealing, then there is the second option, which is to continue to annoy me and consequently get your ass beat. The choice is yours."

Releasing him completely I tossed his wallet at him, laughing to myself as he fumbled to catch it. The barista had my replacement coffee ready as I approached the counter. I slid him the twenty.

"Thanks, Brian, keep the change. Sorry for the mess," I said, my smile sweet.

He chuckled, "No problem, see you next time."

I walked straight to meet Luke, bouncing on my toes as I explained to him what had happened at the coffee shop the moment he walked into the training center. He laughed proudly.

"I wish I could have seen it," he said with a smile.

"I'm just glad I'm retaining what you are teaching me. It fucking worked and I feel more confident now for sure."

"It will work most of the time but remember; small precise movements and always be ready to adapt. It's not a flawless thing, especially with someone who is trained to fight back."

I nodded, repeating it to myself in my head; *small precise movements, be ready to adapt.* I would have to be more conscious of my surroundings now that there's a Russian in the picture. Not that running into one meant they were coming for me again, but I wasn't going to take any chances. My brain got plotting. I'd train with Luke, train after work, and do a parkour run each day. Double runs on the weekends. Last time I had to run for miles before I got to the location where I knew I'd be safe. *This time, you will be ready.*

In the S-Rank break room at work, which reflected a living room, I joined my coworkers. We worked for a company called The Core. The legal side of the business offered security to companies and people, mainly celebrities. Then there was the illegal side that was off the books. It offered services such as private investigating, helping with blackmail, thievery, getting leverage, and also... revenge.

I joined The Core at the age of seventeen. They allowed me to start early when I passed their skills tests at my young age. It also helped that I was trained by a fellow Rogue for two years and was a skilled shooter. There was no need to work my way up, the boss placed me on the S-Rank team after I put my skills on display for him. That meant I was a member of the "off the books" group. It was small and made up of only six people. We were each considered independent contractors even though technically we were a team. Most of the time we each performed our tasks separately for our lead to join the pieces together for the client, whom we never met.

The top of our group was the boss. We never saw him, spoke with him, or even knew what he looked like. Only knew his nickname, Big Frank. He handled the paychecks and who knows what else. Leaving the rest up to Spencer.

Spencer was "the mastermind" behind the operations. He met with the clients and had the final say if their cases would be presented to the S-Rank team. He would then, upon our approval to take the case, construct the mission. He was an excellent strategist, always thinking three steps ahead and analyzing each possible outcome. Even if you were trained you couldn't beat the man at chess; he thought so far ahead.

Elliot was "the hacker." If you gave him a computer, he could tell you anything you wanted to know. He could even take over surveillance and electronic security systems. Shit, I've seen him hack a stranger's cell phone for its photos. His hobby was creating cool ass gadgets for us to use on our missions. If you needed something electronic you went to him.

Scarlet was "the chameleon." She spoke seven different languages and was a master of accents. Her beauty could be altered and still look natural. She was one of those girls who could pull off any hair color, outfit, or persona. It helped that she had an abundance of aliases and was a great actress. She had also just begun training with Luke to work on her self-defense skills.

Luke was "the ninja." Gathering recon and intel on people was his thing. If you couldn't find someone, say they went off-grid or disappeared, he could find them without a problem. He was a trained fighter and skilled gunman. Although if you ask him, he'd prefer fighting with his fists rather than any other weapon, said it was more fun. If you needed a weapon or bodyguard, he was the guy to call.

Then there was me. I was "the rogue." You wanted a safe cracked, a file stolen, or needed to break in somewhere you called me. I stayed agile by doing parkour. I was a great escape artist and my petite figure measuring in at just five foot two inches was a benefit most saw as a downfall. The challenge of thinking outside the box to get into places exhilarated me. Each safe or lock was like a puzzle that I was determined to solve.

By learning multiple languages and knowing how to defend myself I'd become more independent in the field. My teammates were encouraging as we all strived to become well-rounded members. I was even teaching Scarlet and Luke how to crack simple codes and pick simple locks in exchange for what they were teaching me.

I was in the middle of getting translations from Scarlet when Spencer walked over almost giddy from a meeting with a client.

"We have a mission." He smiled. "Conference room, five minutes."

Quickly finishing up we walked into the conference room. It was a secure room that could only be opened by a retinal scanner that had been programmed by Elliot. Inside there was a high-tech table that doubled as a touch screen computer. One of the walls was also a touch screen monitor that was linked to the computer in the table. As we filed into our normal spots, my excitement began to grow, feeding off Spencer's. He sat a couple of folders down on the edge of the table.

"Ready for a good one?" he asked. "This is a damn big job, guys."

"Let's hear it then," Luke said, while he smiled eagerly.

"There is a benefit happening in one week. During this benefit there has been a rumor that this man," Spencer slid his finger across the table, sending a picture of a man up onto the screen on the wall, "is going to attempt to sell the project blueprints for a military-grade autonomous vehicle. His name is Adam Williams. He was one of the lead engineers that produced the technology."

"Wait," Scarlet started, "shouldn't the military or C.I.A. be taking care of this? I mean, you are making it sound like it's a government thing."

Spencer's smile widened, as he continued, "This project was highly classified. Due to the...discretion we are known for among our clients, we've been given this contract by the government to take care of the issue."

Simultaneously we all leaned forward in disbelief. It piqued my interest and we all agreed to take on the case without Spencer having to say another word.

"Great, here's the plan," he explained. "Adam Williams disappeared two days ago. Luke, I need you to retrace his steps and start with his last known whereabouts, which is this address. Elliot, I want everything on this guy, emails, texts, finances, all of it. He dumped his cell phone already so we can't trace it, but here's all the information we have on him so far." He slid him a manilla folder. "Scarlet, you are going to the benefit under an alias as a potential buyer. Get to know your character." Giving her a blue folder, he finally turned to me, and said, "Mia, you are going to steal the blueprints before he has a chance to sell them. For now, tag along with Luke to gather more information on this guy."

My body lit with adrenaline. Each time I got to steal something or break in somewhere I got excited like I'd just won the lottery. Yes, I know this isn't normal but hey, when you grow up like I did, nothing is normal anymore.

"Then why am I going to the benefit to buy it?" Scarlet asked. "Won't I be buying nothing since Mia is going to steal it first?"

"The government wants the identities of the buyers. You will need to be fitted with a camera to get the images, which Elliot can get for you."

We nodded as Spencer stood up from the table.

"Oh, and the benefit is being held by the mayor. I need daily updates on progress."

As we walked out Luke turned to me, showing me the address Spencer had given him. I typed it into my phone.

"9:00 pm?" Luke stated.

"See you there."

I was pumped! I had to get some energy out, so I went on a parkour run before heading home to change. By eight I was ready to go. I threw my long eggplant purple hair into a ponytail. The people that inhabited the coastal city of Ashport, California were that of flavorful hair choices. This meant I was free to display my hair without it being a factor in my identification. I did make sure to wear a shirt that had sleeves long enough to cover my half sleeve of tattoos on my left arm. I didn't want any part of it visible as it could later be used to identify me.

Arriving five minutes early, I watched from a distance until I saw Luke come around the corner. *Here we go*, I thought excitedly. We snuck up to the apartment where Adam Williams last lived before he "disappeared." Luke put on gloves, trying the doorknob. It was locked. I gave him a sly smile as I put on my own gloves. It wouldn't be locked for long.

Stepping inside we quickly realized we were not the first ones here. His place had already been turned upside down. Furniture and papers were scattered across the floors. Drawers were tossed, clothes were everywhere, and his mattress was flipped. The cushions were cut open like someone searched the inside of them. Me, being a thief at heart, began searching all the places a safe could be, hoping whoever it was didn't find it while they were here. We were there for an hour. I was searching the vents for...well, anything. My last one was in the bathroom...nothing. *What the hell? There was something there, I could feel it.*

"There's nothing here. Whoever turned this place before us either found what they were looking for or are in the same situation we are," Luke admitted.

I hated being beat. Letting out a growl I looked up. *Oh shit, he had a drop ceiling in his bathroom.* A smile crossed my lips as I glanced back at Luke. He looked at me, furrowing his brows as he watched me climb to stand on the toilet seat. I reached up, standing on my tippy toes. I was still too short. Dammit.

"Look above the drop ceiling," I ordered, jumping down.

The anticipation grew as it felt like he moved like a turtle. Then again, he was a good size man at five foot eleven trying to climb onto a small toilet seat. I rushed him as he laughed at me. Pushing up one square of drop ceiling he shined his light in the space above.

"Well fuck, Mia, remind me to hire you not only to steal shit, but hide it as well."

Reaching up he pulled something toward him. Hearing it slide across the ceiling made me jump up and down. It was a small wooden box, the size of a three by five index card holder. A tiny lock was on the front of it. I took it, wanting to pry it open right there. Before we could make another move a voice sounded from the front door of the apartment.

"Adam? Wow, what happened?"

The voice was getting closer. I gave the box back to Luke, peeled off my gloves, and stuffed them into my pocket. I transferred my emotions, which gave me the ability to trick my mind into feeling whichever emotion I wanted in the moment. It was something I'd learned how to do when I was much younger through what I'd experienced. After putting it to use throughout the remainder of my life thus far, I'd come to master each emotion. With a wink I ran out, now feeling panicked and overwhelmed by the disheveled apartment.

"I'm not sure what happened," I cried, reaching out to hug the stranger. "The police are on their way. How do you know Adam?"

The man, baffled by my actions, awkwardly patted my back to comfort me.

"Hey…it's okay," he said softly. "I'm his neighbor. I saw the door cracked. Are you Adam's girlfriend or something?"

"Just a friend, I visit when I'm in town. We just uh—hang out—if you know what I mean. He texted me like two days ago but didn't text me back tonight. That's not like him, you know? I'm so worried, do you know where he could be?"

"I'm sorry, I don't," the man sighed. "Have you tried him at his cabin?"

I shook my head. "We've never met there. We always meet here or in my hotel room. Where is his cabin?"

"It's out off of 350 South. Cabin twenty-something, I believe."

I hugged him, 'relieved' at the new information.

"Oh, thank you. I'll go check right now, I'm so worried about him." I looked at the trashed apartment, and asked, as earnestly as I could, "Would you umm-mind walking me down? I'm kind of freaked out."

"You don't want to wait for the police?"

"I do, but I'd rather find Adam and make sure he's all right." I sighed, "Can you wait for the police? I can give you my number and you can give it to them when they get here?"

His eyes lit up when I mentioned giving him my number. He agreed without a second thought, handing over his phone for me to enter my information. I put in the number to the local library under the name Megan.

"So can I still walk you down...Megan?" he asked, smiling a little.

"Please?"

I wrapped my arm around his and let him flirt with me for a bit until I saw Luke walk out behind him.

"Thank you again, call me tomorrow." I smiled.

Luke was waiting on me in his car two blocks away. I'd transferred my emotions back to normal as I walked to where he was. I jumped into the passenger's seat, holding my hand out for the box.

"I'm impressed Mia, you were very convincing."

"Scarlet has been teaching me a thing or two," I admitted, "she deserves the credit."

Picking the tiny lock, I lifted the lid of the box. Inside was a piece of paper. I put my gloves on, picking it up. There were just a bunch of numbers on it.

"Mia," Luke said, stunned.

"What?"

I looked over to see he was looking in the box. When I looked down, I saw a gray and black zip drive. Our eyes snapped to one another's. There was no way it would be that easy. Either way, it would have to wait until the next day for Elliot to look at it.

A FEW MORE SECONDS

WE WERE WAITING ON SCARLET the next day in the conference room. She walked in ten minutes late, a coffee for each of us as an apology for her tardiness. Spencer got the meeting rolling, calling on each of us to give him updates. I handed the zip drive over to Elliot who enthusiastically plugged it right into his laptop. Spencer examined the piece of paper.

"The numbers on this could be a bank account," he stated handing it to Elliot.

"I can run it, but first"—he typed something on the keyboard—"I want to know what is on this little zip guy."

It took him all of forty-five seconds to break into the password-protected file. He mirrored it onto the wall monitor for us all to see.

"It's just a bunch of names and pictures," Scarlet stated. "Oh,

I bet you those are the potential buyers and that zip drive is an insurance policy."

"He's smart," Luke stated.

"Look at this one," Elliot said, bringing up another file.

It was the picture of Adam Williams. But the name attached to it was Matthew Johnson. Elliot began ferociously typing, his eyes going wide.

"Is that his alias?" Scarlet asked.

"No, Adam Williams is his alias, this is his real identity."

Spencer walked around to get closer to Elliot's screen. He leaned in to be even with Elliot's face.

"I want everything," he ordered.

"That paper with those numbers is not a bank account attached to either name. But I'm running it through a decoder now. Matthew Johnson," he continued, bringing more things up on the wall monitor, "thirty-two years old, went to M.I.T., originally from Chicago. Disappeared after he graduated. His bank accounts haven't been touched since he started living as Adam Williams." His computer started beeping. "That's weird, a safety deposit box was rented out under his real name five days ago. It's located at the Credit Union here on Main Street. I'm going to flag the account so that when he requests access we will be notified. He's got a cabin which we know about. Let me do some more digging."

"So, what's his plan?" Luke asked, leaning back in his seat with his hands resting on the back of his head. "Why keep your real bank accounts open?"

"If you're asking me, I bet he created this alias just to sell the blueprints. Once he gets the money he probably plans to return to life as his real self with a cushy new lifestyle," Scarlet guessed.

Spencer looked at me. "Mia be ready. That zip drive with the blueprints has to be in that deposit box. If he makes the pick-up, I want you to make the grab. Until we get more information have a go-bag ready and stay close to headquarters."

We all lived close to headquarters. It was nice to be able to go home even when we had to be ready to move. If I ran, I could make it to headquarters in six minutes. I stopped by the coffee shop on the way home. It was peaceful to get to read my book for an hour or so. Realizing that I was reading and not stopping at words I didn't know encouraged me to continue.

The sun was beginning to set in the sky, indicating that most of the employees would be gone at The Core. I closed my book, giving Brian a wave over my shoulder as I made my way back. Like clockwork, the training floor was empty. I made my way into the trainers' room where the ice bath was located. I filled it with fresh ice before stripping down to my sports bra and athletic shorts. I checked the time on my watch before climbing up the step to get in. *All right Mia girl, just like last time but a bit longer.* With a deep breath, I sunk down to my shoulders in one swift movement. The water was so cold it pricked my skin, sending alerts to all my nerves wanting to stop the motion. My breaths became more rapid with the shock of the temperature. I closed my eyes, trying to focus solely on my breathing for a few minutes. I took a long, slow breath, holding it a few seconds before releasing it.

My thumb pressed the 'start' button on the timer I had brought up on my watch. This time my deep breath was as large as I could make it before completely submerging myself in the water. The prickling feeling swarmed my face, invading every inch of me. In my mind, I ran through random facts to keep my thoughts coherent. My lungs started to burn from the inside. *Just a few more seconds, girl.* I counted to six in my mind before exploding out of the water. I gasped for breath; my eyes glued to my watch as I rapidly blinked away the water. *Controlled breaths to slow your heart rate.* I started my breathing, in for a count of five, out for a count of five. My body was shaking as I'd been in the ice bath for six minutes.

I could do better than the time I'd just got. I concentrated on my breathing again, sitting in the freezing ice water for a couple more minutes. My hands began to feel as though they wouldn't work as I attempted to tap the reset button on my watch. Finally getting it restarted, I submerged myself once more. The longer I was under the more my nervous system rang with alarms. My body started to shiver under the water. *You can beat it; you can beat HIM,* I kept telling myself. It wasn't until someone yanked me from the bath that I realized how long I'd been in there. My gasps were shallow and fast as I collapsed to the ground.

"What the hell are you doing?" he asked.

I glanced up at him for only a moment before rolling over to stand back up. My body shook involuntarily from the cold and my fingers wouldn't cooperate completely, but I'd managed to pull on my dry clothes over my wet ones. The man standing before me I'd not seen before. He had short, chocolate brown hair. His big brown eyes swirled with worry as his eyebrows pulled together.

"Why did you pull me out of there?" I snapped.

"You were in there for almost eleven minutes. That's a great way to get hypothermia."

He was watching you, Mia. I squinted my eyes at him, still shivering. I needed to get warmer. Without another word, I turned to walk out to the training floor. I started to jog in place as well as my legs would allow.

"Why were you in there so long?" he asked, moving to face me.

"Doesn't matter." I stated, "Why were you watching me?"

"It's dangerous to be in an ice bath that long alone. What if you would have died?"

"Then I would have died cold." I shrugged, getting down into a plank.

"Just tell me why you did that," he demanded.

"Fuck you. I don't even know who you are. Go away."

"I just saved your life!" he yelled, baffled.

"You didn't save shit, the only thing you did was interfere with my training!" I shouted back. "Leave me alone!"

"What's going on?"

Both of our heads snapped up to see Elliot standing there. He had a steaming mug in his hand and a blanket slung over one shoulder. I got to my feet as he walked closer.

"This asshole just pulled me from my ice bath, demanded an explanation on why I was in there, and then claimed he saved me. Now he won't go away."

"He will leave you alone now." He stated, glaring at the guy. "Here, I made you some tea for when you finished."

"Thanks."

I reached out to take the mug, my fingers having a hard time with the demands my brain was making. *Just grab the damn mug, Mia.* Elliot guided my hands around the mug. The warmth bringing heat back to the tips of my fingers.

"You know she does this?" he asked, his eyes wide.

"I do." Elliot nodded, wrapping me up in the blanket. It was warm like he had just gotten it out of the dryer. "Ready?"

"Yes. Let's get to work."

We left the guy standing there dumbfounded as we made our way to the secure conference room. Elliot knelt in front of me, rubbing my arms gently to warm me back up.

"Who was that guy?" I asked.

"His name is Dante and he works here."

"He's an asshole."

This made him chuckle, "He can be." He plopped down in his computer chair. "I think I found something about your real identity."

My body froze as I scanned his screen for a hint. He'd been helping me trace myself back to my childhood. I had never known my real name as my parents sold me for drugs when I was a baby. I somehow ended up in foster care and was on the hunt for my real name. *This is it Mia, time to finally find a piece of who you are.*

"Tell me."

"It's nothing super solid, but I think Mia is your real first name," he stated. "I don't know why your real identity is so hard to find. I've never come across information that was this locked down. I traced back all your foster families and Mia is the most consistent name in all of them."

"That can't be a coincidence, right?"

"Well, it could be the name given to you at birth or it could be the name given to you by the first people who took you in. Either way, I think it gets us a step closer to who you are. I also found who your first foster family was."

"Can we talk to them? Where do they live? Somewhere local?" I asked.

His frown made my heart fall into my stomach.

"They died after they gave you up to the next family." He sighed, "I'm sorry."

I shook my head, sipping my tea. "It's all right. It's a step closer, though, right?"

"It is...I promise I won't stop digging until we find out who you are."

"Thanks, Elliot," I mumbled. "I appreciate you doing all this for me after hours."

"Don't mention it." His smile was warm.

We sat together as he worked a bit more on the case we had. I kicked my feet up on the desk, leaning back in my chair. I rocked it side to side, keeping him company until he was ready to call it a night.

The next morning, I was disappointed Williams hadn't moved on the safety deposit box. The benefit wasn't super close but why wouldn't he get it ready? We were walking out of our morning meeting when Luke nudged me with his elbow.

"Want to train for a bit? I know it's an off day, but I'm bored just waiting around."

"Hell yeah, I do."

We walked down to the training center that was on the second floor of the building. It took up the entire floor and had many different weightlifting options, a CrossFit rig with pull-up bars, a track that snaked around the outside of the floor to run, and a sparring ring. Anything you could ever want to work out. After a short warm-up, we jumped into the sparring ring. A half an hour later, Luke was teaching me how to disarm someone who had a gun pointed toward me. It was exhilarating and I could have practiced it for hours. He explained each of the three strategies he recommended before focusing on one with me.

We were taking a water break when the same guy from the night before sauntered over. No longer so angry with him I could see now that he was built, his muscles visible under his tight-fitting black t-shirt. One of his forearms had tattoos claiming it. About the same height as Luke, I wondered if they knew each other. They didn't speak, but they met each other's gaze momentarily. He smiled, lazily leaning against the ropes of the ring.

"Want to spar with me?" he asked, looking directly at me.

I glanced at Luke, wondering if I was ready to spar with someone else who was probably trained. *He had to be trained to work here, right?*

He shrugged. "You could take him, Mia."

I smirked, and said, "All right, come on."

Luke moved to stand on the outside of the ring and the guy climbed in.

"I'm Dante, by the way," he said with a smile.

Not giving him anything but a nod, I tried to anticipate which move he would make first. *This was going to be great payback for last night.*

"Aren't you going to tell me your name?" he asked.

"My name isn't important in a fight."

I swung at him with my right arm. He dodged my punch, returning one of his own with a laugh. We sparred for another twenty minutes before the S-Rank alarm sounded throughout the training center. It was just a red light that lit with an alarm clock-like sound. The only ones who knew what it meant were the actual team. To everyone else, it was an annoying alarm to signal a meeting.

Without another word, I slid under the ropes and took off running with Luke. We met in our conference room. Elliot was there already.

"Here." He handed me a tiny device to put in my ear to communicate with the team, an 'earwig,' "Scarlet is already headed to the bank. She is going to give you a description and tell you which way he exits. I put a flag in his folder to stall the bank teller, so we have six minutes to get down there and then however long it takes for him to get the drive. Luke, you are back up and will be with me in the van. Oh, here," he repeated, and handed me a grey and black zip drive. "Replace it so he doesn't notice."

"How do you know this is what the one with the blueprints on it looks like?" I asked.

"I'm guessing. It's the same kind that you two found in his apartment," he admitted. "I hacked the camera system so I will let you know which pocket he puts it in."

Piling in the car for the seven-minute drive, we were silent. Focused on the task at hand. I was going over all the ways it could go wrong in my mind so I could have an exit strategy just in case. Scarlet came over the earwig.

"He's going back now."

I jumped out, walking around to the side of the bank and into the alley. I began to stretch like I was going for a run. Since I was already sweaty from training it was the perfect cover. I was getting antsy almost ten minutes later. What was taking him so long? All he had to do was pick it up, put it in his pocket, and—

"Right front jacket pocket," Elliot said.

"Walking out now. Red jacket, grey baseball cap," Scarlet verified. "He went left out of the building."

"Understood," I stated with a smile.

This was perfect. I put the phony zip drive into my right hand. Jogging up behind him I moved to his right side. Then I "tripped" into him, reaching my left hand into his jacket pocket, and grabbed the drive. He reached out to catch me from falling. I dropped the phony drive to the ground in the tussle.

"Oh my gosh, I'm so sorry, I wasn't paying attention. Are you all right?" I asked.

"No, it's okay." He half-smiled. "I'm fine."

He instinctively put his hand in his pocket to check for the drive. When he didn't feel it, he began looking at the ground frantically for it. I picked up the phony drive.

"Is this what you are missing?"

A relieved smile appeared on his face. But when he reached for it, I pulled it away teasingly. "I will give it back on one condition."

A worried look splashed across his face as he rubbed the back of his neck with one hand. "What's that?"

"What are you doing, Rogue?" Luke asked in my ear.

I blatantly checked him out, teasing, "I want your number."

"All right." He blushed at my advance.

When I reached back for my phone, I slid the real drive into my pocket. After getting his phone number I gave him back the drive and walked away giggling.

Back at headquarters, we traced the number he gave me under his alias 'Adam Williams.' Turns out, he gave me a legitimate number for his new cell phone. Now we had an additional way of tracking him. I punched Luke in the arm playfully.

"What was that for?" he complained.

"Doubting me, 'what are you doing Rogue,'" I mocked him.

He laughed, shaking his head. Elliot looked at the zip drive like it was a precious metal he was examining. Once he confirmed it was the real deal, we had a short celebration and grabbed our things to head out. Until Elliot's computer started going insane with noises that sounded like an alert had popped up. All of us stopped at the door, waiting for information.

"Go home." He waved us off, saying, "I still have to decipher this code."

He didn't have to tell us twice. We scurried out of there like mice being chased by a hungry cat.

Three days later and it had been eerily quiet on the Williams case. We still met each day, planning the benefit infiltration. Now that Scarlet's alias was not on the list of buyers, we had to figure out another way in. With two days to prep, my task was done, and I was bored. On the bright side, Luke was training me more frequently even though he was still working on his tasks. I was working on a second strategy of disarming someone with a gun.

Elliot came running into the break room urgently rushing us into the conference room. The moment the door shut he started talking a million miles a minute. No one could understand him, so we all stood there, staring like he was an alien speaking a different language.

"Slow down, Elliot," Spencer finally said, "take a breath."

He closed his eyes and inhaled deeply, holding it for a second before letting it back out. We all glanced at one another; eyebrows raised.

"Okay, look what I figured out," he took the paper with the numbers on it to the middle of the table, shining a blacklight on it to reveal words. We all leaned in to examine it closer.

"What's it say?" Luke asked.

"The zip drive Mia took off Williams was only half of the blueprint. This is the location of the other zip drive containing the other half. Some of the numbers in the list are crossed out with invisible ink. That leaves—"

"Three two-digit numbers, it's a safe code!" I connected.

My body got a jolt of excitement as I rubbed my hands together eagerly. This meant I was back in the game.

"Where and when?" I smiled.

Elliot's shoulders fell. "That's the issue. This location is the same as the benefit. It's guarded in a secure government building."

"Are you doubting my ability?" I asked, crossing my arms.

"No, there's no time. The building has eight offices, six bathrooms, and two libraries, and that doesn't even count the kitchen, closets, and main ballroom. The benefit happens in a day and a half. Plus, during the day the rooms are occupied by government officials."

"But that means—" Scarlet started.

"Someone involved is a government official," Luke finished.

"Exactly." Elliot nodded.

As I stood there, I kept glancing back at the numbers that were crossed out with invisible ink. 1574. They had to be there for a reason. Everything Williams did so far was purposeful and calculated. It was four digits which meant it was too short to be a safe code. Unless he omitted the zeros and it was 15, 07, 04. But the safe code is already on that paper, why would there be two?

"Elliot, bring up the blueprint of the building the benefit will be held at, will you?" I asked, waiting as he did just that.

Walking to get closer to the screen I poured over it. There had to be a reason for them.

"What are the office numbers?"

After typing a few moments, he started listing them off, "28, 29, 30, 42, 43, 48, 49, 50."

"What's going on in your mind, Mia?" Spencer asked.

I turned back to the paper, pointing at the numbers.

"The crossed-out numbers must mean something. Like a number to something or an address, anything."

"What's this room?" Luke asked, pointing to an unlabeled room on the blueprint.

"That...," his brows furrowed as he read his screen, "just looks like a closet."

"But?" Scarlet smiled.

"But look at this picture from the surveillance cameras inside. There's a keypad outside the door. Why would they have a secured closet?" he asked, confused.

"It's not a closet and I bet you the keycode is one, five, seven, four. You have to let me try it, Spencer," I begged. "That second zip drive is in that room."

Silence filled the room as he marinated in the new information. None of us said anything as we waited. I watched him closely as his eyes moved from the piece of paper to the blueprint on the screen. Finally, he shook his head. My shoulders fell, knowing he wasn't going to let me attempt to get into that room.

"Too risky," he stated. "Let me think on it, meet back here in an hour."

DEATH DIDN'T SCARE ME

I MADE MY WAY TO the coffee shop, feeling disappointed. I wanted in that damn room. Sitting down with a huff in my regular spot I sat there a minute. Then I felt eyes on me. I let the group know in the secure group chat Elliot created for us.

> eyes on me, regular coffee shop

CHAMELEON:

> on the way, description

I got up, ordering a scone. As I waited, I pretended to look around bored, my phone in my hand. The asshole from the training center, Dante, was there with another guy. When he saw me, he shot me a warm smile. I gave him a small nod. Maybe I was paranoid. Picking up my scone, I turned to see Adam Williams sitting by my coffee at the table.

it's Williams

NINJA:

on the way

Sliding my phone into my back pocket I sat down, pretending to have just noticed him.

"Umm, hey," I smiled keeping a calm demeanor.

He leaned forward. "You have something that belongs to me." He said through gritted teeth, "I want it back."

"I don't know what you are talking about," I lied.

"Maybe this will help you remember." He scooted closer, revealing a gun pointed at me under the table. "Let's take a walk, shall we?"

I got up, letting him guide me around to the back of the building into an alley. There, he pushed me against the building to face him. It was broad daylight, surely someone would see him with a gun pointed at me, right? My adrenaline began to pump through me and my heart rate quickened.

"Where is it?" he snapped.

Play dumb, Mia-girl.

"Where is what?"

"The zip drive," he demanded, and stepped closer, the gun

now inches from my chest. "Tell me what you did with it."

I could see he was getting increasingly agitated. His hand was shaking almost like he didn't really want to use the gun in his hand. His finger wasn't even on the trigger...yet. But desperate people do desperate things, and I knew this from experience. My mind was analyzing the possible escape routes. I thought I saw someone poke their head around the side of the building out of the corner of my eye, but I wasn't turning away from Williams to check.

"I gave it back to you, what are you talking about?"

When he stepped toward me again he put his finger on the trigger. I said a silent prayer that this would work as it had in training. Using my left hand, I smacked the barrel of the gun while simultaneously using my right hand to hit his wrist in the opposite direction in one swift movement. The gun flew from his hand, skidding across the concrete alley. He let out a yelp, shaking out his hand as he went for the gun. I kicked his feet from under him and took off running. I ran back to the front of the coffee shop as Luke and Scarlet were going inside.

"Run!" I yelled to them as I flew by.

They were quick to follow and I didn't stop until I was sure he wasn't behind us anymore. Once we made it safely to headquarters, I explained what happened. Spencer was pacing as I spoke, his mind—I'm sure—was going crazy analyzing all the new information and possible outcomes of the next moves we would take.

"New plan," he finally said, "tomorrow night, we all go to the benefit. Scarlet, you keep your eyes on Williams while Luke, you silently tail him. But stay out of sight. Mia, you are going to break into the secure room and replace the drive with another phony. Elliot, we need eyes around the building, hack the cams and we all need earwigs."

"Shouldn't I go tonight? Why would I wait for the benefit?" I asked.

"Too risky, he's going to be watching and waiting. If we do it tomorrow, we will have constant eyes on him. It's safer this way."

It made sense, but it also made me nervous. He knew what I looked like which meant if he saw me, the whole operation could be blown. Scarlet gave me a one-armed hug.

"You got it, Mia, and we got your back."

After Spencer dismissed us, I went home to change for Rush Park, which was fifteen minutes from my apartment. It was a place that had obstacle courses for those who liked parkour. Which was my favorite way to let loose, running, flipping, and jumping over anything and everything. I saw the regular group of runners there when I approached. One even brought his giant speaker, blaring music as they ran the course.

"Hey M," Enzo greeted me with a bro-hug.

He was one of the guys that ran with me each time I came. Most of the time we found ourselves hanging out next to the course while the others ran it before running as well. Although we didn't hang out aside from here, running with him was a fun break from reality for me.

"Hey Enzo, you just get here?"

"Yeah. I was hoping you'd show up."

"Why?"

"You challenge me to try new paths and jumps. It makes it more fun to run," he explained. "How was your day?"

"Good, work was long. Ready for this run."

"Let's get started, then."

We ran together for an hour before watching the others go through the different obstacles. After doing a couple of other things to get a workout, I was thoroughly drenched with sweat, laying in the grass, when Enzo joined me. He had a small bowl of ice cream in each hand he'd bought from the guy with the ice cream cart.

"Chocolate or strawberry?" he asked.

I sat up. "Strawberry, thank you."

"I figured it would be the best way to end a long workday." He gave me a grin.

"What do you do for work?" I asked, taking a bite.

"I own a real estate company. I own properties up and down the California coast that I rent out as well." He explained, "I'm more into the business property side though, not traditional housing."

"That's impressive, how old are you?"

"I'm twenty-three, but I can't take all the credit. I didn't start the company; my father did. I just took over for him."

"Oh, is that what you've always wanted to do?"

He paused, looking out at the park in thought for a moment. By the way he took his time to answer it felt like no one had cared to ask him that before.

With a small smirk, he shrugged his shoulder. "No, but the

older I got the more it intrigued me."

We watched as some of the guys ran their final routes for the night. There were no more questions, only teasing jabs back and forth between us and the other runners. The sky darkened as the sunlight started to dwindle.

I stood, announcing, "I'm heading out."

"Do you want a ride home?" he asked. "I've only ever seen you walk here."

Nope, not a good choice girl. No one can know where you live. I shook my head.

"Thank you for the offer but I enjoy the walk."

He nodded. "I'll see you next time then, M."

"See you!"

No matter how much I had worked out that previous night, I got zero sleep. My mixed emotions of being nervous and excited took hold of me, fighting for dominance in my body. I thought about transferring my emotions to that of relaxation but I only did that when there was no other option. Besides, in the past I'd been able to work off no sleep for a day or two before I crashed.

I reported in with the crew, changing into my all-black outfit that consisted of high-waisted skin-tight jeans, a sports bra, a T-back tank top, and a tight leather jacket. My shoes were black combat boots. My lock-picking tools were tucked safely in the inside pocket of my leather jacket.

"Just for clarification, I'm going in unarmed, correct?" I asked.

"Correct," Spencer stated.

Scarlet, Luke, and Spencer were dressed to the nines. The guys wearing sharp suits and Scarlet was in the most beautiful green shimmery gown. They looked so fancy, but I was glad I could wear something comfy as I was going to be crawling around this 'closet.' Who knew what would be in there once I got inside?

"Why can't I wear something comfortable like Mia?" Luke complained, "I'm not supposed to be seen either."

"Your chances of being seen are higher and you need to have the ability to blend in. Mia won't be seen at all, no matter what. Deal with it." Spencer laughed.

We started making our way down to the garage where our two cars would be waiting. The van for Elliot and me, and a town car for the rest of them. When we all walked past the sparring ring of the training center a guy let out a whistle to catcall me. I flipped him off as I continued to walk, rolling my eyes. He jumped down approaching me with angry eyes. The group slowed to a stop in front of me at the disruption.

"You better watch who you flip off, *piccola*," he threatened.

Piccola was Italian for 'little one.' A fire ignited inside me. *Who does he think he is, talking to you like that?*

"Then I suggest you watch who you catcall asshole," I snapped back.

He attempted to backhand me like it was an instinct to do so whenever someone spoke back to him. I moved just enough he missed; his eyes widened in shock. A mocking laugh escaped me. I turned to walk away. My reaction didn't seem to sit well with him.

He yanked me by my arm to bring me back to him. I pressed the thumb of my free hand into the pressure point between his thumb and pointer finger. As his grip weakened, he let out a yelp. I pulled my arm away. I watched in satisfaction as he shook his hand to get rid of the numbness.

"I have a job to do. I don't have time for your bullshit," I stated.

That was when he reeled back to punch me with his full force. I was ready to dodge it but instead, a strong arm came from behind me, stopping him mid-swing. I thought it was Luke.

"Enough, Emilio," he ordered.

His voice was strong and dominant. *That is not Luke, girl.* I turned; it was Dante. Emilio snatched his hand away from him.

"Did you hear the way she spoke to me?" Emilio spat, shooting daggers at me with his eyes.

"I did," Dante nodded.

Shit did this mean I was in trouble? *Well, we regret nothing at least.*

"But had you not catcalled her she wouldn't have felt the need to flip you off from the start. Go back to your training."

After a low growl aimed in my direction, Emilio walked away reluctantly. Dante looked at me, laughed, and shook his head.

"Good luck," he nodded to the group behind me as he walked away.

Dumbfounded, I continued with the group down to the garage. It sounded like he knew where I was going. Which wasn't possible. Right? The lower workers didn't know S-Rank existed. Unless he wasn't a lower worker! Was there another level above S-Rank? The thought crawled to the back of my mind as I jumped into the van with Elliot. We parked three blocks away, waiting for my signal to head inside. Elliot got everything online and a-go in the van in three minutes. He was so talented. I admired his abilities.

"Williams just walked in, Mia go," Spencer ordered. "Scarlet, eyes on Williams at all times."

I hopped out of the van, sneaking my way around to the back of the building. It took me a little while as the guards were walking around to protect the mayor. The kitchen door was propped open courtesy of Luke. He was waiting on me in the main hallway. Once I got there Elliot guided me to the secure 'closet.'

"Code should be one, five, seven, four," Elliot stated.

Sure enough, the little green light appeared and the sound of the door unlocking made me grin. I pushed the door open slowly, taking a single step inside. When I turned on my flashlight it seemed like the room was just a tiny office for someone. My search for the safe started immediately. I found it with ease but when I saw it my eyes got wide.

"We have a problem," I whispered. "This is a biometric safe."

"Which means what?" Scarlet asked.

"It takes a fingerprint to open it, not a combination," I explained. "But then why would the note have a combination on it?"

Either this is a bogus safe and there was another one in this room or the combination was just to trick us. I bit my lip, pulling the small safe toward me to get a better look at it. As I checked the sides, I saw a keyhole. I held my flashlight with my mouth as I made quick work of the lock. Smiling at my success was short-lived as I opened the door to reveal an empty safe. Feeling around, it seemed as though the inside was much smaller than what it should be when looking at the outside of it. I slid my hand across every side, the back of it, and then the inside top of it, feeling a button. What else do you do with a button? *Press that shit, Mia.* I did. The back of the safe popped open.

"What the hell?" I whispered. "This is one cool ass safe. Can I just take the whole safe with me?"

"No, you may not, Rogue," Spencer stated.

"But I want it," I frowned, sticking out my bottom lip to pout even though he couldn't see it. My voice feigned sadness, like a child. "It's badass," I whined.

"How are you going to sneak an entire safe out of the building right now?" Luke laughed.

"Hey," I stated, "when I want something, I get it. Don't doubt my abilities. I can sneak this safe out twenty times without anyone noticing."

"No Rogue, how much longer?" Spencer chuckled.

"You're no fun, Mastermind. Give me ninety seconds," I said, but continued to pout.

I crawled onto the floor to look at the backside. There, I saw that beautiful combination dial just waiting on me.

"Combo, Hacker?" I asked.

"Seventeen, twenty-seven, eleven," Elliot stated.

"Williams is on the move. Thirty seconds, Rogue," Scarlet warned.

"Well shit," I mumbled.

My heart was racing as my fingers twisted the dial to put in the correct combination. The adrenaline was making me even more thrilled to be in this situation. Swapping the identical drives, I closed the backside of the safe. I was pushing the safe back when I saw a shadow at the base of the door.

"I need twenty seconds, or I'm made," I whispered, panicked.

Scarlet to the rescue, flirting with him outside the door. I shut my flashlight off, hiding in an even smaller broom closet.

"Go," I whispered.

Instinctively, I took a step back when Williams walked in. Stepping on something that was probably a broom I almost fell. Then whatever it was moved and a hand that was not mine flew up to cover my mouth. Another locked around my waist. My heart was pounding as whoever was behind me pulled me against him. He was big and muscular. I knew that for sure just by the feel of his hard body on mine. *Oh shit, this is where you die.* All I could do was stand there and wait for Williams to leave. My entire body was tense. Had he been in the closet the entire time?

When Williams left, I didn't hesitate to jam my elbow into the ribs of the guy, throwing open the closet door and bolting out. I heard him chuckle, stepping out behind me. I couldn't see anything as the room was pitch black with no windows. The only light was coming from under the door and it wasn't enough to illuminate anything. I didn't dare look at this beast of a man with my flashlight. When my back hit the wall I swung. What baffled me even more was that he caught my arm mid-swing.

"Are you always this feisty?" the faceless voice laughed in the darkness.

"Is there someone in there, Rogue, do you need backup?" Spencer asked.

The guy leaned down to my ear. I could feel his presence so close to my skin. It sent a pleasurable tingle across my cheek.

"We are on the same team, *cattivella*."

Cattivella; Italian for *trouble-maker.* It made my heart pang. I hadn't been called that in a long time. His voice was smooth and smokey. It made the hairs on the back of my neck stand on end as a thrilling chill traveled down my spine. With that, he took a step away, and I no longer felt him near me. A cold air replaced the heat that had been radiating from his body. I walked to the light coming from the door.

"Negative on the backup," I whispered, "package is secured, let me know when I'm clear."

"I'm here, let's go," Spencer ordered.

I cracked the door open, sliding out and making my way back to Elliot. We waited another hour in the van before our mission was complete. As we got back to headquarters, we debriefed in the conference room. I was being uncharacteristically quiet, my leg bouncing in rage at what'd happened. They all noticed and immediately called me out on it.

"Okay, there was a guy in the room with me. He said we were on the same team. He was there the entire time. He could have killed me. He felt so damn strong."

"What did he look like?" Scarlet asked.

I shrugged. "I don't know, it was too dark and I wasn't about to shine my flashlight on him. He was taller than I am but that eliminates no one. I tried to swing at him when my back was against the wall. He laughed and caught it. I don't even know how he saw it; it was so dark in there. I don't know if I should feel mad that I wasn't fast enough, strong enough, or just be mad that I didn't think to clear the room first."

"So, either way, you should be mad," Elliot stated, "just putting that out there."

"Thanks for that Elliot," I sighed. "Are we done? I'm going to train."

"Yeah, I'll see you all tomorrow."

In the locker room down on the training center floor, I changed into workout clothes. The training center was quiet and empty. I made sure to check the surrounding areas and bathrooms to make sure that Dante wasn't stalking me again. After being satisfied I'd found not a single soul, I made my way to the sparring ring. I sat my phone and gun on the edge of it. I played my music from my phone. It wasn't the normal kind of music one would think to listen to while working out. Instead of it being the upbeat pop style, I preferred to listen to songs with a slower beat. Songs with brooding lyrics. The background beats that accompanied the lyrics were melodic in the electric piano merged with jazz kind of way. It got me into my place of peace.

I leaned my hands on the side of the ring, closing my eyes for a moment. *First step in preparations for the Russians: keep a clear head.* I walked over to the mirror on the wall, staring into my eyes to watch my pupils dilate before coming back to their normal size.

I wasn't sure why, but it wasn't preventable. It happened each time I transferred my emotions. After years of practice, controlling what I allowed myself to feel was something that I'd become an expert at.

My steps were swift as I walked to the punching bag. I let loose on it until my breaths became so rapid it felt like my lungs were going to burst in my chest. *Push yourself harder, it won't be as easy to escape them this time, girl.* With my hands on my hips, I turned with my back to the punching bag. Desperately thinking of a way to get myself into fight or flight mode, my eyes fell onto my gun. With steady hands I curled my fingers around the grip, lifting it from its place on the edge of the ring. *This might work.* I felt my heart rate increase as I thought about what I could do to raise it even higher. The metal barrel was cool against my skin as I pressed it against my temple. I felt my heart start to become frantic in my chest like that of a caged animal.

I turned, facing the mirror. It was one thing to feel what was happening but seeing it in the mirror painted a different picture. It was like my brain was realizing the seriousness of what I was doing. *Push your limits, girl.* My finger moved slowly to the trigger. I'd expected a sharp involuntary inhale and a quickening of my heartrate in response. Instead, the only thing that happened was a slight dilation of my pupils. Aside from my hectic heartbeat in my chest, the thought of pulling the trigger didn't faze me. *Are you not scared?* Oh shit, death didn't scare me. That realization was what made me get the reaction I needed. I gasped. My breaths became fast, feeding my body with oxygen as a rush of new adrenaline hit me like a brick wall. I placed the gun back down before I once again let loose on the punching bag.

It wasn't until I heard a noise to my left that I froze in my spot. My eyes started to scan the room, seeing no one. Nothing was out of place or had seemed to move since I began training. But someone was here with me. Thinking I could draw them out, I walked to the middle of the room, away from the punching bag. With each step, I sang the song playing from my phone just loud enough for them to hear. This would give them the impression I was just taking a break. It would make them believe I was distracted. It was intentional that I turned my back to the direction of the noise. I crouched down, placing one knee on the ground as if I were lacing up my combat boot. My fingertips were touching the floor and I closed my eyes, humming the song to myself. *Now we wait.*

There was a moment when the hairs on the back of my neck stood on end. I felt a presence behind me. *There's more than one... two...no, three.* Now that I was focused on their proximity I waited until they got close enough. Then I kicked my leg out as hard as I could, sweeping the feet out from under the first one to my left. As he fell on his ass I took my knife out from my boot, swinging it at the guy in the middle. He leaned back to avoid being hit by the blade.

"Whoa! Calm down, Rogue. It's me."

My shoulders fell, groaning. It was Dante.

"What do you want? Were you stalking me again?"

"I don't stalk you," he complained. "This is Arturo." He motioned to the black-haired guy, he was helping off the floor, "and Salvatore," he added, pointing to the dirty-blonde-haired guy on the other side of him.

All three of them were buff as shit and each had a couple of tattoos. Arturo and Salvatore were clean-shaven whereas Dante had a short beard, no mustache. Arturo was taller than the other two, but only by a few inches. They were all smiling at me, which made me instantly annoyed. I rolled my eyes.

"What do you want?" I asked.

"What are you doing?" Salvatore asked.

I narrowed my eyes at him. "Cut the shit, I know you were watching me."

"Why did you put your gun to your head?" Dante asked.

"None of your business. Any other questions?"

"If you feel the need to commit suicide, please don't do it at work," he snapped.

"Well, no shit. The last thing this place needs is a police investigation surrounding it." I bent down, putting my knife back into the holster in my boot. "Thanks for the tip, though."

He sighed, moving closer to me, and whispered, "Look, if you are feeling suicidal, we can talk about it."

I snorted, "What are you, a therapist? I'm not suicidal. It's a training tactic."

"How is that a training tactic?" Arturo asked.

"If you don't know, then consider yourself lucky."

"Who are you?" Salvatore asked.

"Do you work here?" I ignored his question.

"Yeah, we oversee S-Rank missions. We're the ones behind the scenes and make up the extraction team," he answered.

"Then you know who I am," I pointed out, "why are you bothering me?"

"Why are you training so hard? And for weird things? First the ice bath and now the gun to your own head? What's going on?" Dante asked.

It wasn't his question that caught me off guard, it was his tone. It was soft, like his eyes at that moment. His head tilted to the side as he took a small step toward me. I crossed my arms over my chest.

"That's none of your business either. Why do you suddenly have an interest in me?"

My brows furrowed. *Could they be working for him?* My eyes widened as my feet backed away from them. I reached back for my gun, pointing it at Dante.

"Who sent you to spy on me?"

"Mia, please."

"Tell me!" I growled, switching my language to Russian. "Was it him?"

They were taken aback by my sudden change. Dante reached up, scratching his temple.

"I don't know what you just said," he admitted. "I don't speak Russian."

He knew it was Russian, but can't speak it? I yanked my phone from the ring with one hand, my eyes never leaving them. With it shoved into my back pocket I took a step to the right as if to walk around them. They remained frozen in place.

"Stay away from me," I ordered before running to the door.

I'd get my things that next day. The employees would be there and they wouldn't dare make a move. If they did, it would be a blood bath, I'd make sure of it.

That night I researched Dante on my phone. I'd done my research on The Core before moving from Florida. It didn't make sense. I was pointed to this company under the impression of safety. If Dante was working with the Russians, then I wasn't safe at all. Although all I had to go off of was his first name and The Core it didn't take me long to find a picture of him and the two men in suits at some banquet posted online. The comment on it only confirmed they were Salvatore and Arturo. His name was Dante Luciano and he had connected ties to organized crime. My stomach tightened as I sat up in bed. *Organized crime, just like the Russians, right?* I swallowed the lump in my throat as my eyes scanned the rest of the article. When my eyes fell onto one word, the tense feeling that had its grip on me lessened: Italian. *He was Italian, not Russian, girl.* Falling backward on my bed I took a deep breath. Did this mean The Core was also Italian organized crime? There wasn't any mention of that in my initial research of the company itself. *Are you safe there if they are in the same business as the Russians who are after you?* I closed my eyes. Something was coming, I could feel it.

SLEEP

THE NEXT MORNING CAME IN the blink of an eye. I was late to get my coffee, unable to read as I did each morning in the coffee shop. My eyes darted back and forth as I made my way to work. They could be following me, I had to keep my eyes peeled.

Inside the S-Rank breakroom, I choose the opposite couch. It allowed my back to face the wall so I could have a view of the entire room. My leg bounced as I observed the others doing their normal morning routines. Scarlet had walked in with a cheery smile on her face, taking the cushion next to me.

"How late did you stay last night?" She asked. "You look like you haven't slept at all."

"Is that your kind way of telling me I look like shit?" I tried to tease, bringing my coffee cup to my lips.

She smiled, "all right, we don't have to talk about it. Was it a guy, though? I've never seen you with a man. Or are you interested in women?"

I choked on the coffee I'd just swallowed.

"No, it wasn't a guy. I don't date." I take another sip, and paused before continuing, "If I did, though, it would be a man."

"Damn, I was excited to live vicariously through you. Don't get me wrong, I knew I'd have to pull all your teeth to get you to tell me about him, but it would have been worth it." She gave me a wink.

My attempt to smile was weak and I became quiet. She got out a book and began to read. I sat there, scanning the room as my thoughts sucked me in. *Could they be working with the Russians?* Why else would they start to bother me? It couldn't have been a coincidence that right after my run-in with the Russian guy at the coffee shop he starts to watch me.

The door to Big Frank's office flew open and Spencer busted out. It wasn't unusual for him to be there before us, especially when we had a case. When his smirk took over his lips, I knew what that meant.

"We've got another one," he announced.

We made our way into the conference room without question, taking our normal spots around the table.

"What have we got?" Elliot wiggled his fingers readying them to begin typing if he needed anything.

Spencer flicked his pointer finger across the glass tabletop, bringing up a picture on the screen that covered the wall. Spencer said something, but my mind was still going through the interaction with Dante. There had to be a tell if he were working with them, right? No one is that good. *He did recognize Russian.* True.

He could have lied when he said he didn't understand, just to make sure—

"Mia?"

"What?" I glanced up at Spencer.

"I said we were tasked with a heist." He paused. "Are you all right?"

"Yeah, sorry."

I brought my attention to the screen. On it was a picture of a small safe with a dial lock. He waited a second before continuing.

"Our client wants to steal whatever is inside this safe. He won't give us any indication of what it is that we are stealing, but it's a small safe so it can't be that large."

"Where's it located?" Luke asked.

"The address they've given is to a building just outside the city. It appears to be a warehouse for the incoming shipments of artwork the museum handles. From what I suspect it's going to be heavily guarded. Elliot, you are going to be our eyes. I'm going to have you hack into the security cameras. You will need to disarm any systems they have before we move. Mia and Luke, you two are going in. Luke, your task is to secure the perimeter. Mia, you're going to steal whatever's in the safe. Scarlet, you're going to be in the van with Elliot and me, just in case we need another pair of hands...or a distraction." He leaned his fingertips on the table, and said, "It happens in two days."

"What can we do before then?" Luke asked.

"Elliot's got that covered. I can give you the blueprint of the building to study. That way you know your way around without having to be guided. Other than that, I'm going to try to figure out what's in that safe. It's bothering me."

With that, he dismissed us. Luke, Scarlet, and I went down to the training floor. I helped him coach her on moves for a while. Then he asked if I wanted to spar. Due to the small amount of sleep my body had, my coordination was off. It didn't take long for Luke to punch me in the side. I was too slow to block it. Wincing, I took a step back.

"You're done, Mia," he stated. "You don't seem like yourself."

"I'm fine. I just, need some air."

I bent down under the rope of the ring, heading to the roof. The Core wasn't the tallest building in the city, but it was tall enough to look down on others. I let my eyelids fall shut, concentrating on my breathing. The air was warm with just enough wind to not make it sweltering that day. It'd only been ten minutes before the door behind me screeched open.

"Mia?"

I turned to see Elliot. He had his hands in his pockets as he walked over.

"What?"

"What's going on?"

"Nothing, I just wanted some air."

"Scar said Luke punched you."

I rolled my eyes. "We were sparring, he got lucky. I'm all right, really. Don't worry."

"Do you need some ice?"

"No." I let out a sigh, putting my hand on his shoulder. "I'm fine,

Elliot. Thanks for checking on me. Come on, let's get back inside."

He said nothing more but walked with me back down to our floor. Scarlet and Luke weren't anywhere to be seen when I walked back in. I sat down on the couch in the spot I had that morning. My eyes flickered from the elevator to the staircase door. *They're not going to come for you in the middle of the workday, girl.* I wouldn't put anything past them. Who knows what they would stoop to after last time?

It was the end of the workday and I'd realized I hadn't so much as glanced at the blueprints of the building we were supposed to infiltrate in only two days. Everyone had gone home for the night. I took the blueprints, spreading them out on the table in front of me. When I looked at a blueprint my mind envisioned a maze. Instead of solving the maze for one route in and out, I always planned for three. Two of them I shared with the team so they would know the routes. The third one was an insurance policy that only I knew about. But as I sat there, staring at the blueprint, I couldn't get my thoughts straight long enough to plan a single route. I fisted my hair in my hand, giving it a tug as a growl escaped me. *This is stupid, you need sleep.* No, I have to be ready just in case. Maybe I can figure it out tomorrow. I placed the blueprints back in the secure conference room before taking a different way home than usual.

That night I went through my backpack I kept ready. It contained a few changes of clothes, an extra magazine of bullets that would go into my gun, a wad of cash, and some fake identities so I could start over. In the smaller pockets were a few granola bars, zip-ties, a short rope, a lighter and a pen that contained invisible ink. I picked it up, twirling it in my fingers as memories of using it to write secret notes with Giovanni flashed through my mind. We'd shared a notebook, passing it back and forth to one another each night. He'd shown me how to pass the pen to him with the same amount of stealth as someone who could pickpocket. It was our way of communicating things we didn't want to say in front of his parents. The notebook like unmonitored text messages. I felt the corners of my lips tilt up at the memory. I'd lost the small black-light that used to be attached at the end. Hell, I wasn't even sure if it still had ink, but the thought of throwing it out caused my heart to twist inside my chest. I tucked it back into my bag, shak-ing away the memories to refocus on the present. I spent the rest of the night readying the apartment. I walked through it, making sure everything I wanted to be hidden was. By the time I was done, it was time to go back to work that next morning.

I grabbed a coffee and headed into the locker room on the training room floor. The dark circles under my eyes were even darker today. My head throbbed, screaming for me to shut the lights off. I leaned down, splashing cold water on my face in hopes it would wake me up a bit more. It was time to get focused. I took the elevator up to our floor, heading for the blueprints.

After two hours of staring at them, I'd managed to make one route. I rubbed my eyes, feeling them burn when my eyelids shut. Resting my chin on my hand I continued to stare at the blueprints.

It wasn't long before I felt my eyelids becoming heavy, drooping at their own will.

"Didn't you get any sleep last night, either?"

I snapped up, seeing Elliot standing in front of me. He was leaning on the table, his eyes swirling with worry. Coming to my feet, I stretched.

"I just need a break. I'm going to take a walk for lunch. I'll be back in a bit."

Leaving him no room for negotiation, I walked away.

The fresh air hit my face as my feet carried me away from The Core. I felt like a zombie padding down the sidewalk. My destination was unknown but my feet carried me on a familiar path as my mind began to shut down. Eventually, I found myself at Rush Park, hearing Enzo call my name as he ran over to greet me.

"Whoa M, you don't look so good. You should sit down." He wrapped an arm around my waist, guiding me to the bench. "When's the last time you ate something?"

I heard his question, but I couldn't formulate a response. It was as though my words were stuck in my mind, which was no longer in control of my vocal cords. He put his hand on my shoulder.

"M? Hey?"

I blinked a few times, gathering myself.

"Yeah?"

"When's the last time you ate something?"

"Uh—I don't know." I swallowed, my throat suddenly dry.

"Let me buy you lunch, there's a sandwich shop on the corner we can go to."

He got up, motioning for me to join him. I stood, too fast, feeling dizzy. *You're dehydrated, all you've had is coffee for two days. Take care of yourself or you're not going to escape them.* I reached out, grabbing Enzo's arm to steady myself. He gave me a minute before latching onto my waist. Anyone walking by would see a couple going to lunch together. In reality, I felt like I might be stumbling if he hadn't helped me. He sat me down at a table inside the sandwich shop, bending to be eye level with me.

"What do you like?"

It was an odd question. Instead of asking what I wanted, he asked what I liked. It made my brows furrow. I didn't answer, feeling fuzzy again. It was like I could hear him and physically move around but my mind wasn't there. Like it was stuck in neutral.

"Mia," he said softly, putting his hand on my cheek to get my attention. "I'll be right back, okay?"

I gave him a nod. I watched as he walked up to the counter, ordering for us. He filled a giant cup with water and ice. When he set it down in front of me, he stuck the red straw through the lid.

"Drink this, it'll help," he stated.

I brought the straw to my lips, suddenly feeling parched. It was like I couldn't get enough and before I knew it, my cup was empty. Our order number was called, pulling him away again. When he got back, he took my cup without a word, refilling it for me. He then unwrapped my sandwich, sliding it to me before moving on to his own. I picked it up without a word, taking the smallest bite. I wasn't sure how my stomach would handle it after barely eating.

"What's going on?" he asked. "Are you in trouble or something?"

"No, work stuff," I managed to squeak out.

"You have to take care of yourself, no one's work is that import-ant, M. You're no good to anyone dead and that's what you'll be if you continue," he claimed.

"Yeah, I—" I began, bringing my water back to my lips to take another long drink, "I've been having trouble sleeping."

"Because of work?"

I nodded, my mouth full with another bite.

"There will always be work. You have to leave it at the office, M. It's hard, I get it. Believe me, I do. I'm addicted to my work as well, but you have to draw that line." He paused, then asked, "Can I help with any of it?"

"No." I cleared my throat. "This helped."

That made a smile cross his lips. "You scared the shit out of me, I thought you were sick or something."

I felt a little stronger than I had after eating something. We walked back toward the parkour park together, stopping at the entrance.

"I have to head back to work."

"Do you want a ride back?" he offered. "Disclaimer though, I rode my sports bike here today."

You'd get there faster and wouldn't have to look over your shoul-der. I gave him a small smile.

"Sure."

"Where do you work?"

"The Core."

"Oh shit, you do security?"

"Yeah."

He put on a pair of sunglasses, helping me onto the back of his bike. I had no idea what to do once I was on it. I heard him chuckle, holding his hands back for me to take. When I did, he threaded them around his torso.

"Hold onto me."

I leaned into him as the bike below us roared to life. The world around us whipped by as we sped down the street. It was a short drive compared to the walk. He pulled over outside the front door.

"Thanks, Enzo." I climbed off, more gracefully than I'd expected.

"Be careful M, take care of yourself. I'll see you next time."

The growl of his bike echoed around us as he sped away. I still felt exhausted but moved back inside. *Okay, just go upstairs and get your routes done. Then you can go home and try to sleep.* Yeah, like I'll be able to sleep with the Russians around.

A yawn escaped me as I entered the S-Rank lounge. The blueprint was where I left it. I sat down to stare at it some more. Scarlet and Luke came to check on me a few times throughout the day. My body started to shift back into neutral at times. I tried to stop and stretch or splash more water on my face. It only got worse. I checked my watch to see it was almost seven at night. I had one route down and maybe half of a second. A frustrated sigh escaped me as I rubbed my eyes.

"Mia, why are you still here?"

It was Elliot. He'd just come out of the secure conference room. My eyes locked back onto the blueprint, avoiding his eyes like the plague. When he sighed and walked away I thought he was going to leave me alone. Then he came back, holding a steaming mug of tea. I took it without a word, thinking it would get him to walk away.

"Come with me," he said, holding his hand out for me.

I took it, slowly coming to my feet. He brought me down a back hallway. We came to a stop at a door with the letters "E.L." on it. He pressed four numbers on the keypad, then took his glasses off so the retinal scanner could get his right eye. The door opened to a modest size room. On the wall to the right hung four monitors above a desk with two keyboards and two computer chairs. To the left was a giant sofa and bean bag. Along the back wall were bits and pieces of tech gear. I assumed this was his room to experiment with tech things for us. A soft blue hue lit the room.

"I don't know what's going on, Mia, but you need to sleep." He motioned to the couch, and said, "If you keep it up like this you're going to get hurt on a mission."

When I didn't move, he pressed his hand gently against my lower back. Guiding me to the couch, I finally collapsed into it. He pulled the blanket off the back of the couch, draping it over my shoulders.

"I'm not leaving this room, all right? Just rest for a few hours."

He's right, just rest. I sat there for a little bit, sipping on the tea he'd brought. He got to work on the computers. When I could see the bottom of the mug, I laid on my side, my eyelids falling shut. I felt him move to sit on the edge of the couch, rubbing my back for a minute before sleep consumed me.

"Why hasn't she slept?" a hushed voice asked.

"I don't know, I didn't ask. Why don't you leave her alone, Dante?" Elliot whispered back.

"Because, Elliot, it's my job to make sure she's all right."

"Well, you're doing a damn fine job. You're going to wake her up, she needs to rest before the mission tomorrow. Go away."

"Not until you tell me what you two are working on after hours."

"That information is between the two of us. If you want to know then I guess you'll have to ask her yourself."

"Oh yeah, that'll be a great conversation. The last time I started asking questions she had her gun pointed at me. I'm pretty sure she also threatened me in Russian."

"You probably deserved it then." The taps of his keyboard sounded. "Go away. I'm working on something."

"What do you want me to tell the boss, then?"

"Tell him she's resting and to leave her alone."

"He's going to love that."

The sliding of the door sounded before I heard Elliot let out a sigh. I heard him get up, feeling him walk over toward me. He adjusted the blanket so it was covering my exposed arms. After that, I let sleep take me once more.

I stretched, feeling better than I had before. Checking my phone, I saw it was almost nine in the morning. I shot up, needing to get ready for work. It was then I took in my environment. I was still in Elliot's office. He was asleep on the bean bag.

"Elliot," I called, my voice still groggy from sleep.

"Hmm?" he answered, not opening his eyes.

"It's almost nine in the morning."

His reaction was the same as mine; he shot up from his spot. I chuckled, stretching before standing up.

"I needed that sleep."

"I could tell, you slept almost fourteen hours." He replied. "I'll text the boss and let him know we will both be late. You should go home and get ready. We've got work to do."

It was a quick shower and change before I was back at work. Elliot handed me a coffee as I walked into the S-Rank lounge. The blueprint was ready for me, and, with a well-rested mind, it didn't take me long to find my three routes of entry and exit. The building was essentially a giant box. The room where the safe was appeared to be just another square-shaped room that was centered on the main floor of the building. It contained three points of entry. Two doors were on the main floor of the room. It also had a loft in it. If you went up the short flight of stairs on the left side of the room, the last door was there along the back wall of the loft. It was outside of that room where the hallways became a jumble of twists and turns.

"All right, what is route one?" Spencer asked in the secure conference room.

Elliot brought the blueprints up, showing the first route I'd given him on the screen. Spencer studied it methodically in silence. His hand came up to rub his chin while he processed it. I knew what he was doing, looking for problems. It was his job to find the problems with the plan and strategically come up with solutions or alternatives. When he was satisfied with it he turned back to me.

"And the second?"

Once more, Elliot did the same thing. After settling on our secondary escape, all we had to do was wait. Luke and I went down to the training floor.

"Hey Luke, will you teach me how to get out of a pin?"

"What kind of pin?"

"One where I'm pinned to the ground."

"Depends, are you feeling better?"

"Yes." I smiled. "Much better."

"All right, then let's get to it."

The ring was being used by Dante and another giant of a man. He had his shirt off while he traded punches with Dante. The alternating thin and thick black lines of a tattoo created what looked like something tribal. My eyes were glued to it, intrigued, and wanting to see if it stretched around to the front of his chest.

"Mia?" Luke called, snapping me out of my trance. "Want to run until they are done?"

"Sure."

We'd run a mile before taking a break to check if the ring was open. They were getting out as we came around the corner. I let Luke lead the way, my eyes drifting back to the tattoo guy. *He's going to catch you staring Mia, stop it!* Too late. His electric blue eyes struck me like a bolt of lightning.

"Rogue," Dante chimed, "you look well rested."

I squinted at him, aware that Luke was watching our interaction from inside the ring. The conversation he'd had with Elliot while I was supposed to be sleeping in his office replayed in my mind. *He was trying to gather intel on you.* I took a step closer so I could lower my voice enough that Luke wouldn't hear me.

"I'm going to say this only once, Dante," I kept my voice even and calculated, "what Elliot and I do after hours is none of your damn business. Tell your boss if he has an issue with it, he can speak with me directly."

By the way his mouth opened and then shut, I could tell he didn't know what to say in response. Tattoo guy had a grin on his face as I turned to leave them standing there. I climbed into the ring, ready to work out some newfound irritation.

"Everything all right?" Luke asked.

"Everything is great." I nodded. "Now teach me how to get out of a pin."

After an hour, we ate something together as a team in the S-Rank lounge. Before I knew it, it was time to get ready for the mission.

I went into the locker room, feeling uneasy about it. It was a contrast to how I felt on every other mission I'd been a part of. It wasn't because I was fatigued or unfocused, it was my gut. I couldn't pinpoint what or why I was getting this feeling, but something felt off. I wore my same all-black outfit as normal. Spencer had been very specific that I was to go unarmed again. My only mission was to get in, get the thing in the safe, and get out. I normally followed his lead, leaving behind my firearm and knife. This time, though, I made sure my knife was tucked into my right combat boot. I put on my shoulder holster for my weapon, hooking it onto my belt. An extra magazine of bullets was attached to the right side of it, my gun on the other. This mission was different—I could feel it. I pulled my black leather jacket over it, concealing my weapons perfectly. I patted my breast pocket, feeling my lock-picking tools ready and waiting. I pulled my eggplant purple hair into a ponytail.

"Ready?" Scarlet came in, and complained, "I can't believe Mastermind is going to make me sit in the van. I feel like I'm in time out."

I snorted, "I think it's because you're not as far in your self-defense training. Don't worry, I know you'll get there, Scar. For the record, I feel the same way when you guys get to do something fun without me."

She put her hand on my shoulder. "Well, we do make a good team altogether. Think about it, when I learn how to fight or shoot, I'll be right there with you." She winked. "I got your back from the van tonight though."

"Thanks." I took a deep breath, then said, "Let's go."

NOT ALONE

THE FIFTEEN-MINUTE DRIVE FROM THE city to the
location was quiet. I put my headphones in, listening to my music
to help get me into my zone. My concentration was on the routes
I'd take. But the anticipation inside of me grew, causing my leg to
bounce involuntarily. Elliot nudged me with his elbow. I pulled one
earbud out.

"You all right?"

As he asked the question Scarlet and Luke turned to look
at me.

"I'm fine, just getting in the zone." I put my earbud back in.

He didn't say anything more the rest of the ride. When we
pulled over on the outskirts of the area we got ready. Elliot gave
each of us an 'earwig' to communicate with. I silenced my phone,
sliding it into my jacket pocket and zipping it shut. Spencer was
giving Luke and Scarlet one last run down when I jumped out of
the back of the van. Elliot pulled me to the side.

"What's wrong?"

I chewed on my lower lip. *You know you can trust him.* He wouldn't give away information he found while searching me. Finally, I motioned to my ear, not wanting the others to hear.

"I didn't activate them yet."

"I have a bad feeling about this mission, Elliot." I pulled my jacket open to reveal my firearm. "A really bad feeling."

His eyes scanned my face as his hand came up to run through his hair. He gave it a tug at the back of his head.

"Do you want to turn back? We can go back to headquarters just say the word."

"No, I just. I don't know. It's probably nothing."

Luke jumped out, holding a black drawstring bag for me to take.

"For whatever's in the safe. Ready?"

"Yeah, let's go." I put my arms through the strings and pulled it onto my back.

Elliot met my gaze once more, giving me a nod. He'd have my back. With one last glance, we started the short trek to the building. It was surrounded by woods on two sides. The other two were roads that remained untouched by tires since the place closed for the day.

"What was that about?" Luke motioned back to where Elliot and I had been standing.

"Oh, nothing. Just wanted to tell me good luck."

He grinned, and said, "Like you need it."

The statement brought a hint of a smile to my lips. We crawled under the fence that surrounded the property. It had barbed wire around the top of it. The tan metal-sided building was similar to that of a warehouse. Hunching over, we ran to the side of the building. The loose gravel crunched under our feet as we made our way to the first plan of entry.

"I've got control of the cams; they are on a loop. You are good to move freely, security won't know the difference," Elliot said over the earwig, "the key code to the door is two, nine, three, zero."

I put on a pair of gloves, pressing the numbers. The mechanism whined, unlocking the door for us. We stepped inside, following the winding path to the room the safe was housed in. Luke stopped just outside the door, giving me a nod. He was to monitor the hallway that snaked around the outside room, keeping out any security officers that may happen to do a round to check on things.

The moment I went through the door I knew this was going to be more complicated than what we had anticipated. The entire left wall of the room consisted of glass windows. Anyone walking by could see inside. My eyes scanned the room once more to spot any other areas I could be seen. I'd come through the first door. It had no window, just all metal. *At least they can't see you from behind.* The other door to the back right had a small square window in it. To my left, there was a set of metal stairs that led to the loft where the third door was waiting, unguarded. My eyes searched the area, seeing wooden boxes of all sizes scattered and stacked around the room. I used them for cover, taking advantage of the blind spots they created. The safe was on the left side of the room farthest from any door.

"Luke, the safe is in front of the giant glass windows. Monitor that side more frequently." I whispered, so he would hear me through the earwig.

"Copy that."

The safe was on a small table, just waiting there for me to unlock it. I snuck to it, taking out my earwig. I replaced it with the small stethoscope from my lock-picking tools. Spinning the dial clockwise, then counter-clockwise, and finally clockwise again until I heard the two beautiful clicks each time. I replaced the earwig, putting away my stethoscope.

"I'm in," I whispered.

"What's in it?" Scarlet asked.

I twisted the handle, pulling open the door to the safe. I saw a manila envelope, the size of a piece of paper. My steady hands picked it up, taking the bag off and putting it safely inside.

"An envelope. Feels like there's short papers of some sort inside. Package is secured, I'm on my w—" I stopped myself. I heard a shuffle behind me.

My muscles tensed as the others began asking questions through the earwig. I felt my heart start to pound harder in my chest. The room wasn't dark, but it wasn't bathed in complete light either. There was this soft glow from one light above and that was it. A security light.

The hairs on the back of my neck stood on end. *You're not alone.* I felt eyes on me, scanning the glass window to see Luke. His brows were furrowed, giving me a questioning look. I took a step back, away from him.

"Give me a second," I stated.

My eyes closed, focusing on the sounds around me. When I heard footsteps my heart dropped. I knew it. The mission was a set-up. When I opened my eyes, I saw three men standing around me.

"Oh shit, we need backup now!" Luke ordered, his voice panicked as he took off.

I transferred my emotions to that of determination. It was my most focused emotion that I relied on when in a fight. Then I glanced around at the three men.

"Gentlemen." I gave them a wicked smile. "How may I help you?"

"You're coming with us."

The Russian accent gave me all the assurance I needed. *He was here for me.*

"The primary escape door has a chain around it. I can't get in!" Luke said, panting over the earwig. "So does the secondary."

Dante and three others came running down the corridor. Two of them I recognized from the other night, Salvatore and Arturo. The other one was the giant he'd been sparring. I could tell by the tattoo that spread down his arm. They stopped at the big glass window. I met Dante's eyes for a moment. He gave me a nod as if to go ahead with what I was planning.

"Oh, where to?" I asked the men around me, raising one eyebrow.

"You know where. He's waiting, let's go." sneered the one to my right.

"First, I need to apologize," I stated.

"Apologize?" the one in front of me asked, brows furrowed.

"Yes, to Mastermind." I explained.

"For what Rogue?" Spencer asked through the earwig.

"Master—" one started to ask before I kicked him square in the chest.

He flew backward, smashing into the nearest wooden box. The other two hesitated for only a moment. I took that moment to roll backward, away from them, getting into my fighting stance. They traded a look, coming at me together. I ducked under one's swing while punching the other in the stomach. I wasn't far enough away when one kicked the back of my knee. I fell, rolling onto my back just as the other one straddled me. He put his hands on my throat, squeezing. I heard Luke yelling in my ear, giving me directions on how to get out of the hold. His words were just sounds to me as I reached into my jacket. I took ahold of my gun, pushing the barrel against the man's chest. When I pulled the trigger, the shot echoed through the room.

"You're armed?" Luke said in disbelief.

I didn't have time to think, pushing the guy's body off me. I rolled to see the other ones coming at me. Firing two shots I took both of them out. Coughing, I rubbed my throat as I went to the glass where the guys were standing.

"Meet me at headquarters. Take the team with you," I ordered, hearing a door above me open.

"We're not leaving you," Luke stated.

I closed my eyes, leaning into the rage I felt for this Russian asshole. I could feel it overtake me as my body felt more powerful. When I opened them, I stared straight into Dante's eyes.

"Headquarters, go. I will be there."

This time my voice was more commanding. I'd said it with finality. I put my gun back in its holster. Dante gave me a nod as more Russians began running down the stairs. I backed up, scaling the wooden boxes. *If they are coming through the door upstairs, that must be the exit.* Not looking back, I leaped from the highest box I could reach, to the metal railing of the walkway above. It took me a moment to pull myself up. The sounds of their footsteps running back up the stairs gave me the adrenaline I needed to move quickly. I ran out the door, turning left as our secondary route determined. I took an immediate left and then right. At the end of the hallway, there should have been an exit door.

My feet froze in their tracks as I rounded that final corner. I could see the door right where it was supposed to be. In between that and myself, were three Russians.

"Going somewhere?" one taunted.

They were waiting on you. I turned, taking my third exit route. Since I had to backtrack I ran into two of the Russians that I had encountered before. They'd come back up the stairs to cut me off. I rolled forward, pulling my knife from my boot as I did. When I stood up, I shoved the knife into the stomach of the one in front. I pushed as hard as I could so he would fall backward. When he did, he became a blockade to the one behind him. I yanked my knife back, taking a left turn to sprint down the hallway. My third route was clear of any Russians or teammates.

When I shoved open the door to the outside of the building I ran straight into a hard chest. An evil laugh sounded.

"I found her. South side, exit nine," he stated, grabbing ahold of my arms.

It was like he was strangling the life from my arms. My knife fell from my hand. I kneed him, aiming for his family jewels, but instead getting his thigh. It at least loosened his grip enough for me to attempt to run. He used that to his advantage, shoving me to the ground. I let out a yelp as the tiny rocks dug into the palms of my hands and cheek.

"Rogue!" Elliot said through the earwig.

"I'm fine, get to headquarters!" I growled.

The guy punched me in the gut the moment I stood upright. Another yelp in pain escaped me, but it only made me angrier. I thought there was nothing beyond rage, but in that moment all I saw was red. That's when I threw an uppercut to meet with his jaw so hard my knuckles hurt. He stumbled backward, giving me another opportunity to punch him square in the chest. The moment he started to cough I knew I'd knocked the wind out of him. He wasn't going to be able to chase me. I turned, taking off through the woods.

I didn't stop running, even when it felt like my lungs were on fire. We were ten miles from the city. Once I broke through the trees, I started walking down the main road back into town. I took deep breaths, counting to seven before exhaling to get my heart rate down and control my breathing. I checked my phone; I'd been moving for twenty-five minutes. A car sped past me, screeching to a stop. My body tensed as the driver opened the door to get out. I prepared myself to run again. That was until I was met with the familiar chestnut brown eyes and copper brown curls I'd met all the time at Rush Park. *Enzo.*

"M? What the hell?" he made his way to me, leaving his driver's side door wide open, "I thought that was you. Why are you so far out of the city? What happened, your cheek is all bloody?"

I reached up to touch it, although I already knew what state it was in. I hissed when my fingers brushed the open scrapes on the once smooth skin. *Quick, think of an explanation.*

"I—" I cleared my throat. "I went on a run and got kind of lost in the woods. I tripped over an exposed tree root, that's why I was walking."

"You went on a run this far from the city? Where did you park your car?"

"I don't have a car, I ran here."

"Mia we're at least an hour outside the city on foot." His eyes widened, flabbergasted.

"Don't remind me." I tried to joke.

"Come on, at least let me help you get your cheek cleaned up and your hand, you've got blood there too." *But that blood isn't yours.* He motioned for me to follow him. "I have a first aid kit in my trunk."

I tensed, a few hundred possibilities running through my mind. *He could shove you right into the trunk.* Then how would I escape? This sounded like just another situation I need to work on getting out of during training. *But this is Enzo, we run with him almost every day.* Did we even have time to clean up my cheek? How close were the Russians now?

"Wait," I started. "I'm fine, I'll get cleaned up when I get home."

"M, I really think you should clean it now. It could get infected or something."

"Then I'll clean it on the way back. Just bring the first aid kit to the front seat," I negotiated.

"Deal."

He opened the passenger side door for me to hop in. My eyes stayed glued to him as he opened the trunk, retrieving a black box before joining me in the front seat. When we got going on the road I opened the kit, getting out the antiseptic wipes. I used the mirror on the visor to gently clean my cheek. A hiss escaped me as the sting rang through the side of my face. I then wiped both my hands as my palms were decorated with similar scrapes and the blood of the Russian I'd stabbed.

"What's your address?" he asked as we crossed the city limit.

"You can just drop me at work. I left my things there thinking I'd be back long before this," I lied.

"Are you sure? It's getting dark and I know you walk. You could have a concussion from your fall or something."

"I'm all right, Enzo, and yes, I'm sure. Thank you for being so concerned about me."

"Well, I can't have my favorite woman get hurt. Who would I run with then?"

I snorted, "We run with three other guys and two other women; you'd find someone I'm sure."

He turned to meet my gaze at a red light. "But they aren't you."

It seemed like he wanted to reach out for my hand. His tone

was full of want, which set off every red flag in my mind. *This is starting to sound like he's interested. Time to uninterest him.* A quick direction change should do the trick.

"Yeah, I am pretty badass, right?" I joked and sat back in the seat. "I guess I would miss having a partner that beats me all the time too."

It worked, he laughed. "You don't beat me *all* the time."

"I'd say it's at least eighty percent of the time, but who's counting?"

He shook his head, a grin stretching on his lips as he continued the drive to The Core. When he pulled to the front, he put it in park and turned on his hazard lights.

"Can I have your number, just in case this happens again and you can call me?"

My throat suddenly felt like it was constricting. *That's a huge no from me, girl.*

"I don't run with my phone on me," I explained. "Also, I don't give out my number to anyone that I don't work with."

His brows pulled together. "You only give your number out to coworkers?"

"Yeah, I only use my phone for work." I continued, "Also, I can guarantee I will not ever find myself in this situation again. I now know to run only in familiar places."

"But what about friends? You don't talk to them or call them to hang out?"

I opened the door, getting out before leaning into the space to meet his gaze.

"I don't. I see them when I see them. Just like I'll see you tomorrow at Rush Park." I gave him a smile. "Thank you for the ride."

"Wait!"

He opened the compartment between the front seats, pulling out a pen, then he opened the glove compartment. My eyes landed on the familiar metal of a handgun. *Why does he have that?* He didn't even flinch that it was there. Instead, he dug out a notepad. He scribbled something down then tore off the top sheet, handing it out for me to take.

"Just in case you ever need me." He explained, "I'm one call away, M, coworker or not."

I reached out to take it, seeing a smile creep across his lips.

"Do you always carry a gun?" I asked motioning to the weapon with my head.

"I do. Does that scare you?"

A laugh escaped my lips. "Not in the slightest. Have a good night Enzo."

"You too, M. See you tomorrow."

I closed the door, making my way up to the second floor, heading straight for the locker room. Once I was inside I checked my cheek in better light. It was no longer bleeding and the blood that had leaked through after I'd cleaned it was dry and crusty. I took the sling bag off my back, retrieving the envelope. *Was there something in it or was it just a prop in the plan the Russians had for me?* I opened it with steady hands, peering inside to see three photographs.

The first one was from a long time ago. It was of Giovanni and I walking in the park. A fire reignited inside me as memories of what this Russian douchebag did. Now my hands were shaking with anger as I flipped to the second one. It was of a couple holding a baby. I didn't recognize anyone in the picture. Turning to see if there was anything on the other side of it I was met with just a white background. I flipped it to the back of the stack, looking at the third one. It was of me and a friend from childhood. I vividly remember him being my first friend the moment I entered kindergarten. He ran right up to me, asking if I wanted to play. *His name, girl?* I was at a loss for that. My brows furrowed. *How are they all connected? This family picture might be a good one to give to Elliot for more investigation.* I put the manilla envelope back in the drawstring bag, folded the pictures to fit into my jacket pocket, and opened the door.

I'd only taken one step off the elevator to the S-Rank break room when I heard loud arguing. I followed the sound to the room where Spencer meets with Big Frank. *You should knock.* I twisted the handle, pushing the door open. *Or barge right in.* The room was hushed as they all looked at me. S-Rank was sitting around the table. The extraction crew, which consisted of Dante, Salvatore, and Arturo stood in each corner of the room. The person I assumed to be Big Frank was leaning back, sitting at the head of the table like this was a casual meeting. On either side of him stood the catcalling asshole, Emilio, and the blue-eyed behemoth that had come in with Dante.

"Mia, your cheek is all scraped up."

Elliot stood up, coming straight for me. I pulled my gun, taking a step back and aiming it for his chest.

"Get out," I ordered.

"Mia, it's me." He shook his head in disbelief.

"Get. Out. Scarlet, Spencer, Luke, Elliot. In that order. Out."

The room was silent as a cloud of tension descended. They all looked to Big Frank who nodded. Out they went, one by one. I put my gun away as they did. I grabbed ahold of Elliot's wrist to stop him before he could get through the door, yanking him close to me. I spun us, planting my hands on his chest to push his back against the door so only he could see my face. Dante took two steps toward us before Elliot held up his finger to stop him. His eyes flickered between mine. I reached up, putting one hand on his left cheek. I knew he put his earwig in his left ear, each time we wore them. Without much movement, I pressed against it with my ring finger.

"You are always there," I whispered. "Only you."

He squinted at me. I pushed down on the earwig again causing a grin to stretch across his lips. It was then I knew he was clear on my instructions. I wanted him to listen to what was about to be said, but only him.

"Always."

I took a step back, letting him scurry off to his private office. I knew he needed some time to shut off the others' earwigs. My gut told me I could still trust him. So far, my gut has always had the right feeling. I mean it's gotten me this far in life. Now it was time to deal with the men in this room. As I met their gazes I could tell they were just as serious as I was about the situation. I moved to sit down at the opposite end of the table across from Big Frank. They were all waiting for me to say something.

"All clear, Mia," Elliot said over the earwig.

"Shall we get started?" I asked.

"Mia, I'm Frank Sartori I—"

"I know who you are."

"Do not interrupt him!" Emilio demanded.

"Fuck you," I snapped.

Emilio opened his mouth to speak but was silenced solely by Big Frank raising one hand. He had a few chunky rings on his fingers that caught the light when he lifted his hand. His eyes sparkled with curiosity while he offered me an intrigued smile.

"Then we can skip the formalities. We were just going over what happened," he explained. "Gentlemen, have a seat."

I rested my arms on the table in front of me. The extraction team replaced the spots of the S-Rank team. No one said anything but their eyes moved back and forth between Big Frank and me.

"Who were those men?" Big Frank finally asked.

"You should know, they paid you to send me in there."

"They paid me for a heist," he stated.

"They paid you for an abduction!" I sneered. "All the research I've done on The Core and Dante states that you are involved in Italian organized crime. So, tell me what you are doing joining up with the Russians?"

He sat up straight in his chair. All the heads at the table snapped to me. My eyes stayed locked on Big Frank's.

"You investigated me?" Dante asked.

"Dante." Big Frank warned before tilting his head to one side, "You are very bold in your accusations, Ms. Clark."

"I don't like bullshit, Mr. Sartori. I find it best to get straight to the point to not waste anyone's time. As you can tell I don't have much longer before they make another move. If you would prefer the term mafia I can use that. Either way, it doesn't change the fact that I'm still wondering why you would team up with the Russians. Why now? I've worked here for four years. You could have made a move on me sooner than that."

"Let me be clear with you, I had no part in the event that unraveled tonight. I would not risk your safety nor that of the team's." He interlaced his fingers on the table, and continued, "It does seem, however, that we both have information the other needs to piece together what happened." He said, "Would you like to go first?"

"Why would I do that?"

"A question for a question, then?"

"As long as I know you are telling me the truth we won't have a problem."

"I'm ready to cross-check anything he says, Mia," Elliot said over my earwig.

"Very well, shall we get started?"

RULE NUMBER ONE

I MOTIONED FOR BIG FRANK to ask his question first. That would help me gauge what information he was trying to ascertain from me. I could then use his lead to guide the conversation to where I wanted it to go.

"What do you know about the men who are after you?" he asked.

I shrugged, "All I know is that they are Russian. Do you know who they are?"

"I do. How long have they been after you?"

"Since I turned sixteen," I answered.

His brows furrowed at my response.

"Why does that surprise you?"

"I guess I thought it was a new infatuation with you. I didn't realize it's been years of them coming after you," he admitted. "It doesn't make sense to me, Mia. You don't know who they are but they've been after you since you were sixteen?"

"I hate to break it to you, but it's the truth. I have no idea why all of a sudden they want me to go with them. What's his name? The head of their organization?"

"Nicholai Petrov. He has two sons and they are based out of New York."

New York? A wrinkle formed between my brows as I glanced at him.

"Why does this puzzle you, child?" he asked.

"Last time they found me I was residing in Florida." I stated.

Why would they be searching around Florida for me if they're based in New York? Or what if they were on vacation and saw me. *Did you do something to antagonize them?* Not that I could remember. In fact, I couldn't recall meeting them before that day they attacked when I was sixteen.

"It appears their only interests are to capture you regardless of where you are. What happened in Florida when they came for you?"

My eyes darted down to my hands as my knee began to bounce. Memories of Florida clouded my brain. Giovanni, his parents, the love I'd felt from all of them. The only place that had ever felt like home to me. *Stay focused, Mia.* I didn't look up until I'd pushed all my emotions from that time away. Bringing clarity and dominance to the forefront. I sat back in the chair, pressing my lips into a thin line.

"Why do you ask?"

"Maybe it'll help this time."

"I don't even know what they want from me, why would it help?"

"You have no idea?" Big Frank squinted at me, his head tilting to the right a bit to gauge if I were telling the truth. "None at all?"

"No." *If you tell them a short version of what happened, maybe they will know.* "All right, I'll give you the short version in exchange for any other information you can add."

"Deal."

"They came in the middle of the night. We ran but they captured the boy I loved and killed his family. They contacted me hours later through his phone. I went to them under the impression of a trade, my life for his."

Big Frank's head dipped; a sigh escaped him. He knew it before I had to say it. That must have been something the Russians were known for.

"They killed him, didn't they?"

I nodded. "They made me watch." I paused; glad I could transfer my emotions as I was sure I would have had a breakdown by now. "Then they turned on me. Told me I was being punished for being with an Italian. They claimed that I needed to be cleansed. I escaped them after four hours and thirty-eight minutes of torture."

"While they had you, did they indicate in any way what they were after you for?"

"I didn't speak Russian at the time. The only time they spoke to me in English was to tell me how filthy I was for loving someone who wasn't Russian. All I know is that they are very persistent. No matter how many times I evade them, they still search for me.

After I escaped them I found my way here. This is the longest I've been able to stay in one place before they found me."

"Are you Russian? From a Russian family?"

"No, that's the thing. I'm Italian."

Emilio scoffed. "Mia Clark doesn't sound very Italian."

Big Frank gave him a glare that told him to shut his mouth. My eyes shot bullets of anger at him. For some reason, he just rubbed me the wrong way. I wasn't sure if it was the catcalling incident or the way he carried himself around me. Like he was better than me because I was a woman. It made me want to puke.

"Mia Clark isn't my real name," I snapped at him.

The table around me became hushed. Every pair of eyes were locked on me as their bodies perked up. Emilio's were angry while the others remained full of curiosity. The gaze of the guy with the tattoo held so much intensity I had to look away. I waited quietly for one of them to say something. By the looks on their faces, I knew exactly what they wanted to ask.

But it was Big Frank who asked, "What's your real name?" He was now leaning forward in anticipation of my answer.

"I came here under an alias so it would be harder for them to find me. Clearly, it worked, it took them four years to find me again. I'm not going to give you my real identity so you can find me when I leave. I'd rather not have the pressure of two families after me."

"No one is going to chase you, Mia. You are free to go anytime."

I shook my head, "I don't mean to go home. Look, after the night I escaped, I made a set of rules for myself. Unfortunately,

I've broken rule number one being here. That means I can't stay. I need to relocate to somewhere that could buy me a few more years."

"What is rule number one?" he asked.

"Don't create leverage against yourself. I learned the hard way that allowing myself to have friends or caring about someone will give these people leverage over me. They will take that leverage and use it without question. It wouldn't matter if it were even a child. That's how sickening they are." I grimaced. "The situation that happened four years ago will only repeat itself if I stay. It's inevitable."

"You are saying they would come after your friends and loved ones you have here. We can protect them if that will ease your mind. Just give me their names and I can arrange it."

I closed my eyes with a deep breath, "Elliot has been a close friend whom I trust, I'm sure they have noticed. Don't let them harm him, he needs protection. They will come for him if they think it's a way to get to me, and let me admit to only you in this room, that it would be exactly that. I'd gladly trade my life for his. He is the only person I would do that for."

"Mia," Elliot said in my ear. "I would never ask you to trade your life for mine."

"If you have nothing else to tell me then I believe we are finished. I'm going to lead them away from here." I stood up, and said, "Thank you for your time tonight. Please consider this my resignation from The Core."

I walked to the door, hesitating before I could grasp the handle. *You should tell them about the rat.* If I did, maybe they could take care of it for me. I was positive they wouldn't let a rat stay in their organization for long. Not only would it look bad on them, but it would also allow the back and forth of information to continue. If he wasn't working with the Russians, I was sure they were enemies. That's what everything else online alluded to. I turned around, walking back to stand next to my chair. I kept my voice low, just in case they were listening on the other side of the door.

"Oh, and one last thing. I'm sure you already know that I am the one who chooses the exit routes for all missions. What you might not know is that the rule of thumb for a rogue is to always have a backup route. I present a primary and secondary route to the team to be approved for each mission. When the Russians swarmed me, I was forced to take the secondary exit route as they had blocked the first. When I turned the corner to do so, they were waiting for me. There were five different ways out of that building yet they were waiting at the secondary exit that had been predetermined and presented to the team."

"What are you saying?" Big Frank asked.

"You have a rat in your organization."

The room was silent, until Arturo asked, "How did you get out then?"

I gave him a twisted smile. "Like I said, the rule of thumb for a rogue, is always have a backup route. I always have a personal backup plan that only I know about just in case I find myself in a situation such as this. I will die before I let them capture me again. Thank you for the past four years. They were quite enjoyable. I think I'll probably miss it here."

I sat the string bag back on the table before finally walking out. It was time to move on. To find a new location to pretend to call home. The rest of the team was sitting on the couches when I walked out.

"See you Monday," I called to them, walking down the back hallway.

If there was a rat and it was one of them, I wasn't going to let them know I was running just yet. That way I'd get a head start on the Russians. I'd wait until Monday for them to figure it out on their own when I didn't show up for work. *Unless Big Frank tells them.* I doubted he would, knowing someone on the team was giving away information on the cases. It would be like giving the rat exactly what he wanted; information on me. I marched down the hall straight to Elliot's office. He opened the door as I walked up to it.

"We can figure this out Mia, you don't have to leave. We can—"

I held my hands up, stopping him.

"Elliot. I can't, but I need you to do something for me because I'm damn selfish."

"Anything."

I pulled the pictures from my pocket, revealing them to him. Placing the one of the family with the baby in his hand I watched him inspect it for a moment.

"These were in the manila envelope in the safe. I need you to figure out who this family is. The three pictures in there all somehow connect back to me. If you figure it out, text me a secure message. I will respond with a time that you can call me on a secure line. That way we're safe to discuss what you found."

"Are you sure? I can still keep digging for your real name as well. I don't mind."

"That's all right, you've helped so much. Just do this one last thing for me. I'll owe you big time and I hope that one day you can collect on that."

A delicate smile appeared on his lips.

"I'm sure I'll figure something out." He shifted his weight between his feet, pushing his glasses back into place with his pointer finger. "Can I—um—give you a hug?"

Instead of answering, I took a step forward, engulfing him in a hug.

"Thank you for everything," I said before pulling away. "If they get to you, have them call me. I'll be there."

He shook his head. "I wouldn't let you sacrifice yourself for me."

I gave him a half-smile, placing one hand on his cheek. "I was afraid of that."

"Be safe, Mia." He took my hand from his cheek, giving it a quick squeeze.

"Oh, I will."

After leaving the one picture with Elliot, I moved into the weapons room. Punching in my code, I stepped inside. The walls to the left and right were full of firearms. The left one was designated for handguns while the right was reserved for the more powerful automatic weapons. The wall straight ahead was full of drawers of knives and other hand weapons such as brass knuckles. I'd need a new knife since mine was on the ground somewhere outside that building. I moved to the exact drawer I needed.

"You know, stealing from the company you work for is a punishable offense."

I turned to see Dante leaning against the doorframe, his massive size claiming most of the space as he crossed his arms over his chest. With an eye roll, I pulled open the drawer that housed knives identical to the one I'd lost. I plucked one from its spot, claiming it as mine. I tucked it into my boot where the holster was.

"I don't work here anymore," I scoffed.

"I feel as though that makes it worse." He gave me a lazy smile before speaking again. "We can help you, you know? If we work together we can fight them off."

My entire body seized at the thought. To think that I would allow more bloodshed over me was something I swore would never happen again. Not after Giovanni.

"It won't happen again, Mia." His voice was soft now; careful as he knew he was toeing a touchy subject. "We won't get hurt like the one you loved. I'm sorry that you lost someone so close to you, I know you must be—"

"Stop," I interrupted.

I wasn't important enough for anyone to go to battle for. Their families didn't need to feel the soul-crushing despair of losing a loved one because of me. It would also require me to tell them the much longer, detailed version of what happened in Florida. *Don't do it.* No. I was going to face these men alone. Eventually, I'd find the one that tortured Giovanni and return the favor.

"Not an option. Have a good night, Dante."

With that I walked straight home, taking the long way just in case someone was following me. I'd managed to keep the location of my apartment a secret from everyone at work, aside from Big Frank who needed an address for proof of residence. I had my checks sent directly to a P.O. box that I emptied and cashed. I had a bank account only under my old name to use for emergencies. The rest was cash that I carried in my go-bag or random places in case of emergencies. I had a wad of cash stashed above the drop ceiling at the coffee shop. Some in my work locker. As far as I'd known, no one had ever followed me home to find out where I lived either. My eyes and ears became hyperaware of everything around me the further I made it from work. Each sound pulled my eyes to it, my heart racing with paranoia. A cold clammy sweat broke out across my body.

I'd locked the deadbolt and the lock on my bedroom door. I pressed my back against the door, releasing the breath I had held since I hit the first step into my building. My knees buckled and my body slid down the door. I knew they'd come. It was only a matter of time before they would find out where I lived. I took the fastest shower of my life to wash the day off. Instead of wearing pajamas to bed, I put on a parkour outfit. Then if they came in the middle of the night again, I'd be ready to go.

Although my sleep had been light I did manage to get a few hours before I got up that next morning. All I had left to do was get the zip drive of information I'd stored out of the kitchen wall. Using a suction cup, I stuck it on one of the tiles that made up the kitchen backsplash. It took some wiggling but out it popped revealing a cubby behind it that would shield my zip drive from intruders. When I tucked it into the smallest pocket of my backpack my eyes fell onto the picture Giovanni had given me. My thumb stroked his face in the picture as my mind took me back to years ago when we took it.

"What are your parents doing?" I asked him as we sat on the couch in the living room of my foster family's home.

"They are talking to your foster parents," he explained.

"Then why did they bring the guy in the suit? Where are they sending me now?"

"No one is sending you anywhere. We are going to let you decide where you go," he said, his brown eyes warm like melted chocolate.

"What does that mean?"

Giovanni's parents and the guy in the suit walked into the room with my foster parents. There was a tension between them. I met the eyes belonging to my foster father, waiting for him to say something. He was the ruler of the house. What he said went and he ruled with an iron fist in that if you didn't obey you'd be punished. I'd learned plenty of times to sneak food into my room I'd shared with another girl—as that was what he withheld most of the time—as a consequence for not following what he said.

"It's come to our attention that you've been sneaking out to intrude on this family's vacation," he snapped.

I stared into his eyes, waiting for my consequence but it never came. Instead, Giovanni's mother crouched down to my eye level.

"How would you like to come live with us Mia?" she offered.

I swallowed. "For how long?"

"Until you want to leave or are an adult."

"You want t-to adopt me?" I managed to choke out, overcome with emotion.

"We would love that… if you'd have us." Giovanni's father smiled. "What do you say, kid?"

I nodded through my tears as they spilled from my eyes. Giovanni took one of my hands, lacing his fingers through mine.

"Do you have anything you want to bring?" he asked. "I can help you pack."

"She can take the clothes on her back, that is all she came with." My foster mother spat, crossing her arms over her chest. "We will not give her anything we have bought as it doesn't belong to her."

"She doesn't need anything you gave her. She will have everything she wants with us," Giovanni growled at them. He brought the back of my hand to his lips, kissing it gently. "Don't worry Mia, you will have everything you've ever dreamed of. I'll get a job if I have to."

I was in a daze the entire ride back to their home. It wasn't until we stood outside their house at the base of their front porch steps that it finally hit me. I'd been given a chance to have a family, one that had already shown how much more they cared for me than any foster family I'd been placed in.

"Turn around and smile!" Giovanni's mom had sung, "we have to remember this moment as your first day in your new home."

Giovanni had tugged me to sit beside him, slinging his arm around my shoulders.

A tear had fallen, hitting my hand. The cool wetness pulled me from my memory.

"Miss you, G. I'll avenge your death, I promise. I just need more information first," I whispered.

I gently put it away with the other two pictures from the manilla envelope. Over the next few minutes, I went over my checklist in my mind, making sure I had everything. With everything mentally checked off, I slung my backpack over my shoulder, securing it onto my back. I found myself standing in the middle of my living room, ready to run yet again. I couldn't believe it took them this long to find me. I reached back, feeling my gun that was safely housed in the front most pocket of my backpack. No matter how many times I checked to make sure it was still there, I was still paranoid I'd leave unarmed. I couldn't take any chances with these men.

Time to say goodbye, Mia.

EGO

I WAS THREE STEPS DOWN the stairway when I heard men speaking in Russian. Their voices carried from the hallway up through the stairwell. "We take her alive, that's what the boss said." Then I heard the click of a gun and another voice responding, "We will see how much of a fight she puts up."

I swallowed hard. *Oh, fuck Mia.* I was going to have to fight my way out of this one.

They looked up the moment I peeked over the banister at them. They were two floors below me and there were three of them. They took off, sprinting up the stairs toward me. *Fuck! Guess you're going to the roof.* I took the steps two at a time. Their hurried footsteps were getting closer. I was going to have to jump to the next building. I'd done it before, just never with the extra weight of my go-bag on my back. Shoving open the door to the roof, I didn't stop, launching myself across the six-foot wide gap between buildings. The amount of adrenaline I had must have given me a boost as I cleared it more than I did before. Rolling forward to my feet I continued to run.

Gunshots echoed as I ran to the next building. They were now trying to kill me. So much for *'we take her alive, that's what the boss said'.* I dove behind an old brick chimney sticking out of the building. I dug my gun out of my backpack, taking a deep breath to steady my hand. They were yelling at me to stop running and come back to them. *Yeah sure, let me just come with you assholes. I did that once and didn't care for the outcome.* Turning back toward them I fired two shots, seeing one guy fall to the ground. I had gotten his shoulder and chest. When the two other men turned to check on their associate, I climbed down the fire escape.

Think Mia, it's not the first time you only had this backpack full of stuff to your name. The plan was to head to the coffee shop and borrow someone's laptop to buy a plane ticket under my old alias. There's no way I could go there now. Places I always went—the coffee shop, the park, and headquarters—were now off-limits. Where did I never go? The beach? It would have too many people. Although I could blend in, there would be a lot of innocent bystanders that might get hurt. Church? There wouldn't be enough people to blend there. Churches got out about five minutes ago and they would be empty soon. I'd be a sitting duck. Regardless of where I went, I had to lead them away from the city. I couldn't let them hurt Elliot or any of the other members of S-Rank for that matter. Rat or not, three of them were innocent. *Dammit, Mia, you let them get too close! Now you care if they get hurt. Why the hell did you let yourself do this again? Did you not learn anything from the last time you got close to someone?*

I hustled around the city blocks just to make it as far away from the Russians as possible. I jogged toward a group of people conversing outside a church. They seemed to be dressed for service. I didn't think churches got out that late? Then again, I'd never been to one. I slowed my pace, hoping to blend with the crowd. As I was scanning my surroundings I noticed Dante, Salvatore, Arturo, and the blue-eyed one in the tangle of people. *Oh great, please don't see me.* I tried to keep my head down, pulling my hood further over my face. When a car came screeching to a stop next to me, it pulled everyone's attention to it. I looked over. *Oh shit, it was the Russian guys from the rooftop...minus one.* When they jumped out, I tried to run. The one in the driver's seat grabbed my backpack pulling me back toward him.

"Time to go," he said in Russian.

I elbowed him in the ribs, causing him to drop his hands. When I turned around, I punched him in his throat. He stumbled backward, reaching for his neck as he coughed. I then struck the pressure point at his temple with the side of my hand, knocking him out with one swift hit. That's when the passenger of the car pulled a gun on me. The crowd behind me screamed and I'm sure began to scatter.

My hood had fallen in the fight and I peeked back to see Dante and crew watching my every move like hawks waiting to swoop in to help. *Great.* Glancing back at the guy with the gun I grabbed his wrist, twisting it back into an armbar he let go of the gun. I picked it up, pointing it at him.

Speaking in Russian so no one else could understand me, I said, "What do you want from me?"

"You were promised to Nicholai Petrov."

Speaking back in English I scoffed. "You can tell Nicholai Petrov he can go fuck himself."

I shot his left knee so he couldn't chase me. He screamed, collapsing to the ground in pain. His hands went straight to his injury as blood poured out of it. I didn't hesitate before turning to take off. Dante stopped me as I ran by.

"Mia," he urged. "We can help you."

I looked him in the eyes, and pleaded, "Stay out of it, it's not safe."

"Just let us help."

I pointed the gun at his chest as he stepped toward me. He stiffened, keeping his eyes locked on mine.

"No one can help me," I stated. "Don't get involved. We are not friends."

I ran into the street, a car coming straight at me. I jumped onto the hood, ran over the top, rolled off the back end, and continued my run without missing a step. I snuck around the back alleys until I found a place to sleep, an empty lifeguard's tower at the beach. Although I wouldn't call it sleeping. More like laying there, hyperaware of every damn sound and movement for hours on end. I had the gun clutched tightly in my hand, finger off the trigger, of course.

That morning I walked around the other side of town for a while. I'd not been on the far side of town in all four years I've lived here. It had a warm aura to it, like it was a community in and of itself. There was less hustle and bustle than downtown. I came across this little Italian coffee shop. My body craved caffeine. I walked inside, keeping my head down and hood up. Ordering a cappuccino and a brioche I sat down at a table. I made sure my back was to the wall so no one could come up behind me. Although I had taken care of most of the men this Petrov guy sent after me, I was sure he would send more. Taking the first sip I managed to steal a moment of peace to myself, letting my eyes fall shut to take in the taste. It was the best damn coffee I've had in my life. I stayed there for hours, watching people come in and out. The others around me enjoyed their coffee, laughing as they went about their simple lives.

I left mid-afternoon and walked toward the library, thinking it would be pretty cleared out at this time on a Monday. Just enough for me to blend in. I was right. I headed back to the computers to buy a ticket to New York. They would never assume I'm going straight to the heart of their own territory. They wouldn't even be looking for me there. It was my thought that I'd be able to evade them further. They would be monitoring the flights out for the next few days. Instead of an immediate flight, I choose one for three days from now.

After successfully printing the ticket under my old alias, I started my walk back to the other side of town. It gave me an odd feeling of being safe—one I didn't completely trust but welcomed nonetheless. A tiny bookstore off the side of an alley caught my eye. I hid out there 'reading' until they closed. I knew better than to sleep in the same place twice, so I walked until I found a dimly lit alley that looked as clean as an alley could be. I sat behind a dumpster, making note that I would need to buy a new hoodie after being by the horrendous smell of rotting garbage all night.

The next day I walked by a boutique and bought a new hoodie, with cash. I waited until I could get out of there to change into it on a side street. I tossed my old hoodie in a random dumpster I passed. I went back to the little Italian coffee shop. Just like the day before, I got a cappuccino and brioche. I made sure to sit in the same spot so I could still observe every person who came and went. I noticed a lot of customers were the same as the day before. They must keep a lot of regulars, mostly Italians too. They spoke it in there, then again the little old lady at the counter spoke it to them like they were all friends. I tried to listen to the words just in case they figured out my identity. Although the people after me were Russian I wasn't going to take any chances. After that, I roamed the streets for hours, all through the night. I didn't sleep; instead, I walked.

By Wednesday, even though I knew better, I went back to that coffee shop. The little Italian lady smiled as she greeted me. My eyelids were heavy weights on my face as I walked up to the counter. Hoping the caffeine would help, I attempted to give her a smile.

"Are you new to the area?" she asked.

I nodded, and said, "yes, ma'am."

Keeping my head down I got situated at the same table before digging through my backpack. Retrieving my phone, I turned it on for the first time since I took off. Flipping the button on the side to silent so it wouldn't assault the happy aura of the coffee shop with any noises. I had tons of texts from my teammates in our S-Rank group chat. They all offered to help. *Clearly, it was no longer a secret you were leaving.* They couldn't. It wasn't safe for them. I checked the time; two minutes. I had to shut it back off so Elliot couldn't trace my location. I knew he'd be waiting for it to ping, no matter how much I assured him I'd be fine. Five minutes later as my mind had slipped into neutral, I heard the little old lady behind the counter giving a description of what I was wearing.

"Yes...black hoodie, running shorts...purple hair?" she asked, confused.

My head snapped to her. She was on the phone and I'd been discovered. Our eyes met, and my heart sank. *Shit, so much for good coffee.* I snatched up my backpack and rushed out as fast as I could. I didn't stop running until I found a convenience store. I bought a burner cell phone before walking to the pier. I wasn't sure who the old lady was talking to, but considering she was Italian I was sure it was someone from The Core. I called the secure conference room. A number we were required to memorize. I was hoping I could just leave a message on the line, but they answered.

"Where the hell are you?" Spencer asked. "What happened to 'see you Monday'? It's now Wednesday and we've yet to see you."

Okay, maybe they didn't know everything.

"Who can hear me?" I asked in Russian, knowing Scarlet was there.

"S-Rank and the extraction team," Scarlet answered in English.

"Are you hurt?" Elliot asked.

"No."

"What the hell happened, Mia?" Luke said.

"Where are you?" Spencer repeated.

"Listen, I'm going to keep telling you to stay out of it. I don't work there any longer. Stop tracking my location. I'm leaving California, you won't see me again after this. It's better for everyone this way."

As they started to protest, I growled into the phone. It was time for them to understand why I didn't want them involved.

"Listen to me," I ordered, "last time this happened I just moved across the country and look how long it took them to find me. These are dangerous people and I shouldn't have let you get this close. Stay away from me and don't try to help."

"That's not going to happen," Spencer said, his voice tight. "You are a part of our family."

I laughed darkly through the words, "They killed my only family. The last time they found me they tortured the person trying to protect me to his death. To top that off, they made me fucking watch. I'm leaving and not coming back. Tell your extraction team to go home."

I hung up, tossing the phone into the water below, getting as far away as I could from that spot. Just like last time I had to move, I allowed myself to cry for a couple of minutes so I wouldn't break down completely. Although I was a master at controlling my emotions, I knew that every mind had its limits—even mine. As humans, we could only handle so much. So I gave my body what it needed.

That night as I wiped my cheeks clean of the last of my tears, I steeled myself once again. *Okay Mia girl, time to get it together. Maybe New York isn't the best option. If they found us there we'd be completely surrounded. We should go to a different city. Where are we moving? It only took them two years to find me in Florida, but four years to find me in California.* My eyes widened...I could use the ticket I bought as a decoy. Then I had to go somewhere else though. I could go to Vegas. I formulated a new plan in my head.

Step one: find someone to bribe to go to New York

Step two: using cash, buy a bus ticket to...where? Vegas? Maybe I'll try Las Vegas. It was a big place and I could probably get another four years out of it before this happened again.

Step three: contact my 'ego'

An 'ego' was a person in the underground world that created new identities for people.

Step four: start researching Nicholai Petrov.

At dawn, I started going through the plan once more in my mind. Then it hit me. The information I had on my 'ego' was back at my apartment. *Should we chance it?* It was early, maybe they wouldn't be watching it yet. *They are watching it, girl.* I growled, wondering how many days it would take me to find a new ego in Vegas. The only downfall with that is I'd have to wait to be vetted by a new one. That's how they make sure you're not a cop. The regular guy I went to would get me right in. I had to chance it. The longer my identity stayed Mia Clark the more chances it gave Petrov to find me in Vegas.

I snuck back toward my apartment. I took the back way, staying off the busy main streets where cars could drive by and see me. Quietly taking the stairs two at a time I listened to my surroundings with each step. It was quiet, too quiet. I grasped my doorknob, twisting it to see if it was locked. It wasn't. That meant someone had been there or was still inside. I held my breath as I twisted it, cracking the door slightly to peek inside. Sure enough, I heard voices, but not the voices I expected.

"Why do we have to go through her stuff? I feel like I'm betraying her, like it feels wrong. She's one of us," the voice complained.

"It's to help her. Get searching for anything you think could help us."

Dante. Fucking great. *You're not going to find anything.* I thought to myself. I pushed the door open all the way, walking in like it was a normal day. The sound of the door clicking shut didn't cause them to stop talking as I thought it would.

"Hey boss, we can't find anything. Can we try a different strategy, like, I don't know, calling her maybe?" Arturo asked.

"That wouldn't work, my phone is off," I stated, walking into the kitchen.

They stood there for a moment, dumbfounded. I carried on, walking around them to retrieve a screwdriver from under the kitchen sink. Their footsteps were right behind mine as I made my way back to the living room.

"Mia, can we please talk?" Dante asked.

"That sounds like the start of a breakup," I snorted, sitting cross-legged on the floor in front of an outlet.

The door opened, then shut again. I glanced back to see Salvatore and the quiet one. He met my gaze without blinking, something unusual about his eyes; I couldn't tell what color they were from here. The way he was looking back at me, so intensely, held me frozen for a moment. Although he'd not said a word to me there was an air of dominance about him. It gave off the impression that he may be the one in charge of the group. Dante was just the annoyingly vocal one. Regardless, they were all with me in the apartment which meant more obstacles between myself and the door. *Now you're going to have to escape them.*

"What are you doing?" Arturo asked.

"Getting something I left," I answered as I unscrewed the outlet plate.

"We can help protect you, you know?" Dante stated. "Where have you been sleeping?"

"The streets. Different ones, with one eye open. My plane doesn't leave for two more days. Until then it's me and the city." I shrugged like it was no big deal. "I don't want your help. That's the part you don't understand. I'm sure you could protect me, but damsel in distress is not in my character. Also, I can take care of myself. I'm pretty badass, just in case you haven't noticed."

"How can you take this situation so lightly?" Salvatore asked. "They are trying to kill you."

I pulled the plate out, retrieving the business card for my 'ego' before screwing it back into place. I tucked it into my backpack.

"See that's where you're wrong. They want me alive."

"For what purpose?"

"I have no idea, but I'm not going to stay to find out either." I shrugged on my backpack, and asked, "What were you looking for in my kitchen?"

"Anything that could help?"

I rolled my eyes. "You're not going to find anything. Everything I have on the Russians is always on me. Unless you are searching *me* then you're wasting your time. If you'd like to keep your hands, then I suggest you don't try it."

I moved toward the door. Salvatore blocked my path.

"We can't let you go, Mia."

"You know, I was afraid of that." I sighed.

There was a moment when we were all still before I kicked him in his shin. When he went down, I ran for the door. I ran up the stairs, knowing I could lose them if I jumped rooftops again. Out they came as another chase ensued. I took the steps two at a time, my legs burning as I exerted my muscles harder than I ever have. These guys were faster than the Russians. Just as I had last time, I didn't stop when I flung the door open. Sprinting across the roof, I leaped across the gap between the two buildings. Rolling to my feet I looked back at them to see if they would jump across to me. When they stopped at the edge of the building and looked down at the drop, I knew they weren't going to attempt it.

"Holy shit, you are insane!" Dante shouted as he shook his head in disbelief.

"Stay out of my business," I yelled. "Have a nice life."

"Oh trust me, they will."

My head snapped to see who spoke behind me. It was the Russian guy from the coffee shop. His wide shoulders upright, chest puffed out in dominance. The predatorial glare he was shooting my way sent a chill up my spine. One that wasn't good. I reached back for my gun, finding nothing in its place. Then remembered my gun was in my backpack, shit. *How could you have been so care-less Mia?* I took a few steps back toward the edge of the building.

"Let's go," he ordered. "My boss is waiting."

My brows furrowed. "What does he want with me?"

"He will tell you when we see him."

The back of my legs hit the side of the building. I stepped up onto the edge, looking down at the drop. There were balconies on both buildings that stuck out. That's when I knew my way out.

"I'm not going to see him. He's a Russian asshole."

He stepped toward me yelling "you bitch" in Russian. I twisted, launching myself toward the balcony of my building. Dante and the crew ran to the edge, reaching for me as if they were going to catch me. When I caught the edge of the balcony, I twisted my body to face the Russian again, a sly smirk on my face.

"How does it feel to be outrun and outplayed by a woman, twice?" I spat, flipping him off.

Jumping back and forth between the balconies I finally dropped down to the concrete alley. I walked past the library only to see two guys in all black scanning the area when one pointed at me and yelled, "There she is!"

I took off, sprinted as fast as I could until my lungs felt like they were going to burst. I took every twist, turn, and jump I could to get rid of him. Finally stopping to look around, I had no idea where I was. It was getting dark by the time I found myself in a somewhat familiar alley. Sliding down the wall of the building, I hugged my knees to my chest, and rested the back of my head against the wall.

SHADOW

I FELL ASLEEP. THE REALIZATION made my body scare itself awake with a jump. A door opened to my right as I yawned. Out stepped the little Italian coffee shop lady. I scrambled to my feet as our eyes met. She was going to call whoever she was talking to and tell them she saw me.

"Wait, *piccola,*" she called.

My feet stopped. Not sure why, but they did. When I turned back to face her, she walked up to me. She looked me up and down like she was inspecting me for injuries.

"I was informed I should give you shelter; no one will know where you are here. Please come." She pointed up to the building. "We have an apartment above the shop."

I shook my head, and asked, "Who were you talking to on the phone about me?"

"Dante Luciano...come," she repeated as she put her hand on

my back, ushering me toward the door. "I won't call them. I won't call anyone, just rest here."

Fuck. Dante...again. When will he leave me alone? Better yet, *why* wouldn't he leave me alone? I doubted he just wanted to help. Everyone had an underlying motive. But I let her show me up to the apartment. The moment she was gone I scanned the entire place, making mental notes of all the doors and windows. Then I checked every window to see which ones would be best to exit out of in the case of someone coming to bust down the front door.

I locked the deadbolt, heading to the bathroom. I locked that door as well, so whoever came would have two doors to get through. My backpack slid down my shoulder, landing on top of the toilet seat. I pulled one of my three outfits out to change into. It was time for a fresh set of clothes. The shower had shampoo and body wash already. Searching through each cabinet in the bathroom I finally found the towels. The rest of them were empty. The shower felt amazing. Coming out of it I felt more optimistic and determined. But a knock at the door caused my body to tense and go on high alert. Slowly reaching for my gun, I stood up, tucking it into the back of my shorts.

"Piccola?"

It was that little lady. Her voice was pleasant and soft. She gave me a warm smile when I opened the door for her.

"Come, get some coffee and food."

I grabbed my backpack, pulling the bottom of my sweatshirt down over my gun. My hood covered my hair and shielded my face from anyone who would be down there. After getting my things I sat in what was becoming my regular spot. It wasn't until I looked around to scan the area that I noticed the entire place was like a ghost town. I started to panic, especially when she sat down across from me. Instinctively, I reached for my bag. Her face fell.

"Don't leave, rest here."

"It'll put you in danger," I argued, and started to stand.

She laughed, causing me to pause, "Oh *piccola*, if you only knew the life I've lived. Then you wouldn't be worrying about me."

I sat back down. "How do you know Dante?"

She took a sip of her coffee, "A question for a question, that's my price."

It was the same exact thing Big Frank had said. I was momentarily taken aback by it, chewing on the inside of my lip. I twisted my ceramic mug on the table as I did. If I agreed, she could give me information about how she's connected. But then she'd ask questions on behalf of Dante. *Or would she?* I met her gaze as she waited patiently for me to answer.

"All right." I nodded in agreement.

"Dante is my grandson's right-hand man. They grew up together. He's like a second grandson to me. My turn; why are you running?"

Her question was straight to the point. She didn't ask my name or where I was from. Instead, she asked that. It also told me that Dante didn't give her specifics. Either that or she didn't ask.

"To survive. Are you Big Frank's mom?"

Her lips turned into a smile as she chuckled.

"Big Frank is my son, yes. Although when his father was alive he was Little Frank," she noted with a wink. "How did you put our relationship together?"

"When I had a meeting with him about our mission, he said the same thing you did. A question for a question."

"He got it from his mamma." She chuckled.

Her bright demeanor made me more relaxed; I even cracked a smile. One that disappeared the second she started asking more questions."

"*Piccola*, so many people want to help you, why choose to run? Why not accept the help?"

She wasn't pressuring me to change my mind about accepting help. Her tone was absent of persuasion or force, but full of wonder.

"They don't need to be involved. I don't even know why these people are after me." I sighed, digging in my bag for the picture I carried with me. "Look." I slid her the picture. "I was fourteen in this picture. The boy next to me, his name was Giovanni. He tried to help me fight these people and—" my breath caught in my throat.

She reached out to hold my hand. I steeled myself, pulling my hand away. No tears were going to spill from my eyes as I transferred my emotions to that of feeling indifferent.

"They made me watch as they murdered him," I said as I took the picture back. "I won't let that happen again. I stay alone, I fight alone, that way they have no leverage against me."

She nodded like she understood. I could see she had pain in her eyes, but she wasn't going to share it with me. I finished off my brioche and coffee as she waited for me to ask my question.

"Why is Dante so hell-bent on helping me?"

Her eyebrows flickered up to her forehead. She took a sip of her coffee in an attempt to hide her smile. When she sat it back down she was quiet for a moment.

"There are times when people just want to help a friend. There are other times they are being pushed to help due to someone asking them to do so."

"Which category does Dante fall under?"

"I believe both. He wants you safe and his boss also wants you safe. He's going to at least try to do everything he can to show you he can help you."

I rolled my eyes. "I don't want help."

"I understand. I will be sure to relay the information."

"I appreciate that Mrs. Sartori."

She chuckled, "Please child, call me Nonna."

I retired to my temporary room after that. Sitting on the bed I stared at the picture of Giovanni and me. He had given me the picture the day before the Russian guys came for me. Living with him for those two years was the only time I could ever remember feeling...loved. My life had become satisfyingly normal. From going to school to hanging out with Giovanni at the park. His mom even taught me how to bake and his father taught us parkour tricks. They accepted me even when I got angry and never deprived me of food when I argued. Even while I went through the teenage phase of thinking I was an adult and could make my own decisions regardless of what they told me, they didn't bat an eye. At the end of every day, there was no doubt in my mind that they loved me, they made sure of it. I put it away, covering myself up in bed. My backpack and gun slept next to me that night, just in case.

The next day, I walked around the beach, offering two women the ticket before a third excitedly agreed. I gave her $500 cash to not only forget my face but to sweeten the deal. Walking to a bus station I bought my bus ticket for Vegas. Hopefully, the Russians would follow the plane to New York since it would cause their trackers to ding. *Oh shit, that means it would also ping on Elliot's.* I sighed, finding another store to buy a burner. It took two rings on the secure line for Scarlet to answer.

"Why New York? And who is Mia Davis?"

Elliot was a better hacker than I'd expected. I'd bought the ticket under my old alias. *Does this mean he's digging into your past?* I couldn't help but laugh, of course, she would ask that.

"Relax, is Elliot there?"

"I'm here," his voice was relieved and ready to help, "what do you need?"

"Just you, no one else."

"All right, hold on, I'll call this number back on a secure line from my office."

I hung up without another word, walking to a new location while waiting. I sat down on a bench, watching the people walk around me. They went about their day not caring who was around them. Who might be watching them. The violent vibration of the phone in my hand snapped me out of my fog.

"Hey," I answered, "are you alone?"

He paused, then said, "Yes?"

I laughed. "You're a terrible liar, Hacker. Who is with you?"

"The extraction team. They can also hear you."

"Really Elliot?" Dante complained.

"What? She probably figured as much. She's not naive." He argued, "tell me what you need Mia."

"Find anything for me?" I asked.

"You want me to tell you right now?"

"Yes."

"I am running their faces through facial recognition. I haven't gotten anything yet. By the styling of their clothes, the picture appears to have been taken about twenty years ago."

"Let me know the second you get something," I tell him. "I'm leaving soon and my phone will be off for a while. I'm going to get a new one with my new identity. Then I'll text you a very specific sentence so you'll know it's me."

"What sentence?"

"You'll know it's me."

"All right, what else can I do?"

"Nothing at the moment. Thanks, Elliot."

"Be safe, Mia."

"Safe is my middle name."

"Oh, I was under the impression it was badass."

I laughed. "That too. Oh, and Dante?"

"Yeah?" his voice moved closer to the phone.

"Thanks."

"Don't mention it."

"I have to go. Bye, Hacker."

"Bye, Rogue."

I hung up, turning it off and putting it in my backpack. The sun felt good on my face, but I knew I had to hide it again. My bus left in two hours. I had left the little old lady a note and some cash. I wasn't going back there. I decided to wait it out a couple of blocks from the station.

As we boarded, I sat all the way at the back of the bus, next to the emergency exit. Then no one would be behind me. This also meant that I could see every person, every movement, and being by the window, everyone that approached the door to get on. Wiggling back and forth in my seat to get comfortable I watched out the window. It was going to be a six-and-a-half-hour ride to Vegas. I welcomed it with open arms since I didn't have to worry about being attacked on the bus. Even getting an hour of light semi-paranoid sleep.

My first task off the bus was to contact my 'ego.' Then I could start over again with a new name. I called him only to find out that he retired and was no longer in the business. *Can anything else go wrong?* I now had to find a new one. That only opened the door for the Russians to search for me under my old name, instead of having a new one to cover my tracks once they see my decoy was a decoy.

I walked down a couple of alleys looking for a backstreet bar. Finding one, I stepped inside. It was dimly lit and full of smoke. I sat down at the corner to keep my eyes on the door. I ordered a drink, waiting for my opportunity to ask the bartender about an 'ego.' It was crazy the kind of knowledge bartenders had. Customers would freely tell them things in confidence. When I finished my drink, he walked over with a smile just like I knew he would.

"Would you like another?"

"Actually, can I get an 'ego'?"

Surprise crossed his face for half a second before he nodded. He put down a napkin, then sat a shot on top of it. I slid him some cash, taking the shot. I balled the napkin in my hand, walking out before reading it.

1792 Willow Dr.

Suite E

Two days @ 2:00pm

Fuck yeah, he was faster than the previous guys I used. Hopefully, he was cheaper too. Next, I had to find a hotel that would allow me to use cash only. Most wanted a card for 'insurance purposes' even if you paid in cash. I was ready to call it a night and sleep on the street when I found a motel. It was sketchy as hell and I was almost positive I saw a drug exchange happen in the parking lot. But hey, it's better than the side of the street. And who was I to judge after the life I lived? Walking over to my room I pulled my hood down. It was a freeing and short-lived moment of peace.

Sitting at the table in my room that night I found myself staring at the picture again. Did he know what was going to happen? He had to have known; his videos implied it. Why would he give me a picture taken from that day? Maybe it meant nothing, and I was just trying to make it mean something.

By eight thirty I was going stir crazy, wondering if it would be safe to go on a walk. *Like you haven't been walking for the past five days aimlessly around the city.* A knock on the door caused me to grab my gun. I went to the door, listening for voices. Silence. When they knocked again, I looked through the peephole. Fuck. My. Life. I swung open the door.

"How long have you known my location," I asked.

Dante gave me a smile, and answered, "Since you boarded the bus. Caught you on the bus station camera."

I sighed in defeat, at least it would be entertainment for the night. Stepping aside I let him in. He sat down at the table. I joined him, watching him look at the picture on the table.

"Who's this?" he asked. "Is it Giovanni?"

"How do you know his name?"

"Nonna." He grinned. "She said you talked about him with her." *Curse that adorable old lady.*

"Yeah, that's him." I glanced down at my hands and cleared my throat. "Why are you here?"

"To bring you back home."

"I don't have a home."

"Yes, you do. It's with The Core. Whether you want to admit it or not, you have a lot of people who care about you. We all want to help."

"You shouldn't want to help. I understand the S-rank crew wanting me to come back but you and those other guys I don't even know! Besides, no one in that building knows who I really am. It's better to just make a clean break again."

His brows furrowed as I let out a frustrated groan at myself. Why did things just spill right out when I talked to him?

"Mia," he said softly. "I'm your shadow."

He said it like I should know what it meant. But I had no fucking idea what he was talking about. I rubbed my temples with my fingers. The situation was becoming more complicated and it was the last thing I needed. The more they followed me the easier it would be to find and track my movements through them. I let out a frustrated sigh.

"My what? What the hell is going on?"

"Every member of S-Rank gets assigned a person who helps keep tabs on them while they work; their shadow. We are on call for every mission and we also make up the extraction team if needed. My job is to help keep you safe if things go south. Which you are not making easy on me."

"You weren't the guy in the closet from the mission before last. Was that another shadow? Do I have two?"

"No, just me. My boss shadowed you on your last mission."

"Big Frank shadowed me?"

"No, not *the* boss, *my* boss."

"Who's your boss?"

"His son."

"Why did he shadow me?"

"To make sure you were safe." He paused to let me process what he'd just told me before continuing. "Look, the point is, you're making my job harder than it has to be. The Core has the extraction team for this reason, you don't have to run. We can handle it."

"These Russians aren't after me because of anything related to the Core!" I gritted my teeth. "Leave Dante, and don't come back.

You don't want to get into my mess and I don't want you complicating it any further."

He stood, handed my picture back to me, and nodded toward my backpack.

"Get your stuff, time to head back for the night."

"I'm not going back."

"Yes, you are. We have a plan and need you there."

I crossed my arms in protest. "Get out," I demanded.

"Okay," he said, and rolled his eyes, walking to the door.

I thought he was leaving, but when he opened it, in walked Arturo and Salvatore. I hurriedly put the picture in my backpack so they wouldn't see it. Arturo began to approach me. I aimed my gun at him, causing him to freeze. The entire room fell into a tense silence.

"What are you doing?" I asked.

"Mia, put the gun down," Dante ordered.

"I don't follow orders from you. Get out—all three of you."

"Come on Mia, I don't want to fight you, just come with us," Arturo said.

"Get out!" I growled.

He moved fast without hesitation, knocking my gun from my hands. I kicked him in the leg as he stepped closer. I threw myself across the bed, rolling to my feet in a fighting stance. Arturo groaned, mumbling something under his breath I couldn't hear. He swung but it was slow, almost like he wanted me to block it. I did, flawlessly punching his side and turning around to make my way to the door. His two strong arms came from behind me, encircling my own at the elbows. *Shit Mia, don't hold back if you want to get out of this.* I kicked my legs up, meeting with Salvatore's stomach to send him backward. The force caused Arturo, who had a hold of me, to also fall back. I rolled over him, getting to my feet just as he did.

"Mia please, I don't want to hit you," Arturo begged.

"Then move out of my way and you won't have to."

"I can't do that, our boss wants to speak with you."

"I don't care to speak to him."

I swung, and he blocked it. Then the reverse happened. His movements were faster, like he wasn't holding back this time. It was getting hard for me to keep up. I wasn't sure how long I lasted, but I missed a block and his fist met with my jaw. It knocked me off balance, sending me crashing into the wall before hitting the floor. I shook my head in an attempt to regain my composure. I got to my feet, angrier than before. My fists were clenched so tight my nails dug into my palms. I transferred all my emotions into rage, fighting harder than I ever realized I could. That was until all three of them stormed me at once.

I ended up with my hands zip-tied together and slung over Arturo's shoulder. Dante collected my gun and backpack from the floor.

"This is kidnapping," I spat.

Arturo shoulders rocked as he laughed under me. "We've done worse. I don't know why you insisted on fighting. There were three of us and one of you.

"I should have shot you when I had the chance," I grumbled.

"Lesson learned for what I'm sure will be a next time," Salvatore quipped, opening the car door. "Time to go home."

A FUCKING ROGUE

THEY HAD A DRIVER. THIS meant that I was stuck in the back with the three big-ass men that came for me. Each time we stopped for gas I told them I had to use the bathroom to see what their mechanics would be. What I didn't expect is for all three of them to escort me to and from. They also checked the bathroom for other people each time before I went in there. It was going to be harder than I thought to get away from them.

My eyes scanned the area, noting all the options I had to evade them once the car was parked back at The Core. Then I went through each scenario of me getting out each way. It came down to who I was fast enough to beat, Arturo to my right or Dante to my left. Sal was behind me, so he'd be stuck in the third-row seat, and useless, as I took off.

"Stop plotting," Dante ordered.

"I'm not plotting anything…except your murder right now." I squinted at him.

This only made him chuckle. Arturo had been silent the entire time, glancing my way every so often.

"How is your jaw?" he finally said.

"That's none of your concern," I snapped.

"Oh, but it is." Salvatore grinned, patting Arturo on the back of the shoulder. "How do you think the boss is going to react when you tell him you hit her?"

Arturo's face twisted. It wasn't fear that flashed through his eyes but regret. He ran his hand down his face as he let out a sigh. It appeared he was carrying a heavy weight on his shoulders by the way his body was slouched over. *Was it guilt?*

"I'll take the consequences given. I just hope it's not death."

I thought he was joking but the serious look on his face told me he wasn't. It was then I noticed how tired he looked. The dark circles under his eyes were just the first indication. His bloodshot eyes were the next.

"Mia." Dante pulled my attention to him. "Just hear us out before you attempt to run."

"I'll think about it."

"What would make you stay?" Salvatore asked.

I gave his question some thought. Would anything make me stay? If I felt safe I'd stay, right? I looked down at my feet. *What did safe even feel like?* I don't think I remember what it was like to be carefree. To not have to watch my back or cover my tracks.

"Nothing."

"You have friends here." Dante smiled, nudging me with his elbow. "You said you don't do friends, but there are quite a few people that want to help and protect you."

My stomach dropped; this was not what I wanted to hear anymore. I didn't need anyone to sacrifice themselves or chance death to protect me.

I met his gaze. "No one needs to die for me. I'll turn myself over before that happens and they know that. Which is why I don't have friends."

I felt like I was slowly suffocating. The closer we got, the more I tried to calm myself, taking slow, measured breaths. We pulled into the garage at headquarters. The dread I felt inside my body was heavy, weighing me down to the seat. My knees were pressed together tightly, my zip-tied hands resting on them close to my body. The weight lifted as the cool outside air hit my face. Dante chuckled as my eyes lit with excitement. He was blocking the doorway, his figure so large he took up the entire space.

"It's cute that you think you are walking," he said with a smile.

"I know how to walk, asshole," I snapped. "Let me walk."

"Hell no, you're going to run and not only are you fast, but you do some crazy shit when you run."

"Yeah, like jump buildings and scale down the balconies," Salvatore added.

He leaned against the door. "My job is to know where you are and help to keep you safe. I lost your location for almost an entire week. My boss gave me shit about it every five minutes until I found you. It's not going to happen again."

"It will if I want it to."

He reached his hand out for me to take as he shook his head. When I didn't move, he looked past me.

"Arturo," he said, and nodded toward me.

Hands grabbed my waist, pulling me backward across the seat. Next thing I know I'm upside down slung over his shoulder. He didn't put me down until we were on the fifth floor of the building, which was also the floor I worked on. His hands stayed firmly on my hips as he sat me gently onto my feet. Dante pulled a knife from his back pocket, flinging it open in one swift flick of his wrist. I tensed, taking a step backward. I wasn't scared that he was going to kill me, but memories of the intense pain from my previous torture wracked my brain. My body hit the wall as they all stared at me.

"It's just to cut the zip-tie," he explained. "Mia, I'm not going to hurt you."

"I don't trust you," I said, surprising myself with my honesty.

He shook his head, one hand coming up to rub his chin.

"Why should I believe you? So far all you three have done is stalk me, go through my apartment, follow me to Vegas, and kidnap me."

"We were trying to help you," Salvatore stated. "If we wanted to kill you, you'd be dead by now. We just spent six hours in a car with you, stop being so stubborn."

I glared at him, hesitating before holding out my hands for Dante to cut me loose.

"Just hear us out, then you can run and we won't follow you," Dante offered.

If I could run, then fine. I'd stay and listen to their bullshit.

"Fine, deal."

"We have to meet with our boss now. Emilio is going to wait with you." He glared at Emilio, who came out of the office door. "Don't touch her unless she bolts."

They disappeared into the office where Spencer usually met Big Frank. It was quiet for a minute. I let out a sigh, taking a step to sit on the couches. Emilio stuck his hand out, forcefully pushing me back against the wall by my collarbone.

"I'm just going to sit down," I explained. "I'm not running."

"Did I tell you that you were allowed to sit down?"

The hell? I wasn't sure if it was the fact that he was suggesting I needed his permission or that those words were coming from him, but it pissed me off.

"I don't need your permission. I'm going to sit down."

I smacked his hand away, making it two steps before he grabbed ahold of my ponytail. He yanked it back toward him. A small yelp escaped me before I could regain my composure and punch him so he would let go. I tried to hit that soft spot on his chest but missed.

"Women do as men say," he spat, squeezing my cheeks with his hand.

I shoved him away. "Fuck you, asshole."

He charged at me, swinging a punch. I dodged it, taking a swing of my own and missing. After another swing, I made contact with his chin. That's when his fist met my face, busting open my bottom lip. I took a step back, trying to regain balance when he grabbed me in a chokehold. He was squeezing tight and I felt my face start to prick as it got harder to breathe. I didn't know how to get out of a choke hold.

"You do as I say *piccola,* or I kill you," he threatened. "I don't appreciate being spoken to in such a way by a woman."

Think Mia, get us out of this. I rammed my elbow into his ribs as hard as I could. Just as I did the office door opened and out walked the guys. I fell to my hands and knees coughing as I gasped for air.

"Hey!" I heard a loud thud and looked up. Someone was pulling Emilio off of me. "If you ever touch her again, I will cut you into a million pieces and toss you into the ocean."

Note to self, don't mess with this guy. Something in his voice sounded familiar, but it was darker. I could have sworn I heard it before. I got chills from it, making me feel excited as I stood up. I wiped the dripping blood from my face with the back of my hand.

"She tried to run, boss," he said squirming under the guy's grasp.

Fury brewed inside me and I wanted to punch him again.

"You are a damn liar," I snapped. "I made a deal with Dante. I wasn't going anywhere but the couches to sit down, which is what I told you I was doing."

There was a silence before he met his boss' eyes again.

"She's an unnecessary distraction boss," he spat.

The guy holding onto him threw him toward Dante like he was a rag doll.

"Take him to the conference room," he ordered.

When he turned to face me, I connected that he was Dante's

boss, Big Frank's son. The quiet one that had exuded that dominance. Although I hadn't gotten a good look at him in the chaos of everything going on. Now that he was standing in front of me, my eyes widened as I took in the sight of him. I'd recognized that he was big, but boy, was I underestimating his size. Up close like this, he was built like a house. At least six-foot-two, if not taller, with broad shoulders. His tanned skin was decorated with tattoos. His chestnut brown hair was trimmed shorter on the sides, leaving the top longer to messily fall as it wanted. Contrary to his hair, his beard was neatly trimmed, every hair in perfect place. His cheeks were chiseled, cutting sharply to have that strong, attractive jawline that would make you swoon. His sapphire blue eyes looked down at me with worry.

"Are you all right, *cattivella?*"

My jaw fell open slightly. There was that smooth voice I thought I heard peeking through.

"You're the guy from the closet?" I further connected.

He gave me a lopsided smile. It wasn't perfect but pulled me to it like a moth to a flame.

"Yeah, my name is Matteo. Are you all right?" he asked again.

"I'm fine," I wiped my face again.

"The bruise on your jaw is older, it didn't just happen. Who hit you? Did you have another run-in with the Russians?"

"That's none of your business."

"I hit her," Arturo admitted behind him.

I saw Matteo's jaw clench shut, his fists balling tightly at his sides.

"What were my instructions?" he said in a gruff voice as he turned to face him.

"To bring her back alive and unharmed," he repeated from memory.

"Then why did you hit her?"

"Because I refused to go with them and I pulled my gun on him," I answered for him.

Matteo glanced back at me. "Why?"

"I don't need or want your help," I stated. "Can I go now?"

"No, first come with me."

I followed him out of curiosity. He led me down the hallway into a room I'd never been in before. It looked like a doctor's office. He motioned for me to sit on the counter. I washed the blood off my hands in the sink before jumping up. As I turned to face forward, he was waiting in front of me. His body only inches from my knees. I looked into his eyes. His left had a second ring of color around the iris. It was almost gold in color. I leaned forward, my own eyes squinting to examine them closer. He didn't move away; instead, he put one hand on each side of me on the counter and leaned in even more. The heat coming from his body snapped my thoughts back to the present. I sat upright, putting the distance he was trying to close between us once more.

"What are you inspecting?" he asked as he smirked.

"Do you know your left eye has two rings of color in it?"

"Yeah, I see it every time I look in the mirror," he teased, as he held out a paper towel. "Here, put this on your lip for a minute. Tell me what happened out there with Emilio?"

"Can't you just watch the cameras?"

"I could, but I want you to tell me."

Sparing no detail, I told him everything that happened. When I was done, he asked to see my lip again. It had stopped bleeding now and was just sore. Reaching up into the cabinet behind me, he pulled down some ointment. His body was now only inches from mine. When his torso brushed the side of my leg the good kind of nerves washed over me. Something I hadn't felt in a long time. My heart started to beat faster at his proximity alone. He glanced up as he put some ointment on a Q-tip, only to stop and stare straight into my eyes. My mouth suddenly felt like the Sahara. I tried to swallow, seeing his eyes flicker to watch my throat bob as I did. His eyes darkened, almost like a storm was brewing inside. An intense warmth took hold of me. From my toes to my head, it invaded me, spreading like wildfire. *Oh no you don't, Mia. You shove those feelings this god of a man is causing right back down.*

"Hold still." His voice was gruff and demanding.

As his hand got closer to my face with the Q-tip, my heart matched the pace of a racehorse. *This can't be happening, girl.* I grabbed his wrist to stop him. He glanced from my hand on his giant muscular man wrist back to me, a humorous look on his face. I took the Q-tip out of his hand before letting him go.

"I am perfectly capable of applying it myself."

His reaction: to let out a chuckle as he put the supplies away. I jumped down using the mirror above the sink to apply the ointment. In the mirror, I could see his eyes watching me intensely.

"Staring is rude," I pointed out.

The corner of his lips twitched up. "I don't give a shit."

I rolled my eyes, tossing the used Q-tip into the trash before following behind him to the conference room. I noticed his demeanor switch from soft and kind to dark and cold. It was a different kind of dark than in the clinic. This one was dangerous and charged with aggression. When we walked in, he ripped Emilio from the seat by the collar of his shirt before dragging him out of the room. This left me with Arturo, who handed me my backpack as I sat down. He was sitting next to me, his head hung low. Neither of us said anything for a minute. I twisted in my chair back and forth as I waited for something to happen. He rested his elbows on his knees, letting out a deep breath.

"Mia, I'm sorry I hit you."

"Don't be. Everything is fair when we are fighting. It's survival and I get it."

His head fell. "But I—"

I reached out, putting my hand on his shoulder to get his attention.

"You didn't want to, but you had to. I understand and trust me when I say I'm not a fragile little girl. I can take a hit."

He said nothing more, just gave me a nod before moving to the seat on the other side of me.

"I'm fucking pumped," Salvatore said, smiling as he walked in.

"For what?" I asked.

"Just a bet we have going." Dante shrugged, following behind him.

I squinted at him, and asked, "What bet?"

"Oh, you'll see." Salvatore grinned.

Matteo finally decided to grace us with his presence again after thirty minutes of silence between us. When he walked back in I noticed he had on a different t-shirt than the one he left with. The others hushed, giving him the room. He leaned back in his seat, placing his arms on the armrests of his chair.

"I want to help you, Mia. The only way I can do that is if you tell me what I need to know," Matteo explained.

"What do you need to know that I didn't share with your father?" I leaned on the table, perking one eyebrow up.

"For starters, what is your real name?"

My body tensed. I crossed my arms over my chest, leaning back away from him in my seat.

"It's Mia."

"Mia what?"

"Just Mia."

"Right and I'm just Matteo. If we know your real name we can dig more into why they are after you. Don't you want to know?"

"Yeah, but I can find out on my own without your help."

"Can you?"

"I've gotten this far in life on my own. I'm sure I can handle investigating them before I confront them," I explained.

"Before you confront them? You're going to go after them?"

"Him. I'm going to go after *him*," I corrected. "He's going to die a very painful death. One where he begs for me to kill him just to make the pain stop."

"Who is '*he*'?"

"None of your business."

I couldn't answer him because I didn't know his name. The only thing I remembered was his voice. It'd been absent of emotion while he was torturing me. A fuzzy image of his face appeared in my mind. It was probably because they had drugged me while they tortured me. He had to be high up in the organization to be allowed to torture and interrogate people. The solid thing I did know, was that it wasn't Nicholai Petrov. He was too old, this guy was somewhere around my age. Big Frank did mention he did have two sons. *It could be one of them, girl.* I just had to find them on the internet to get a look at their faces.

"You can't possibly think going alone won't end with your death, as well."

"It might, but at least I'll make sure to kill him first. That is my only goal."

"Why are you so careless with your life?" he snapped.

"Why the hell do you care?" I snapped back, "I'm just an ex-employee to you. In fact, we haven't even officially met until today."

"Your resignation was never filed."

"That doesn't answer my question." I rolled my eyes. "I have a plan, one that involves me not being here with you. I need to get to work if I'm going to stay ahead of them. You are wasting my time. I have a meeting at two in the afternoon and now I have to figure out how to get all the way back to Vegas."

"A meeting with who?"

"That's not your business either."

"I want to help you." He sneered. "Just tell me what I want to know."

"Why? I was fine on my own." I checked the time on the clock on the wall. "I agreed to hear you out on a plan, not to answer a bunch of questions. So, either tell me your plan or this meeting is over."

Matteo's lips pressed into a thin line. I watched his jaw tick as he clenched and unclenched it. He must be used to people doing what he said. Joke's on him, I didn't freely do as others asked unless I had some part of it in my favor.

"You tell me what I need to know, I put you in a safe house, we take care of your problem, you are free to go. So, tell me what I need to know," he explained through gritted teeth.

I stood up, swinging my backpack over my shoulder. That wasn't going to work for me. That Russian, whoever he was, was mine to kill. Teaming up with them meant they might kill him before I even got the chance to graze his pale skin with my knife.

"No thanks," I stated. "Is that all?"

"Sit down, you're not leaving," Matteo ordered.

"Yes I am, you can't keep me here. I don't work here anymore. Plus, even if I did, you're not my boss. I don't have to listen to you."

I walked to the door. When I tried to turn the handle and felt it resist, I laughed to myself. They locked the door. I had never come across a door that wouldn't unlock from the inside with just a twist of a dial. In its place, there was a keypad and a keyhole. I took my lock-picking materials out of my backpack before starting to work.

"It's a high-grade secure lock," Matteo gloated. "Just sit down and talk to me."

I shushed him, listening intently to the lock. With a couple more movements I heard the faint sound of the lock clicking open. I smiled to myself as I stood up to walk back toward him. With one hand on each of the arms of his chair I leaned down to make him uncomfortable. His eyes squinted at me, yet his body didn't move away. My face was only mere inches from his. This time, though, I didn't let the closeness get to me.

"There are many things no one knows except me and one other person. That other person...is dead because of me. I don't open up and talk to people because it gives my enemies leverage. Thank you for your offer, but I decline it." I grabbed the handle of the door, turning back to him. "Oh, and Matteo?" I paused, opening the door. "Don't doubt my abilities, I'm a fucking Rogue."

"Well, I won the bet," Dante stated. "It took her less than a minute to pick that lock."

It brought me satisfaction to watch as Matteo's lips part in surprise. With a smirk, I walked out. I figured I wouldn't get far before they came to me with a different angle. Instead of wanting to help, maybe they'd force me to take their assistance. No matter what was to come, I was mentally preparing for it.

ALWAYS BE READY

SURE ENOUGH, THE PADDING OF footsteps behind me told me someone was coming with an offer.

"Mia wait," Dante begged, "please stay."

"No, I kept up my end of the deal. I heard you out, now I can leave. That's what we agreed to. I don't understand why everyone wants to risk their lives for me. Don't follow me anymore. The Russians are my problem, not yours."

He stopped walking and released a defeated sigh. I continued my way to the elevator, bending down to retrieve my gun from my backpack. *We can't risk not having it on us again.* I did a quick check to make sure it was loaded with one in the chamber. The elevator dinged, opening for me. I stepped inside turning to see Matteo step inside with me. *Great.* He waited for it to start moving before flipping the power switch to stop it.

"Let's make a new deal." He searched my eyes for the curiosity he knew I'd have. "I will tell you everything I know about the men who are after you in exchange for one week of you in the safe house under my protection."

My heart fell into my stomach.

"How many times do I have to say it?" I groaned. "I don't need anyone risking their lives for me. I decline your protection. If they get to me then I don't want any leverage that it could bring. All of you need to get that through your heads. I don't understand why you won't just let me go."

"They will find you again, Mia. Don't you want to be done with them, done running? The way you make it sound is that you've been running your entire life. Don't you want to be able to enjoy life? Have friends and do things with them without worrying about the Russians?" His face softer now; there was a shine to his eyes. "Just one week. You'll gain all the information we have on the men chasing you. I won't ask you to give me any more information than you already have unless there are extenuating circumstances."

I flipped the power back on. The elevator jerked back to life. We were silent. I kept my gaze on the closed doors, although I could feel his eyes on me. He had moved to lean against the side wall like it was a casual everyday thing that was happening between us. The more I thought about what he'd said the more I debated my next plan of action. I bit my lip. *He made it sound like he knew more about the Russians than his father shared, Mia.* That could give me more information to track where they were when I was back on my own.

"Who would be in the safe house with me?"

"Just us four guys and the staff."

The elevator lowered to the garage. He was still studying my every breath intently. When the doors finally opened, I took a step forward to leave. I hesitated before taking another. What could one week hurt? Then I'd maybe figure out why they were after me to begin with. I met his gaze at last, those eyes of his, before stepping back toward the center of the elevator as the doors slid shut again. He pressed the button for the fifth floor. The corners of his mouth twitched upwards in a smile he tried to hide.

"I have conditions to the offer," I stated once we were back inside the room with the guys. "They are non-negotiable."

"Which are?"

"First, I want to keep my gun with me. *If* this all gets taken care of, I want my job back. Lastly, if you capture the one I want, I get him. He's mine, no one else's."

"I have no intention of keeping your gun from you, you never officially resigned, and your interactions with him will be monitored."

"Define 'monitored.'"

"One of us will be there just in case as backup."

"Fine. Deal." It was better than nothing. "Hold on."

I dug around my backpack, feeling inside for the napkin the bartender gave me and my cell phone. I turned on my phone, searching, and then dialed the number of the bar on the napkin. Their eyes were glued to me as they planned on listening to what I was about to say. When the bartender answered I smiled.

"My two o'clock ego is repaired."

I hung up without waiting for him to say anything. My phone had pinged while I was on the phone, Elliot had texted me stating the Russians hadn't followed my decoy. It didn't come as a sur-prise to me. There was a rat somewhere on the S-Rank team. *Or extraction, team Mia, keep your guard up.* They had to have shared that it was a bogie going to New York.

"How many identities do you have?" Dante asked.

"I don't have to answer that," I said, matter-of-factly before turning to Matteo. "Can we get on with it now?"

"Yes." Matteo nodded. "Let me tell you what we know. They are Russian mafia, sometimes they use the term Bratva. The day you left, after the mission went south, I got a phone call. Elliot recorded it for me." He sat his phone on the table, pressing play.

"Matteo, you asshole, stay away from my Mia."

I shot to my feet, my chair rolling back, crashing into the wall. My eyes locked on the phone. That voice. It was his voice. My throat became dry as I listened in.

"Excuse me?" Matteo asked.

"You heard me, stay away from her. She was promised to my father. She's mine and will stay that way. I don't need your interference."

"Fuck you, I'll interfere if I want. I don't take orders from anyone let alone a Russian bastard who can't run his own family's company. Rumor has it your father might pass you up for your younger brother. That must show you what a disappointment you are."

My hands were trembling as the sound of his voice rang through my body. It shook me to my core. Images of *that* night flashed through my mind. It suddenly felt like there was no air in the room. Matteo paused the recording.

"Mia, are you all right? You're shaking." He stood, gently touching my shoulder.

I slapped his hand away. "Don't touch me." My fingers ran through my hair, pulling my ponytail out to redo it. "Press play."

"Are you sure?"

"Press play, Matteo."

He didn't say anything else, just reached over to do as I said.

"You Italian bastard, you have no idea what you are talking about. I'm taking over, it's my right to be the head of the family. When my love joins me, I'll be sure you're our first stop in the destruction we will bring on the five main Italian mafia families." He laughed dryly. "To think I almost lost her to another Italian kid. I took care of that real quick. No one can have her but me."

"So you think. I'm under the impression she doesn't want to be with anyone."

"Oh, she will come to me willingly, don't worry. Well, I must go, we will be reunited soon, her and I. It'll be the best day of my life. Aside from the day I murdered that Giovanni kid."

The line went dead as he hung up.

"What does he mean, you're going to bring destruction on the Italian mafia families?" Matteo asked me.

Although I heard his question, my rage had taken hold of me. This fire inside of me made me want to go straight for him. Knowing I wasn't invincible, I closed my eyes in an attempt to calm down. *This is one step closer.* I transferred my emotions to calmness. It washed over me, like a wave crashing ashore, taking my anger with it. When I opened my eyes I was met once more with theirs.

"What does he look like?"

"Answer my question first, please," Matteo demanded. "Do you know what he means?"

"No, I have no idea what he's talking about. Now show me what he looks like."

It took him all of fifteen seconds to show me a picture on his phone. There he was, golden blonde hair that was pulled into a short ponytail, clean-shaven, with a proud nose. There was a familiarity in his hard features. I squinted at the picture in front of me. Where have I seen him before?

"Do you know him?"

"I don't know. I mean he's the one that I have plans for if that's what you are asking. He's the older son then."

"Yeah. I bet the rumors are true. His father was thinking about dismissing him from his position as the future head of his family. It would allow his younger brother to take over."

"Why?"

Matteo shrugged. "I guess it's because he's doing things that his father doesn't agree with. Or because he can't follow through on much. Such as his threats against myself or them." He motioned to the men sitting around the table. "Or you," he added.

"I told you all not to get involved."

The ones around the table started to chuckle at my statement.

"Why is that funny?"

"His family and mine have been at odds since the conception

of our names. We're enemies, Mia, and always have been. It's not because of you."

"That's why helping you isn't as big a deal as you make it out to be. He threatens our lives daily and we're all still here. The only thing we are adding into the mix is you," Dante explained further.

"What's his name?"

"Igor Petrov." Salvatore answered.

I didn't recognize the name but that didn't stop me from wanting to murder him any less.

"Come on, you must be tired. Let's get you to the safe house so you can rest in a bed," Matteo stated, his voice soft once more. "Dante, go get the car."

Without another word he got up, snaking by me to head down to the parking garage. I reached down for my backpack.

"Would you like me to get that?" Matteo asked.

"I didn't peg you to be the gentlemanly type, Matteo." I raised one eyebrow at him, "I got it thanks."

"I can be a gentleman!"

"Can you, boss?" Arturo asked, turning to Salvatore. "Have you seen it before Sal?"

"Maybe when his sister or mother is around. Never to a woman he's not related to, though," Salvatore stated, leaning to Arturo like he didn't want us to hear. "Maybe he thinks she's delicate."

"Good point." Arturo rubbed his chin. "Do you think she's delicate, boss?"

He glared at them. It was a look that could have killed them in their places. His foot moved only one step in their direction and they were scurrying out of there. Their cackles could be heard down the hall. I couldn't fight the smile it brought me to see their interaction.

"Why does Arturo call you boss?"

"He says it has a ring to it. He refuses to call me anything else except for times his emotions get the best of him. That's when I know something serious is going on," he explained. "How is your lip feeling? Do you need any Tylenol?"

"It's fine, doesn't hurt that bad. What happened to Emilio?"

"Nothing, what do you mean?" A frown formed on his forehead as his brows pulled together.

"Did you kill him?"

"No," he snorted. "He's fine. I just sent him home."

"Right, and that's why you had to change shirts?" I scoffed.

He looked down at his shirt as if he didn't remember changing. One of his hands came up to run through his hair. When he stopped at his neck to rub the back of it he smiled.

"I mean, okay, I probably broke his nose first, but *then* I sent him home," he finally admitted. "Come on, Dante should be up front by now."

Matteo opened my door, letting me climb in. Before I could slide into the middle seat an eerie feeling took hold. The hairs on the back of my neck stood on end. They must have felt it, too, because we all stopped moving and fell silent. Listening to our surroundings, I looked back at Matteo, who was still standing outside of the car. Dante started to climb into the driver's seat. My heart stopped as I saw the red dot of a laser on the center of Matteo's chest.

"Sniper!" I yelled.

There was no time to think. I launched myself toward him. I wrapped my arms around his neck to act as a physical barrier. The reason behind it was a loss to me. Maybe deep down I thought it would be my fault if he got shot. He was there that late because of me.

He stumbled backward at my impact as the shot was fired. I felt the bullet hit my arm, and I let out a yell. Adrenaline quickly took over as it pumped through me, numbing the pain. Matteo grabbed ahold of my hips, lifting me into the SUV. The tires screeched down the road as Dante sped away. We kept our heads down. Matteo had his arm around me as if to shield me from any more shots as we crouched down in the backseat.

Once we were sure we were in the clear, we sat up. I could feel the hot blood dripping down my arm. Should I shut my pain off? *No, it would be suspicious if you did that. Just deal with it.* I pulled my t-shirt over my head. I began to tear my shirt with my teeth and hand. Probably not the best idea as I was in nothing but a sports bra in a car full of men. All my scars would be visible to them now.

"Here, let me help."

Matteo took my shirt from me and tore it the rest of the way. He gently fed it around my arm, tying it loosely, then pausing as he met my eyes.

"Ready?" he asked

I nodded and he pulled it tight around my wound.

"FUCK!" I yelled then punched his arm.

"What was that for?" he snapped.

"Pulling it so tight! It's a graze. A deep one, but just a graze."

"How do you know?"

"I've been shot before. I know what it feels like when it hits you like they intend it to," I explained, "the bullet isn't in my arm."

The car was quiet for the remainder of the ride. Matteo's demeanor was cold as he stared out the window. I watched as his lips pursed into a thin line as he sat there with his thoughts. He was tense but I wasn't sure if it was because he almost just died, or because Igor was finally following through on his threat.

Dante turned off the main road down a long side road with twists and turns. When we pulled into a circular driveway, I peeked out the window. This was not a safe house, but a gorgeous mansion tucked way back into the woods.

"This is your safe house?" I asked.

"It is a house that is safe. Hence a safe house," Matteo stated. "Come on, we need to clean up your arm."

As we stepped out, I looked up at the stone and wood exterior in awe. It was almost like an elegantly oversized cabin. There were two floors above the main level. The front had a porch that was the same length as the house itself, with stone pillars spaced evenly apart from one another. Two guys stood outside the front door and two more on each side of the house. As I followed Matteo and Dante to the front door, I noticed they were armed. *Okay, maybe this was a safe house.* An older man opened the door for us.

"Welcome home, Mr. Sartori," he greeted Matteo.

"Thanks, Al," he grumbled.

We walked into a giant foyer with grey slate tile. The white double staircase had black railings and steps. I followed it up with my eyes, taking in its beautiful craftsmanship. A hallway led straight through the bottom of the stairs. Hints of a large living room were at the end of it. A dining room was to the right and because it was open, I could see parts of a beautiful kitchen in the far back corner of the house. To the left was a room with a fireplace and larger than normal couches.

A hand touched the small of my back. Instinctively I grabbed the arm attached and reared my arm back to punch whoever just touched me. Catching myself only when I realized it was Matteo and I had stopped walking. Dropping my arm with a sigh I glanced at him.

"Is your first instinct always to defend yourself?" he questioned.

"Yes."

"You can let your guard down here. With me. These guys." He motioned to the three behind him, "You are safe, it's okay."

His head tilted sideways, examining me as he waited for my answer.

"Another rule for a rogue...always be ready."

He opened his mouth to say something else, then must have decided against it. Instead, he motioned for me to follow him. This time I didn't protest, trailing him to a room similar to the doctor's office at headquarters. It was much better supplied than the other one. Even had a connected room that looked like an operating room. Sitting up on the padded table I looked at my feet as they dangled down.

He pulled a couple of things down from a cabinet. He was

silent as he cleaned and wrapped my arm. I bit back a yelp as he did. *Okay, maybe we should have turned off the pain.* Once he had put back the supplies I started to stand, but he cut me off, blocking the door as I took my first step. His eyes were on my exposed skin. It infuriated me.

"Are you done?" I snapped.

"Done what?"

"Gawking at my scars." I rolled my eyes. "Like you've never seen one before. I know they are all over, so you don't have to remind me."

I walked around him, throwing open the door to walk out.

"No, I wasn't—wait—Mia!" he called after me.

I turned, slamming the door in his face.

"Fuck you, Matteo," I muttered as I marched up the stairs.

I was mad at myself for getting into this situation. Why did I have to be so damn stupid? I shouldn't have taken this deal. I could have been halfway back to Vegas by now. Now I had to stay a week with an annoying ass giant of a man. I growled to myself. Dante was talking to the guys as I walked up to him.

"Where am I sleeping?"

"Follow me," he stated.

We walked up the stairs to the second floor. My anger blinded me from taking in what I was sure was a beautiful home. Neglecting to admire any of it, he stopped one door short of the one at the end of the hallway. I stepped inside, flipping the light on.

"My room is at the other end of the hall. Matteo's is down here on your side. If you need anything."

Great, Matteo was next door.

"I won't," I said, before shutting the door and locking it.

Turning to inspect the room I was given, I let out a breath as I tried to calm myself. The bed could fit at least four people and was set in the center of the wall to my right. Across from it on the left wall were two doors. Behind one, was a walk-in closet that was as big as my bedroom in my apartment. The other opened to a bathroom with an all-glass stand-up shower, soaking tub, and sink. Two huge windows were on the wall across from the door. I went to them, peering out to see how far the drop would be, just in case. It seemed like a decent fall, but doable in an emergency. Letting my backpack slide off my shoulder to the floor next to the bed I kicked off my shoes and fell sideways onto the plush mattress. I covered myself with the heavy blankets as I thought back to Giovanni. I allowed myself three minutes to cry before I forced them to stop spilling from my eyes.

Exhausted, I fell asleep quickly.

TRUST

NOT SURE HOW LONG I slept, but it was mid-afternoon when I woke up. The sounds of birds chirping outside my window woke me. I laid there for a minute letting the events of what happened the previous day come back to me. My emotions followed with them until I was ready to get up.

All right Mia girl, time to get some answers. Only six days left here.

Tossing the covers off me I stood up, stretching. My arm pinched a little, but it was better than the day before. I made the bed behind me before getting cleaned up. My last outfit reminded me that I needed more clothes. If I left, I'd need an escort. Unless I just...borrowed a car. I shook my head to myself. *Mia, first answer the questions you have.* What was ringing the familiarity alarm about Igor that I can't remember? Not to mention why was he coming after me? The rat was another problem. If it was someone on the extraction team then they had me right where they wanted me.

I first decided to investigate the men that were in the house with me. It would be more beneficial to know their deepest secrets to make sure I had leverage over them if needed. It would also double as a search for the mole. I'd already done a basic investigation into Dante. This time I'd start with their leader, the "boss" as Arturo put it. I dug my phone out of my backpack, beginning my search for information. *Just what does the internet know about Matteo Sartori?*

He was the son of Frank Sartori. *Okay, so Big Frank was his dad, we knew that.* That also explains why Emilio called him boss. He must be above him in the company. There was a lot about The Core connected to his name. As I read article after article, I searched the underground sites. I found one on a site called undergroundrumors.us.org.

"*The Sartori family is an Italian Mafia family with lots of money and power over the city.*" My heart rate quickened as I continued to read the article to myself. "*Matteo Sartori who is slowly taking the reins from his father, Frank Sartori, has his three loyal caporegimes (captains) staying by his side. Dante Luciano, his right-hand man, is referred to as 'the brains' as he is quick to think on his feet and is rumored to be the strategist of the three. Arturo Morelli, also known as 'the enforcer', is the front man for getting things done with, or without, force. Salvatore Russo, whose nickname is 'the fixer' is the one with the ability to clean up any situation particularly when it comes to dealing with the authorities. The unofficial lawyer of the three, if you will. Emilio Palermo, the Sartori family's long-term consigliere (advisor), may retire with Frank Sartori but it has not been specified either way.*"

Oh shit. It all started to make sense. Matteo saying their families were at odds since conception. With one being Russian Mafia and his Italian Mafia. When I mentioned organized crime to his father, he avoided an answer by mentioning how straightforward I was. I put my hand on my forehead. *What the hell was going on in my life?* I wondered if there was any way I could get Matteo to verify the information on this site. *Does he need to?* No. It wouldn't make a difference. It did make me wonder why one of them would be a rat. I typed their names in a note on my phone. I'd have to dig more later. Or ask Elliot, but he was already looking into the picture I left with him.

My body froze. The pictures! I took them out, staring at the one of me with my first kindergarten friend. That's when it hit me. *Iggs.* That's what we called him. His younger face flashed through my mind. I'd seen it somewhere else too, but where? I tossed my phone back into my bag. My eyes fell on my zip drive where I kept all my research material on who I was. Bending down I picked it up, staring at it in my hand for a moment. There were pictures on there of me growing up. My heart started to race, could that be where I saw him? I needed to find a computer. It would have to be without the help of any of the four men here or they would want to know what I was doing.

I grabbed my lock-picking tools out of my backpack, just in case, before I headed toward the door. Cracking it open slowly, I listened for voices. I smiled, welcoming the silence. I closed the door gently behind me. I could see the stairs from my door. My light feet carried me to them, pausing to listen for voices once more. It sounded like they were all downstairs. Maybe there was an office on this floor. I turned, checking the door to my left. It was a library and a big one at that. But no computer or laptop. Walking back toward my room, I tried the next door. It was locked. I grabbed my tools out of my pocket, unlocking the door in less than thirty seconds. I pushed it open hesitantly, peeking in. There it was, an office, complete with a dark wooden desk and cushy chair. On that desk sat the most precious thing in the world at that moment, a laptop.

There was a window off to the right side of the room. Locking the door behind me, I walked to the window, peering out below. It was the same type of fall as the one my room had, grass. Doable, but only in a pinch. The only other door in the room was on the other side of the desk. I walked over feeling pleased when I tried the doorknob and it opened. The only thing behind it was a closet. I snuck to the desk and opened the laptop. I sat my zip drive next to it as I waited for it to load. I wasn't surprised that it was password protected, but Elliot had walked me through ways to get around that many times before. It took me a bit, but when I was finally able to get in, I plugged my zip drive in.

My files popped up in a window, one folder labeled 'I.D.' and the other labeled 'La mia vita' (my life). I had kept a bunch of old pictures and documents in the 'I.D.' folder as I continued my attempts to figure out who I really was. Double-clicking it, I started searching through the pictures for the one I wanted. Zooming in on it to get a better look, I made the connection, my breath catching in my throat. I glanced back down at the photo of Iggs and me in kindergarten, holding it up next to the computer screen. It was him, that was obvious.

"Oh shit," I whispered to myself. "But why? What would he want with me?"

I started clicking through the pictures. He was in all of them until I got to the ones with Giovanni. I moved around so much that maybe we just lost one another. But then why was he in all the other pictures? I don't remember him being in any of my foster homes. So why would he have moved to every location I did? Unless his family was following me. How long had I been a target of theirs?

Voices outside suddenly became louder as someone approached the door. I quickly ejected my zip drive and shut the laptop. I shoved the zip drive and picture into my pocket, searching the room for somewhere to hide. My heart was pounding so hard I could feel it in my ears. There wasn't enough time to make it to the window. My eyes landed on the closet. I ran to the door, shutting it just in time to hear the office door open.

I held my breath, listening to their conversation as they moved through the room.

"I don't think barging into her room and demanding she speak with you is going to blow over well with her," Dante stated.

Of course, I knew the *her* they were referring to had to be me.

"Yeah boss, she doesn't seem to like to talk about herself. Or anything else for that matter. Her temper reminds me of yours."

Arturo; I could tell by his use of the word "boss" instead of Matteo.

"Speaking of, did anyone else notice all the times she showed one emotion and then flipped to a new one just like that?" Salvatore asked, snapping his fingers.

"Big Frank noticed. He guessed she can transfer her emotions," Dante responded.

"But who taught her to do that? See, it's not adding up to me. She could be feeding us a load of bullshit," Matteo hypothesized. "Or what if I'm underestimating Igor and he sent her here to infiltrate our organization? What if he finally grew a pair and is following through on his threats?"

"True, I mean he did have his men carry out a hit on you last night. Also, now that I think about it, there were a ton of Russians at that last mission. It's hard to believe that tiny thing could escape them all and get away with just some scrapes and bruises," Arturo noted.

"Can you have Elliot pull the security footage from that night? I need to see it for myself," Matteo stated. "I can't read her and I don't like it."

Deal with it, asshole.

"Have you found anything connecting her with Igor yet?" he asked them.

"About that…Elliot is refusing to help you," Dante stated. "He's mad because you wouldn't let him see her last night like he asked. He said when you want information—and I quote—feel free to bring her by."

My lips turned up in a small smile. Leave it to Elliot to use seeing me as leverage. *Maybe he has something for you.* I'd have to contact him when I got out of this closet.

"I'm going to kick his ass," Matteo muttered. "Why does he want to see her so bad?"

"I don't know, just like I don't know what he's been searching for with her for the past...however long they've been getting together after hours. Maybe you should ask her?" Dante suggested. "I know you like to stay ahead of our enemies and she's creating a lot of holes in the information we have, which makes you irritated. But if you ask nicely, she might share something that can help you."

"I *have* asked nicely."

"Well..." There was a snort. "You actually just kind of demanded *in a nice* voice that she tell you things, boss," Arturo admitted. "I mean, replay last night in your mind. She only responded when you gave her the option to. Each time you demanded information she basically told you to go to hell."

"Maybe try the question for question strategy. That seemed to work with your dad the best. She answered all the questions with him, for the most part," Salvatore said. "Although I don't know what you did last night, but she came up pissed off at you."

"Yeah, I know. I hate being behind and I was ahead on information on him until her. Now it's like I'm going into these situations blind and I fucking hate it. Last time shit went down and we didn't have all the information we lost a lot of men and women." There was a sigh, "I'm going to go talk to her. Tell Elliot if he finds me the information I need, then he can come to see her. That's the only deal I'm willing to offer." There was a pause. "Did one of you turn my computer on?"

"I didn't," Dante answered.

"No," Salvatore added.

"Not me, boss," Arturo said. "Which only leaves one person."

Matteo let out a growl, "That's it!"

"Remember to play nice," Arturo's voice faded as I assumed he went after him.

I started counting as soon as the door shut. After three minutes, I got up to sneak out. The hallway was clear when I opened the office door. My walk was more like a scurry as I made my way to my room. My first task was to contact Elliot. After texting him for a secure line, my phone rang.

"Hey, Elliot."

"Mia, are you all right?"

"Yeah, I'm at a safe house. Which I think is Matteo's home."

"That's true. All four of them live there."

I took a deep breath, and whispered, "Can I trust them? Is there any way one of them could be the rat?"

"No, they are all clean. You can trust them, Mia, but that doesn't mean you have to share everything with them." He sighed. "I'm just glad you are safe. I'm still working on identifying the couple in the picture. I don't know why it's taking so long. Everything surrounding you is locked up so tight it's like it was done on purpose."

My brows furrowed. "Why would it be done on purpose?"

"I don't know. I wish I did, honest. I won't give up though. It's bothering me that I can't uncover it all. I will call you if I get anything now that I know you are safe."

"All right, thank you, Elliot."

"Anytime."

I hung up, tucking my phone into my pocket before standing. Should I share what I found? *They might have information to add to it that could help connect the pieces.* Then they would ask a million questions. Unless, I gave them a choice: see what I found without asking questions or not see it at all. I straightened my posture, pulled my zip drive from my pocket, and walked into the hall. I heard their voices yelling back in the office they'd been in earlier.

It wasn't until I was closer that I realized it was the three guys yelling at Matteo. I opened the door, stepping inside closer to where they were. Matteo whipped around to face me. His eyes were cold and angry. Darkening into a navy blue, serving as a warning to anyone on the other end of his glare.

"You were in my office," he growled.

"I was," I nodded.

"Doing what?"

"Research."

"On *my* computer?" he asked.

"I used it, yes."

"Or did you take something off of it?"

"What do you have on there that would be of use to me?" I asked.

"Answer my question!" he yelled.

I squeezed my hand tighter around my zip drive. The movement, although small, drew his eyes to my hand. His head tilted to the side as the vein in his neck pulsed at his anger.

"What's in your hand?"

"None of your business."

He took a step toward me. A predator, while I was mere prey. When Salvatore moved to block the door, I knew I'd have to escape them. My eyes darted to the window and then back to where Matteo stood.

"Show me," he demanded, his voice low.

I opened my hand to reveal the zip drive. It was a tactic to buy time as I stepped to square myself with the window.

"Give it to me."

"No."

"It wasn't a question."

When his foot moved to take a step, I bolted toward the window. Jumping through windows hurt like hell so I braced myself as I launched my body at it. My elbow was stuck out to take the brunt of the glass and shield my face. Mid-air, I felt arms wrap around my waist. We both rolled to the ground. Next thing I know, Matteo had me pinned against the floor. One hand firmly placed on each of my wrists on either side of my head.

"Guys, out!" he ordered.

"Matteo, I—" Dante started to protest.

"I said out!" he yelled back at him.

They did as he said. When they shut the door Matteo turned back to me. His eyes softened as he met mine.

"What the fuck were you thinking? You could've hurt yourself in that fall. Or the glass?"

The amount of concern in his voice threw me off. Why did he care so much? We barely knew each other. His earthy scent hit me, making me feel tingly inside. I squirmed under him at the feeling, realizing then that his body was only an inch from mine. His mus-cular...sun-kissed...powerful body. *Oh shit Mia, focus.*

"I don't want you going through my stuff. That was my escape route."

"You went through my laptop," he accused.

"I did not. I only used it to connect something that had been bothering me about Igor. I didn't steal anything from your laptop. Trust me, I don't care about whatever you have on there."

My hand was so tightly squeezing the drive my knuckles were white.

"You want me to trust you, yet you won't trust me. It doesn't work that way."

"You said you wouldn't force me to share information with you."

"Unless there were extenuating circumstances. You hacking into my personal laptop counts as such a circumstance."

He was going to take it; I saw it in his sapphire eyes that pierced my soul. If I offered to show him what I found out, then I could control what he saw. *Now is your chance girl.*

"Okay," I started as he reached for my hand, "to show you I'm willing to trust you. I will tell you what I figured out, in exchange, you will not go through the other folder on my drive nor ask any questions."

"I want five questions." He smirked, relaxing a bit.

"One," I countered.

"Two." He raised one eyebrow at me.

"Fine. Deal."

He raised himself off me, his biceps bulging as he did so. To avoid any more warmth my body produced when being too close to him, I stared at the wall behind him. He stuck his hand up for me to take. When I did, he pulled me to my feet. My arm was now sorer than this morning. It made me cringe a little. Matteo noticed, offering something for the pain. But I wasn't taking any pills from him. I'd rather deal with the pain. He opened the door to his office, revealing Dante, Sal, and Arturo with their ears pressed against where the door was.

"We weren't listening boss." Arturo smiled.

"Yeah, just making sure you didn't need back up," Salvatore added.

"I was listening." Dante grinned with a shrug.

They gathered around the doorway, blocking it with their bodies. It was quiet for a moment as they stood there waiting for Matteo to tell them what to do. They looked back and forth between the two of us as they waited.

"Well, what the fuck do you want?" Matteo finally asked.

"Aww come on boss, we want to know what she found out too," Arturo complained.

"That's up to her."

I was surprised he left it up to me, giving him an incredulous look. They were now all waiting on me to give them a decision. *Elliot said you could trust them. They could have information.*

"You get no questions," I stated.

"How about one each?" Salvatore negotiated. "Then we will answer any questions you have in exchange."

There's why he was indicated as the unofficial lawyer, negotiating with you to give you what you want while also getting what he wants.

I chewed on my lower lip before giving him a nod.

"Do you have a printer?"

Not asking why I needed a printer, they showed me how to print things off. I printed out the map I had of the different locations I'd lived in while growing up. I gathered up everything I needed before turning to the guys.

"All right, let's get started then."

LA MIA VITA

MATTEO LED ME DOWNSTAIRS INTO a larger office that had couches and a big tv on the wall. It reminded me of the secure conference room in the way that Matteo's laptop flashed up on the tv. I opened the first picture of me at the park where I'd noticed Igor in the background. They examined it. I walked up to the TV, pointing to the blonde boy in the background.

"This picture is from when I was younger. That's Igor Petrov in the background. I didn't connect who he was until this morning." I pulled the picture from the mission out of my pocket, revealing it to him. "This was my first day of kindergarten. I vividly remember him asking to be my best friend when I walked in. I used to call him Iggs." Matteo opened his mouth to speak, but I held up my finger to stop him. "It gets even weirder." I circled the first city I lived in on the map with a pen from the desk. "This is where I lived when we took the kindergarten picture. Now flip to the next picture." I waited until the next picture popped up before continuing, "This was taken in the front yard of my second family when I was seven. He's standing outside my house across the street, just watching me. If you look at the map, it's an entirely new city three hours south of the first one."

As we flipped through the rest of them, they saw what I saw. I documented it all on the paper map I'd printed out. Altogether there were five locations where he'd been spotted in the background of my pictures. All spread far across the state of Florida and all at different ages.

"It's weird, right? That means he's been following me my entire life. It didn't just start when I was a teenager. Initially, I thought he just moved around like I did because we were in the same situation. Now though, I know we weren't, which means he had to have been keeping tabs on me, or better yet, his father was."

"Wh—" Matteo started.

"Wait," Dante stopped him, "we only have five questions to get the information we want. We should strategize what questions we need answered most, together."

I sat there as they discussed the situation. Dante really was the strategist. With the new information I'd given them, they had more than five questions. He organized the questions and they all decided which ones were the best to ask first.

"First question, what do you mean he grew up in the same situation as you?" Dante asked.

My fingers ran through my hair as my eyes fell to my feet. I didn't think they'd ask personal questions. *We will be all right, vague answers, girl.*

"I—" I cleared my throat, before answering, "I grew up in foster care and didn't stay with a family for more than a few years at a time."

"Was there ever a time he disappeared from the pictures?" Matteo asked.

"When I turned thirteen."

"What happened when you turned thirteen?" Salvatore asked.

"That wasn't a question in the top five," Dante stated.

"But it could help figure out what he was doing if he disappeared," Salvatore justified his question.

"All right, true."

They turned to me, expecting an answer. I did not want to share but it was a key piece of information. Salvatore was right. Especially if Giovanni had something to do with his disappearance. I knew Giovanni had known something but I wasn't sure how it all connected.

"Mia," Matteo said softly bringing me back from my thoughts, "what happened?"

"That's the year I met Giovanni. I moved in with his family when I was fourteen," I admitted reluctantly.

"How did you and Giovanni meet?" Matteo asked.

Dante palmed his face, muttering, "That's not a top five question either."

"Yes, but we could see if they are connected in a similar way. What if Giovanni was also following her or knew Igor? Or knew what Igor was doing following her around? It's important to investigate him as well."

I chewed the inside of my bottom lip as they once again turned to me for the answer. My eyes dropped down to my hands, picking my nails. The questions were getting more personal than I thought they would. It was starting to make me squirm as everything in me was screaming to lock my mouth shut. I took a deep breath, staring at my hands as I started to explain the beginning of our story.

"I...uh...snuck out of my foster home to go to the beach like I had been doing every night to try to catch the baby turtles hatching out of the sand. He was there doing the same thing." A hint of a smile graced my lips as I thought back. "We were so focused on watching where we were stepping that we smashed into one another. It scared the shit out of both of us. We walked together that night and then met every night after that. His parents invited me along on a lot of their activities and I just kind of joined their vacation. They even celebrated my birthday with me, bought me a cake and everything. It was the first time I'd celebrated it since as far back as I could remember. They told me I could go with them when the summer ended."

"Your foster parents didn't care?" Arturo asked.

"Is that your last question?" I asked.

"No!" He corrected, looking at the guys around him.

"What's your name?" Matteo asked.

The phone in the office rang before I had a chance to answer. Matteo got up to get it. He answered it, only to click a button and hang up. His cold, dark eyes were back. My stomach tightened into a knot. The tension in his muscles was obvious, pulling the guys to their feet.

"Speak asshole," he ordered.

"I'm just calling to see how my love Mia is doing. I know she saved your sorry ass last night. Can I speak with her?"

It was Igor. Matteo glanced up at me.

"No," Matteo ordered.

Excuse me, he did not just make a decision for you? Who did he think he is? I moved closer, standing in front of his desk.

"What?" I asked, staring down at the phone.

The guys moved closer, gathering around the phone. I was confused and angry that he had just called me his "love." I wasn't his and after what he'd done, I never would be.

"Ah my Mia, did you get hit by my sniper? Just say the word and he will face the consequences of his actions. My intention was not for him to harm you, I need you to know that."

"No, I didn't, he's a poor shot just like you," I snapped, "and stop calling me *your* Mia, I'm not yours. Why have you been following me my entire life?"

"You remembered, that means you will figure out your identity soon. We were meant to be with one another to fulfill the destiny our families carry together. Why don't you come back to me? I can answer a lot of questions you have still."

"What questions?" I prodded. "What destiny?"

"Your birth name, the real reason your parents gave you up. I know who you really are, Mia. I know you still haven't figured it out." He paused. "You're not safe with them, anyway. They are Italian Mafia, after all, and they could hurt you."

I laughed sarcastically. "I know who they are. I'll take my

chances. I remember what happened the last time I agreed to come to you."

"Oh come on, love, I only had to punish you for giving your love to that Giovanni asshole. Contaminated that beautiful body of yours for me. I had to cleanse you of that. Besides, I did you a favor, he held you back. He made you soft. He got what he deserved, too, that Italian bastard."

I grabbed the phone, bringing it to my ear. Anger filled me, and I wanted to murder him. My hands were shaking with my rage and I was sure my face was red.

"The next time I see you I'm going to make sure you have every wound you gave him—every stab, cut, and bruise. And when you think it's over, I'm going to put a bullet in every ball-in-socket joint on your body. You are going to be in so much pain you are going to wish you never said his name!" I threatened.

Then I slammed the phone down to hang up on him. I aimed my rage at Matteo, glaring at him.

"Do not ever make a decision for me. This is my life and I am in control of what I do and don't do." I snapped, pointing one finger at him.

I turned on my heel, picked up the laptop, and walked to my room. I locked the door, laying on the bed with the laptop facing me. I needed to hear his voice after that. I was going to have a breakdown if I didn't. I clicked on the La mia vita (my life) folder. In there were videos of Giovanni that he had recorded. Like I did every time, I clicked on the first video, seeing his face take over the screen.

"Hey la mia vita, I know you are going to be sad when you get this in the mail, so watch them as you can. My only request is that you watch them in order. I put them in an order for a specific reason. It's okay if you can't make it through them all right away. I'll be gone if you are watching them, but I hope you will have someone that loves you as much as I do to watch them with. Shit, some of these videos may help him understand your crazy ass,' he laughed, *'so get ready because you are about to watch the story of us."*

The first video ended. I double-clicked on the second one he titled "Rogue Training." It showed us learning all the stuff I knew how to do today. Parkour tricks, lock picking, escaping situations, gun training, all of it except fighting. They didn't teach me much of that. Giovanni taught me a lot of the parkour tricks I knew. His dad was a Rogue too, so he taught us a lot of tricks together.

The video flashed to me jumping from his roof across an eight-foot gap to his shed, running across that roof, and flipping forwards off it. I rolled to my feet, running toward the camera to celebrate with Giovanni. He turned the camera around to capture us in a hug. *"She's a damn badass."* He smiled proudly at the camera.

The next clip flashed to us in a room in his basement. I had a paintball gun in my hand. *"What are we working on today Mia?"* he asked me. *"Sharpening the senses of hearing and touch."* I smiled. *"I get to shoot G with a paintball gun today, basically."* He laughed, and said, *"don't sound so excited about it, cattivella."* I kissed his cheek with a giggle before he set the camera up to view the entire room. I stood in the middle, blindfolded. Starting with touch, Giovanni would hover his hand near me and I would say out loud where he was. Then he gave me the paintball gun. He would go somewhere in the room. A bell would ding and I'd turn and shoot where I thought he was. Afterwards, we walked to the camera together to show off his paint-spattered shirt. "*Well out of ten times, you got me seven.*" He smiled, taking the gun, and continued, "*That means I get seven shots on you, better start running.*" As I ran around the room giggling, I dodged his shots. It ended with us comparing our shirts again.

The next part of the clip was of his dad and I racing to see who could unlock the different kinds of locks faster. There were ten different locks on the table and Giovanni's mom was the judge. When she said "go," we started racing to pick each lock in front of us, stepping aside to the next one each time we got it unlocked. I kept up with his dad for the most part, almost beating him. Giovanni and I raced next, which he said wasn't fair since I just had a practice round. But he did it for me anyway.

The final part of the clip was at night. We were curled up on the couch and I was asleep in his arms. Okay, I was practically on top of him with one leg slung over his body. "*Look at this girl right now, she loves to cuddle. Don't let her badass persona fool you she's a sucker for being snuggled.*" He turned the camera to show me attached to his body like I was an extension of him, his one arm around me, resting on my side. "*I'll tell you what,*" he whispered to not wake me up, "*if someone other than me watches this video with her, you better enjoy this shit, you never know how long you have on Earth. Never take her for granted.*" I woke in his arms, looking at him sleepily, "*G, what are you filming now?*" Hearing his laugh made me smile. "*Uh...nothing.*" I was squinting at him suspiciously, and said, "*Put it away, snuggle with me.*" He flipped the camera back to him, giving it an I-told-you-so look. "*I'll snuggle you to the end of time, cattivella.*" You heard me giggle before the clip ended.

I wiped a tear from my cheek as the second video ended. I missed Giovanni so much, it was like I had a hole in my heart. It would never be filled, I was sure of it. He was the first person to show me love, the *only* person to show me what I was worth, and he was taken from me by a Russian asshole. I clicked on the third video he named "Fun Facts with Mia." This was my favorite video because it made me laugh. Giovanni filmed this one for weeks. He would either sneak up on me or just walk up to me and say "fun fact" to explain a situation we had gotten ourselves into.

In the first clip, Giovanni was grinning as he walked down the hall. "*Fun fact, Mia can sing,*" He then snuck up on me singing in my room. I belted out three complete versus before I saw him filming me. "*G! What is wrong with you? Every time I sing, you film me.*" I laughed. He smiled, and said, "*because you're good at it, the world should hear you. Sing our song, cattivella.*" I smiled, taking his hand, and serenading him. At the end he kissed me so sweetly. I remember drowning in his kiss and he tossed the camera onto the bed as I giggled.

"*Fun fact,*" the next clip started, the camera flashing to me, "*Mia broke both her wrists yesterday. Tell us cattivella, what were you doing that you broke your wrists?*" I held up my purple casts. "*I tripped over the dog.*" I laughed rolling my eyes. "*That thing is trying to kill me.*" The camera went back to Giovanni's face. "*You heard it here. She jumps off rooftops, scales buildings, flips over random shit, and jumps out windows but breaks her wrists tripping over a dog."*

"Fun fact, Mia wants to dye her hair. I told her to let me pick out the color. She agreed but I told her she's not allowed to look at it until her hair is dyed already." He was at the store, pointing the camera at all the different colors. *"Should I get pink? No, she would murder me in my sleep. I'm getting this purple color. Let's hope she likes it."* His mom dying my hair was the next part of the clip. *"G, give me a hint,"* I had begged him. *"No cattivella, you have to wait, just deal with it."* The last part showed me looking at my eggplant purple hair. My smile was wide. *"So how did I do?"* he had asked. *"I love it, G!"* I shouted and attacked him in a hug.

The last clip was of us in a tattoo shop. *"Fun fact, my parents are signing for us to get our tattoos today. What are we getting?"* He put his arm around my shoulders for me to answer. *"We are getting clocks with flowers and I added a hidden G in mine...oh and it's a half sleeve."* Throughout the rest of the video, there were progressions of our tattoos. At the end, we showed them to the camera, Giovanni giving a close-up of his.

The fourth video was named "la mia anima". It started with Giovanni on his couch, by himself. *"Mia I titled this video la mia anima. I know you are working on your Italian so let me explain what that saying really means. La mia anima translates to 'my soul.' I choose to name this video that because"* He paused. *"You breathe life into my soul, I love you with my entire being. You are everything I've ever asked for and I found you at just thirteen years old. I mean we are sixteen now, but damn, I still can't believe it. I know I'm not going to be around to grow old with you, someone else will have to do that. I just hope we can have many more years to come before you have to watch this. But never forget in that giant heart of yours how much I love you, cattivella."* The video was then filled with random clips of us. Laughing without a care in the world, doing parkour, hanging out in the pool. Watching movies or staring up at the stars from their rooftop.

I stopped it at the spot I normally did. Always dreading that if I finished video four, I'd have to watch video five which was the last one he had titled "goodbye amore mio" (my love). I had never watched that video because I knew it was going to tear me apart inside. So instead, I avoided it. I wiped my cheeks as the tears came. Exiting out of everything, I paused. I didn't know what was possessing me to do so, but I copied the first three videos. I pasted them on Matteo's desktop under the name "trust is earned" before taking out my drive. I shut down the laptop, pushing it away from me.

***

An hour later, someone knocked on the door. I was still staring up at the ceiling. With a sigh, I moseyed to the door. Matteo's concerned expression had a hint of something else, I just wasn't sure what it was as he stood in the doorway.

"I just-uh-came to check on you." He scratched the back of his head. "Are you all right?"

Was he nervous? Afraid? *You did threaten Igor with a very vivid death, girl.* But he similarly threatened Emilio, so why would he be nervous talking to me now?

"Do you know why he wants me?" I asked.

He shook his head, saying, "No, but I will do everything in my power to help you figure it out if you will allow me to."

"You only have six days left to figure it out. Then I'm going after him."

"Right, okay, it's a deal then." He looked back at the stairs. "We are going to go workout if you still want to blow off some steam."

"Uh, sure. Do you think there's a way for me to get more clothes? My go-bag only had three outfits and since I had the bright idea to tear my shirt yesterday, I'm down to two."

"You can order more to be shipped here. Or if you want to get out, we can leave since they already know you are here. I just want you with one of us."

"Does tomorrow work?"

"I can arrange that."

"Where are we going to work out?"

"The basement." He gave me a lazy smile.

I nodded, turning to grab his laptop from my bed. Handing it over to him I pulled my lower lip between my teeth.

"Sorry I kind of...held that captive. I did not take anything off it."

"That's okay, I think I trust you now."

"Why did Elliot send you the feed of me escaping the Russians?"

He hesitated before squinting at me. "How do you know about that?"

"I was hiding in the closet in your office during the conversation."

"Then yes, he sent it to me. He said he spoke with you, as well."

"He did."

He opened his mouth, then closed it before opening it again. It was almost like he was unsure if he wanted to say what he was thinking or not. I waited patiently for him to decide.

"Thank you, Mia...for saving my life. I realized in all this crazy shit going on that I never told you that," he finally said.

"Don't worry about it," I said, and I felt myself smile a little.

I waited at the top of the stairs for him to put his laptop back in his office. His eye caught something on me, doing a double take. When he reached for my ponytail I didn't move. He moved it away from my skin. I realized he was inspecting the birthmark on my shoulder.

"Where did you get that scar?"

"It's a birthmark. I've had it ever since I was little." I stepped away from him toward the stairs, and said, "Come on."

In the basement, he opened a big glass door to reveal a smaller version of the training center at The Core. I choose my normal routine of pull-ups, push-ups, and other various body weight exercises. As I stayed to the side, I watch as they lugged heavy weights around. It was the same type of weights used at work. My eyes landed on Matteo as he lifted what appeared to be a couple hundred pounds from the floor to just above his collarbone. It was then my eyes ran down his skin. Sweat dripped down the contours of his shirtless chest and abs. My tongue flicked out to wet my lips without thinking. *Mia, you're staring. Get ahold of yourself.* I shook my head as if to physically shake away all the images of his body playing in my mind. It wasn't until I met Dante's eyes that I saw him watching me with a smirk. I met his expression with a scowl of my own, flipping him off before turning back to my own work-out. *It would be a bad idea to let those emotions run rampant again. Stay focused.* I finished my own thing shortly after, leaving, as they continued to work out.

After a cold shower, I opened one of the windows in my room, raising the screen with it. The fresh air was warm and inviting. I perched on the windowsill, looking to my left I saw a balcony. It was about four feet away. A rush of giddy anticipation grasped me as I prepared myself for the jump. I situated my feet better underneath me before leaping toward the balcony. Catching myself on the rail-ing, I hung there for a minute looking down at what was below me. I rocked my body back and forth until I was able to kick my feet up to the balcony. I pulled myself up and over the railing. There was another floor above this balcony, but it only had a window.

There was another balcony I could jump to that stuck out from the backside of the house. I could see the side of it from where I was standing. But it was at least eight feet away. I'd never made that large of a jump before. I crouched on the railing as I debated it. The ground would be even further away than that if I jumped, but the adrenaline inside me made me want to try. Before I knew it, I leaped off the railing toward the corner of the house where the edge of the balcony was. I latched onto the base of it with just my fingertips.

"Hell yeah," I muttered as I smiled to myself.

"What was that?" Arturo asked.

"It's me," I called, regripping the base with my hands.

I grabbed the wooden railing and pulled myself up to see not just Arturo but all four of them on the balcony. It stretched across the entire back length of the house. Swinging my legs over I stood on solid ground. All four of them had wet hair still from their showers.

"Where did you come from?" Salvatore asked.

"I jumped from my window to the balcony on the side of the house. Then I jumped from the railing of that balcony to here." I smiled. "Why?"

"How many bones have you broken?" Arturo asked.

"From doing stuff like this or just in general?"

"From doing this shit?" he said with a laugh.

"None." I proudly smiled.

"What about in general then?"

"Both wrists, my left arm, three ribs, and I've dislocated my shoulder. All when I was younger. And before you ask, no, I'm not telling you how."

I looked out at the backyard. There was a pool on the other side and a fire pit on the side closest to us. Further out was a field of open grass.

"Can we ask you something about the phone call earlier?" Dante asked.

My eyes fell back to the four of them. Damn my curiosity of parkour, leading me up to the four of them. My stomach tightened in anticipation as to what they wanted to ask.

"You know, being here is starting to feel more like an ongoing interrogation than being at a safe house," I admitted. "You four ask too many questions."

"Only because we are trying to help," Dante said.

"Fine, but I won't promise to give you an answer. What?" I asked, swallowing a lump in my throat.

"Do you really not know your birth name?" Matteo asked.

I looked away, out at the trees that surrounded the backyard.

"My first name is Mia, I'm ninety percent sure," I confessed.

"Have you tried to figure out who you are?" Dante asked.

I nodded. "Of course, ever since I turned sixteen. Elliot even helped."

"That's why he knew you were in the ice bath," Dante connected.

"Yeah."

"How did you know who we are?" Salvatore pipped up.

"I looked you up on an underground website this morning. It had a lot of information about you. You should probably ask Elliot to take it down."

"Like what kind of information?" Matteo narrowed his eyes at me.

"Your names, your ranks, your nicknames and the reasons behind them. Also, it had Emilio's title and job on there. Says you're taking over because your dad is going to retire soon."

"So, does that scare you?" he asked.

I laughed. "No, should it?"

"I guess not. It does most people. They tend to walk the other way when they see us. They think we are just going to start shooting," he admitted.

I shrugged. "Guns don't scare me, people don't scare me, so we're good."

"Then what *are* you scared of?" Arturo asked. "Everyone is afraid of something."

I was quiet, walking across the back balcony. I leaned over, looking down. There was a deck below the end I was standing on, which I could drop down to. Then I could get back inside. I swung one leg over the wooden railing, then the other. I looked back at them as they watched me intently.

"Letting people get too close scares me," I confessed. "Which is why after this week is up, I'm going after Igor...alone."

I dropped down without waiting for them to say anything.

ENJOY YOUR MOVIE

DAY TWO AT THE SAFE house. Five days until I leave for Igor. I grabbed my gun and some cash from my backpack before heading downstairs. I sprawled myself across the couch while I waited for one of the guys to escort me down to the store. The ringing of my phone broke the calming silence of the room. It was the secure conference room number. I smiled as I answered it.

"Rogue."

"They didn't follow your decoy but tell us where you are. We're worried."

It was Luke. I laughed a little. Elliot must not have told them where I was after I spoke with him the day before. He did know there was a rat, so maybe it was to protect all of us. What could telling them hurt? Igor already knew where I was.

"I'm currently with the extraction team at a safe house."

"Oh thank God," Scarlet stated. "How long is it going to take to fix the problem?"

"I'm not sure. But once it's all taken care of, I get my job back."

"When can we see you again?" Elliot asked.

"I don't think you can until this is over."

I listened to them all groan as I pulled my lower lip between my teeth to prevent a grin from sprouting.

"Let us know if we can help speed up the process," Spencer offered.

"I will."

My name echoed from the front foyer. When I rounded the corner, I saw all four of them standing at the front door. Dressed in jeans and different colored t-shirts. They were all some fine ass men, even I could admit that. The keys dangled from Matteo's hand.

"We are all going then?" I asked, confused.

"Boss tried to get us to stay, but we want out too," Arturo said with a smile.

"They have informed me I have made them feel like caged animals," Matteo grumbled. "Even though they can leave whenever they want."

I snorted, "All right, it's a party then."

We went to the mall and I already had preplanned which stores I needed to go into. I had decided to up my load from three outfits to seven in my go-bag. That meant I needed five more of each article of clothing—well, six shirts, since I destroyed one. The four of them hung out around me while I picked out v-neck tops to wear. I then grabbed another pair of jean shorts that were black, two pairs of skinny jeans, a pair of black leggings with pockets for my lock picking tools, and maroon joggers. It took me all of fifteen minutes before we headed to another store. They were walking slightly behind me. As I approached the Victoria's Secret door, I felt them stop.

"Um...Mia?"

I turned, laughing as they all looked terrified to come into this store with me.

"I've never seen four grown-ass men scared of lingerie before. I'll be ten minutes."

They gave me a nod and I smiled, walking inside. I was grabbing a pair of pajamas when I felt eyes on me. I put the pajamas in the mesh bag I was carrying and pretended to look around the store. I tapped my chin with my pointer finger to make it seem like I was debating my next move. It didn't take me long to spot him. He was wearing a bright yellow jacket and black pants, with a black baseball cap on his head. I'd not seen him before, but I didn't doubt he was one of Petrov's men. Standing near an underwear station, he was glancing from his phone to me. I moved to the other side of the store out of his sight, testing to see if my suspicions were true. Sure enough, he stalked over to a new position. I checked out, walking over to the guys where they were leaning up against the wall.

I stood in front of Matteo, getting closer to him than I normally would. I knew from the conversations I had Petrov that it would piss him off even more if he thought I was with Matteo. If he was too angry, he would make a mistake. That would give me an opening to make my move or at least gain information.

"What are you doing?" he asked, peering down at how close my feet were.

I put one hand on the side of his torso, pulling him closer to me as if I were going to hug him.

"Agree with me, then follow me. Yellow jacket," I whispered, smiling at him sweetly, hoping he understood.

I handed Arturo the bag of my purchases. I saw the guy at the entrance of the store from my peripheral. *Time to win an Oscar.* I clasped my hands together with an excited smile in front of Matteo.

"All right babe," I said just loud enough for the yellow jacket man to hear, my voice cheery. "I'm going to run to the ladies room. You four go get us a table in the food court. I want a pizza, pepperoni and extra cheese." I pulled his face down to mine, kissing his cheek.

"What the hell?" Salvatore murmured.

I went to walk away, feeling Dante step to walk with me.

"Dante, wait." Matteo stopped him, saying, "the food court is this way."

Perfect, he got it. I turned down the long hallway to where the restrooms were. It was a stroke of luck that it was empty. *Maybe after all this bad luck we are finally on the upswing of it all, girl.* I walked into the bathroom, seeing a sitting area before you turned down a walkway to the stalls. I hid behind the door, knowing he would follow me. When the door opened and he stepped inside, making a beeline for the stalls in search of me. I caught the door behind him before it shut, snaking back out into the hallway. Matteo and the guys were walking up.

"He's in there searching for me. Ready?" I asked.

We filed in, locking the door behind us. He came around the corner, his brows furrowed. It was when he looked up and saw us standing there that he froze.

"Who are you?" I boomed.

"N-no one." He gulped, stuttering, "but you are...are you... Mia?"

I took slow steps toward him, my shoulders back. Exuding a dominant energy, I glared at him like he was nothing but mere prey to me. His eyes avoided mine, darting around the room instead. He reached up, pulling on the neckline of his jacket like it was choking him. I stepped to his side, leaning into his ear.

"Why are you following me?" I asked, my voice low but controlled.

He swallowed, reaching down for his pocket. I pulled my gun from behind me, pointing it at the side of his head. His body froze. I could see his chest rise and fall rapidly as his breaths quickened.

"D-don't shoot."

"Speak," I ordered.

"I have a picture on my phone of you. Some guy gave me $1,000 cash to follow you, get you alone, and give you a message and a memory card," he blurted out. "I don't even know the guy! He didn't tell me there'd be any guns involved. He made it seem like you were his girlfriend. Like he was trying to surprise you with something, I swear."

"What's the message?"

"He said, *enjoy your movie.* The memory card is in my front left pocket."

"Dante," I ordered.

He knew what to do, walking over to retrieve the memory card from the man's pocket.

"W-Who are you?" his voice shook. "P-please don't k-kill me."

I lowered my gun, tucking it back behind me.

"I'm not going to kill you, but I am going to need you to take a nap though."

Without another word, I punched him in the side of the face, knocking him unconscious.

"Let's go see what's on that memory card," I stated, finally looking at the guys. "Why are you smirking like that?"

"That was hot," Arturo said, smirking at me.

Matteo punched him in the arm.

"Ow, why boss?" he complained rubbing his arm.

"Don't be an asshole."

"You were thinking it, too," he mumbled.

I rolled my eyes. "Let's go."

On the way home I reluctantly agreed to let the guys watch whatever was on that memory card with me. I'd figured if we watched it and they saw something that they could connect back to me they would tell me. My mind spent the rest of the car ride going through all the things that could be on there. Was it more pictures? Or more videos? I brought my bags to my room.

"Dante is setting it all up in the office downstairs." Matteo peeked his head into the doorway. "Should be ready in about ten minutes."

"All right."

He turned to leave.

"Hey Matteo?" I called.

"Yeah?" He reappeared.

"Thanks for trusting me today, at the mall."

He ran one hand through his hair, "Honest truth, I wasn't going to, but Dante asked me to give you a chance after yesterday. I can't say I wasn't impressed. You do know how to handle yourself in a dangerous situation."

"Don't you forget that shit, either."

His head tilted back in a laugh. One that was genuine and inviting. It filled me with warmth, making me grin in spite of myself. *Oh no, focus girl. The memory card.* I cleared my throat, heading toward the door.

"Come on, I've got a movie to watch."

A tense feeling clutched me as I observed Dante use his pointer finger to push the memory card into its slot. A video popped up. We all glanced at one another before I pressed play, seeing Igor staring at the camera, a smug grin on his face. He was older now, his face more mature and defined than when he was a child. Even still, the venom I had for him didn't disappear.

"My darling Mia, I've given what you said on the phone a lot of thought. So maybe this will jog your memory." He leaned forward, toward the camera with a cocky smile, and said "Dostan' menya."

Matteo paused it, and asked, "What did he just say?"

"Come and get me."

Oh, I will, Igor, don't you worry. We all exchanged a look before resuming it. It was now a video of a dark room lit only by a few lights hanging from the ceiling. I recognized the room immediately and my stomach twisted in response. My hand flew to my mouth, scooting to the edge of the couch. I leaned forward to get closer to the TV. The guys turned their gazes to me, at my reaction, I could feel it. My eyes never left the screen in front of me. When the sixteen-year-old boy I loved came into view, attached to a chair, his name escaped me as barely a whisper.

"Giovanni."

In walked Igor and another man. He looked so much younger, with short choppy hair and a boyish face. I assumed the other man was his father. I had not seen this interaction between them. It must have been before I got there.

"*Your girlfriend thinks she's coming to save you. Little does she know she's coming to watch your very painful death.*"

Giovanni laughed. "*I was prepared to die for her the second I figured out who she was. One day, she will figure out who she is too, and then she's going to kill you. I hope she makes it twice as painful. Ona nikogda ne polyubit tebya, mudak,*" he said, and laughed again.

Igor leaned down toward him. "*U neye net vybora v etom voprose.*"

My jaw dropped at what he had said. Matteo paused and asked for the translation. I hesitated, looking at each of them. I was confused for two reasons, which were competing for my attention: I wasn't sure how to interpret what was said, and I was suddenly struck with realization of how little I truly knew of my real identity. My thoughts were going a million miles an hour as I stared back at the screen.

"Mia?" Matteo repeated. "What did they say?"

I swallowed. "G said *'she will never love you, asshole'* and Igor responded with *'she doesn't have a choice in the matter.'*"

Resuming it a second time I heard my own voice on the camera yelling for Giovanni. I sat up straighter now, as Igor came into view, a knife in his hand.

"Tell me, Mia, why do you love such a weak little boy?"

"Fuck you, asshole," the sixteen-year-old version of me yelled in the background.

Igor's nostrils flared, his chest puffed out, and his face began to turn an unnatural shade of red. He pointed in my direction with a knife, and said, *"I was going to go easy on your cleanse after being with him. But just for that, your pain is next."*

I held in tears as I watched him reel back and shove the knife deep into Giovanni's stomach. Matteo paused the video as G let out a painful yelp. I knew at the time Giovanni was holding in his screams because I was there.

"Out," Matteo ordered to the guys. "Dante, take this to my office."

They stood up, Dante taking the laptop from him. When the door shut, he turned toward me. He saw the distraught look on my face and I knew it.

"You don't need to experience that again," he said softly.

I looked into his eyes. "I'm going to kill him. If you get to him before I do, you had better save him for me."

"I will," he assured me, nodding gently.

I was about to break, and I wasn't going to let anyone see it. I stood up quickly trying to get to my room before a single tear fell. Matteo pulled me back to him as I reached for the door handle. His strong arms wrapped me up in a hug. I tried to push away, but he only pulled me tighter against him.

"Let me do this for you," he whispered. "You need to express your emotions. I can tell this is weighing on you."

He was right, I wasn't sure how much more I could keep in. I held this all in for so long, only allowing myself to cry for short times so I wouldn't completely lose my mind. But with everything that was happening, I couldn't concentrate enough to clear my emotions like I'd always done. Something was making me all... fuzzy and I couldn't figure out what it was. I stopped pushing away, and instead, I leaned into him. Still trying to hold back tears, I took a deep breath.

"Cry *cattivella*," he whispered, "let it out."

I don't know why I listened, but I did. Tears spilled from my eyes as I cried into his chest. He rubbed my back gently as I let it all out. When my quiet sobs calmed to slow breaths my body felt how exhausted it had been. I met Matteo's eyes knowing mine were red and bloodshot at the amount of crying that'd just escaped me.

"Who am I?" I whispered, hearing the strain in my voice.

"I don't know." He wiped my cheeks with his thumbs, and continued, "But we will figure it out."

I didn't say anything more. I wasn't sure what more he could do. I had tried everything, even asking Elliot to secretly search all my previous names for me. We always came up with a dead end until the breakthrough of my first name. But that took almost two and a half years of research.

"You need rest," he stated.

When he dropped his hands and moved for the door my body missed his warmth. *Fuck Mia, just go up to your room and leave him behind. This cannot go any further, he's getting too close.*

My mouth betrayed that voice in my head, and said, instead, "Will you walk with me?"

He smiled a little. "Yeah, come on."

"Are they going to be on the other side of the door?" I asked as he reached for the handle.

He looked at the door. "Not if they know what's good for them."

Feet scurried away quickly, bringing the slightest hint of a smile to my face. However temporary it was, I was thankful for it. At my door, I turned to Matteo.

"Thank you," I mumbled.

"Don't worry about it, just rest." He smiled.

Parting in the doorway I walked straight to the giant bed. I threw myself onto it, letting my body sink into a deep sleep.

Day three, which meant four days left at the safe house. I didn't leave the room at all that morning. I was afraid if I did, I might feel some more of those damn feelings toward Matteo. That was something I was trying to prevent. Many men at work and other places had attempted to break the barriers I put up in the past without any luck. What made him so different? Everything was under control until the day before. *For the most part...under control for the most part. What was going on with your emotions?* Maybe I was just on overload after everything happening all within such a short amount of time. I wasn't sure. I decided to start focusing on what I could control. A huge part of that was controlling how much I interacted with the man causing my other emotions to go haywire: Matteo.

By lunchtime, I still hadn't left my room. In fact, the only time I got out of bed was to shower before laying back down. My body felt like it hadn't slept in days. Is this what it felt like the last time I broke? Thinking back on it, I had slept and laid in bed for three days in another safe house once I had finally escaped the Russians.

"Mia?"

It was Matteo on the other side of the door. He couldn't come in. Shit, I was afraid of what I'd feel, I couldn't even see him. He was getting too close and I couldn't let my past repeat itself.

"What?" I called.

"Come eat something, please?"

"I'm not hungry, go away."

He didn't say anything else. I assumed he walked away. It was hours later, and I was now staring at the picture of Giovanni and me. The one I'd carried around since he gave it to me that night. My heart was heavy in my chest as my memories replayed what happened to him. Although all my feelings dissipated the moment Matteo barged into my room, flipping on the light.

"What the hell?" I complained, squinting while my eyes adjusted to the new amount of light, courtesy of Matteo.

"It's almost 8:00 at night. You haven't come out of this room or eaten anything all day. So, get up because you are doing them both now," he ordered.

I sat my picture down on the nightstand, sitting up in bed.

"No, I'm not. Get out."

He walked around to the side I was on. "Yes, you are."

When he reached out to pull me from my bed, I dodged his hand and hit it away. He tried again. I was now out of bed attempting to resist. I swear I saw a smile on his face at one point. He caught me as I tried to jump across the bed. I was over his shoulder only a moment later. As he carried me downstairs to the kitchen, I crossed my arms as I hung upside down in protest. When the other three saw what was happening, I heard them laugh. He sat me down next to a plate of food. I swung at his chest. He caught my fist flawlessly, leaning in.

"The day you hit me will be the day I lose my self-control with you."

I leaned in closer, yanking my hand away.

"You don't scare me," I snapped.

"Matteo! Boys!" a cheerful voice called, breaking the tension between us.

In walked the tiny Italian lady from the coffee shop, Nonna. She was carrying a plate of something with her. When she saw me, her smile widened. I knew then that we were going to have a conversation whether I liked it or not.

"*Piccola,* oh how wonderful! I brought some brioche left over from this morning. You can have the first claim." She smiled.

When she sat the plate down in front of me Matteo reached for one. She slapped his hand away, glaring up at him. I didn't expect her to move as fast as she did, but after Matteo had just forced me out of my room, I took great pleasure in it.

"I said *piccola* gets first choice."

I smiled at Matteo to gloat before picking one up. When she looked away, I stuck my tongue out at him for good measure. The guys laughed behind me. They stopped immediately once Matteo gave them a look that could kill.

"Nonna, you drove all this way out here to drop these off this late at night?"

"You caught me. There was a rumor *piccola* was here. I wanted to come and make sure you four weren't driving her crazy." She smiled at me, and asked, "How are you?"

"She's fine, see." Matteo motioned to me.

His Nonna gave him a stern glare before turning back to me for an answer.

"Okay, I guess," I nodded.

"Boys, time for you to make a quick exit," she stated, pointing. "Outside, front porch."

They began to protest before she took a step toward them. That's when they rushed outside, taking the plate of brioche with them. Sitting down at the kitchen island with me, she smiled.

"What's your name *piccola*?"

"Mia."

"Mia," she repeated. "What's wrong? Something is causing you trouble. I can see it in your eyes."

I sighed, picking up the fork to start eating what Matteo had set out for me. No matter how much I wanted to continue to protest, the plate in front of me smelled delicious.

"I see it was Matteo's night to make dinner," she chuckled, "He's no chef, but he knows how to make a few dishes. Between you and I, his risotto is the best. Don't tell him I told you that, he'd never let me forget it." She winked.

I took a bite, chewing it to buy time before turning to her.

"What scares you, Nonna?" I asked quietly. "More than anything."

Her puzzled expression disappeared as I met her eyes.

"Losing someone in my family," she answered. "What's yours?"

"Letting someone get close again. I lost the person I loved and since then, I'm not sure how to get over that fear of losing someone else. So, I just don't let anyone in. Which has worked...until recently."

"The person you loved, it was that boy, Giovanni?"

I nodded, my shoulders falling. She reached out, cupping my chin so I would look at her.

"*Piccola*, I think if Giovanni could speak to you now, he wouldn't want you to live in that fear. He wouldn't want you to be alone because of what happened. He'd want you to be happy and feel that love again."

"I don't want anyone to sacrifice themselves for me. I'm afraid if I open up, that's what will happen."

"It goes both ways child. You would do the same for the other person. Don't fear it, embrace it. Live life, be happy, don't dwell on what's happened. He will always be your first love and you won't ever forget him. But don't let that loss put a hold on your life. He wouldn't want that."

"How do you know?"

She put her hand on my shoulder. "Because he loved you, *cara mia.*"

Cara mia, my dear in Italian. Yet another term of endearment from her. One that I welcomed. She made me feel weirdly at home. I was quiet, taking another bite of food.

"I'll come back in a few days. We can make dinner together and you can pretend those four men aren't here."

I smiled a little. "Thanks, Nonna."

The guys filed back inside as she left. I finished my food and washed my dishes before heading back upstairs to my room. I had a lot to sort through after talking to her.

YOU'RE FREE

DAY FOUR, THREE DAYS UNTIL freedom. I was out of bed before all the guys. With a fresh cup of coffee, I headed toward the library on the second floor. I walked along the shelves, scanning the books one by one. Pulling the one I wanted from the shelf I snuggled up on the oversized chair. Its cover was plain. Dark navy with just two words printed on it; Cosa Nostra. It was filled with facts of old-time mafia rules dated back hundreds of years. I read for hours; my feet kicked up on one arm with my head on the other.

I must have dozed off, waking up with my book on my chest. I stood up to stretch, grabbing my coffee mug from the table. The house was eerily quiet as I washed my dish in the sink. Opening the fridge, I saw a chocolate cake inside. It wasn't cut yet. *I should wait.* I walked to the bottom of the stairs, wondering where the guys were that they were so quiet.

"Guys?" I called up. "Hello?"

Al came around the corner.

"They stepped out. What do you need Miss Clark?" He smiled.

"Call me Mia, Al," I greeted him. "Whose cake is in the fridge?"

"Anyone's. Would you like me to cut you a piece?"

"Yes, please."

My mouth watered as I watched him cut the cake and put my piece on the table. I ran upstairs to grab the book I was reading. As I ate my cake, savoring each decadent bite, I continued to read at the counter. The book was in Italian and I'd been doing great with mentally translating. It was an hour later that I decided to read outside. I walked through the living room, hearing the guys come in the front door. It slammed shut, the force so hard it shook the walls. *Uh-oh, someone wasn't happy.*

"Find her," Matteo shouted, "because if Petrov lays a fucking finger on her, I'll kill him with my bare hands."

I was standing there, watching the ruckus unfold. Matteo's back was to me as he barked orders at the other three. His entire body tense, fists balled at his sides. They were staring at me like they saw a ghost.

"Matteo," Dante stated wide-eyed.

"What are you staring at?" I asked them.

Matteo snapped around to face me. His lips parted in surprise as his stiff shoulders relaxed. I looked down at myself.

"Seriously, what the hell?" I asked, annoyed when they continued to stare at me, not saying a word.

"Where have you been all day?" Matteo asked.

"Here. Where did you guys go?"

"Mia, we were looking for you," Dante explained. "We couldn't find you this morning. We called your name and everything. You didn't answer."

My brows furrowed. "I didn't hear you call me. I was in the library upstairs. I did fall asleep reading, though." I shrugged. "I made you a deal, I wouldn't just leave."

"I thought you checked the library?" Arturo asked Sal.

"I did, the one on the main level," he stated. "You were supposed to check the second level library."

"Oh, I thought you said you'd check the libra*ries*. Plural," Arturo emphasized, wide-eyed.

"That sounds like great communication." I snorted.

I walked away into the kitchen for a bottle of water. Matteo followed me, keeping a distance as he observed my motions. I thought he was going to say something but never did. Instead, he just crept behind me as I moved to the living room. I plopped down on the couch. He did the same thing and sat next to me, reaching for a book that was on the end table.

"Why are you following me around?"

"Because."

"Because why?"

His eyes closed as he took a deep breath.

"I just need to make sure I know where you are for a bit."

When I read his expression, I saw just how worried he'd been when he thought I'd run off. It almost seemed as though the situation scared him. In the small amount of time I had known him, I'd not seen him scared before, even when he'd almost got shot by the sniper. When I thought back to what he had said when they returned from their search for me I felt it; protected. He wanted to help keep me safe. My stomach tightened into a knot, I had to convince him not to.

"Don't," I ordered. "Don't protect me. No one needs to die for me."

"No one's going to die for you, Mia, I just don't want you hurt."

"So what are you going to do, try to keep me away from him?" I snapped. "Maybe make sure he doesn't get to me?" My anger was steadily growing inside with each word I spoke. "When I leave in three days, don't send Dante or anyone. I'm going to do this on my own."

"We can help, why can't you just accept it?" he growled.

"You are letting your personal feelings get involved with business. Business you have no part in sticking your nose in, might I add." I slammed my book shut and stood up. "You are getting attached and I can't let you do that. I will be staying secluded in my room for the remainder of the time I'm here. Don't even think about coming in to get me again or I will leave and you won't know I'm gone until it's too late."

Without waiting for a response, I walked upstairs to my room. This time I locked the door behind me so he couldn't come barging in. This was for his own good. They would all stay safe and I would get my revenge for Giovanni. If I died, then I died alone. A loud slam echoed through the wall as I had just finished washing my face. Then a knock sounded at my door.

"Go away!"

"It's not Matteo." It was Dante, I could tell by the voice alone.

"What do you want?" I yelled.

"Open the door or I will annoy the shit out of you until you do."

I opened the door to see him with a goofy smile on his face. I rolled my eyes at him.

"What now?"

"Come talk to me."

"Where?"

"My balcony."

"Will you leave me alone after that if I do?"

"Maybe," he said, grinning.

"Fine."

I followed him through his room to his balcony. It was a huge room with a similar layout to mine, with two doors on the left side. But there was a door on the right wall that my room didn't have. I wondered what was behind it. Sitting in the chairs on the balcony I took in my surroundings. The side yard and trees further out were pretty. The sound of the wind through the leaves was calming. I took a moment to breathe it all in.

"Mia can I tell you something?" he said after a moment.

"What?"

"Matteo isn't getting attached to you...he's *been* attached to you. Even before all this went down with the Russians." He paused. "You caught his eye a while ago. You had another shadow before me. I've only been your shadow for six months."

"Six months?" My eye widened; he'd noticed me that long ago?

"He reassigned me to you so he knew you were safe. Also, so he could keep better tabs on you just in case you got into trouble."

"He used you to spy on me?"

Typical alpha male behavior. The information that he was using Dante to spy on me wasn't a surprise. I figured there was a reason he'd assigned Dante, his right-hand man, to me.

"You know who he is. Anyone associated with him gets a target on their back. All our enemies become yours and he didn't want to put you in danger. But when one of Igor's men approached you in the coffee shop, he took that as a reason to be okay with letting you in. You have the same enemies so he wouldn't be putting you in more danger but helping to keep you safe."

"Is that why he was on the Williams mission, not you?"

He nodded, and continued, "He claimed it was because he wanted to make sure you were extra safe on that one. But I think it's just because he wanted to see you in action. He's never chased after a woman before. They either throw themselves at him or fear him. You are the only one I've ever seen that's been able to crack his cold-ass heart."

I couldn't help but smile at his comment, shaking my head to myself.

"I'm not kidding. You should have seen him when we couldn't find you this morning. He was so panicked he was ready to go after Igor, guns blazing. You two are similar and you challenge him, combined with the amount of fight you have in you, well, he admires that. Whether you like it or not, he's going to do everything he can to protect you, even if you do leave alone in three days."

"Dante I—" Looking out at the forest, I sighed. "He's making all these feelings I used to have come back. Feelings that I had with Giovanni. I'm afraid if I let him in I'm just going to lose him like I did G."

"You were how old when everything went down?"

"Sixteen."

"Think of how much stronger you are now. You know so much more than you did. Matteo and, shit, all of us, want to help you, which is more than you had back then. I'm not saying Giovanni was weak, we watched the video last night and his actions showed just how tough he was at such a young age. The point I'm trying to make is that this time, it will be different."

Every one of them wanted to help me because they cared. Even when I tried to shut them out, they were persistent. Should I take that chance again of letting someone in? I was cracking more each day and they were all getting in.

"Fuck Dante, this is hard. You don't get it. I've not allowed myself to feel anything like this for almost five years. I don't even know where or how to start really letting anyone in."

He smiled. "You've already started whether you meant to or not. Let us help you figure out who you are and why Petrov wants you. That's another step, but first, you should talk to Matteo."

My heart pounded in my chest. Was I ready to let him in, really? Shit, my body felt things with him, I was trying to protect him from Igor, he was already creeping into my heart. I growled, frustrated.

"Where is he?"

Dante's smile widened. "His room."

"Oh great," I complained, standing up.

"Can I ask you something?" Dante asked before I walked away.

"What?"

"The ice baths that you do for training, is that because of what Igor put you through when he had you?"

My lips pursed into a thin line. Igor had me hung from my wrists in a freezer for periods on end, causing my body stress. It was a way to torture me without worrying about my escape as my thoughts were consumed by focusing on how to survive.

"How do you know what Igor did to me?"

He turned his head, glancing away from me out at the trees.

"After Giovanni's torture, he recorded yours. We watched it last night," he admitted.

My throat tightened; they'd seen what I'd been through. I wasn't sure whether to be upset or not. They were Italian Mafia so they had to have experienced torture to some degree. Whether it was giving it or being at the receiving end of it.

"Can you tell me why the gun to your head, though?" he asked. "I still can't figure that one out."

"Fight or flight. Put that gun to your head and convince yourself you're going to pull the trigger and it gives you a burst of energy and adrenaline. It's a way to simulate a situation where you need to give it more than you've got."

"You think that helps?"

"We'll find out soon enough."

Without another word, I made the walk down the long dark wood flooring that led to Matteo's room. Taking a deep breath, I knocked.

"What?" he called not coming to the door.

I grabbed the handle as quietly as I could. Twisting it a little I figured out it was unlocked. I opened the door and turned the light on. The light bathed his room, which was twice the size of the one I was in. All the furniture was dark wood. He was laying on his bed, trying to get his eyes to adjust.

"Get up," I ordered shutting the door behind me. "We need to talk."

"Mia, go away."

"Make me."

"What do you want?" he asked sitting up.

"To apologize," I started taking a spot on the edge of his bed next to him.

"You don't have to. I get it, I'll leave you alone if that's what you want," he said, falling back onto his bed.

He kicked his feet up, tucking one hand under his head. His stony expression was plastered across his face. The hard line his lips, the furrow of his brow, and the darkness in his eyes as he stared at the ceiling above him–it all screamed anger. I sat on his bed next to him.

"I do have to apologize. Look, it's hard for me to let people in and—"

"Just stop," he snapped, not even glancing my way. "You don't owe me an explanation. Just leave. I won't chase you or send anyone after you. You're free, I'm letting you out of our deal."

My jaw hit the floor. Along with my heart. I was finally ready and trying to let him in and he didn't want to listen to me. *This is a sign, Mia, get out of there.* I stood up, making my way back to my room. I shoved my zip drive and picture into my go-bag along with my pajamas. I'd crammed in most of the clothes I'd bought before lugging my backpack over my shoulder. Dante was coming down the hall as I exited my room.

"Where are you going?" he asked, his brows furrowed.

"Anywhere but here," I stated.

"You can't, you still have a few days left according to the deal. What happened?"

"Matteo just let me out of it." I shrugged, trying my best to act like I didn't care. "His exact words being *'just leave. I won't chase you or send anyone after you. You're free, I'm letting you out of our deal'.*"

His head snapped to Matteo's door then back to me. I patted his shoulder.

"Stay safe, Dante, and don't follow me."

I was out after that, jogging down the stairs and skipping out the front door. I paused at the bottom of the front porch steps, taking in a deep breath of fresh air. This was it, time to find a place for the night and begin my plan of attack on Igor.

I saw a black luxury car parked out front. The house was a far walk from the city. I walked toward it, trying the driver-side door. It was unlocked. I had fully expected to have to hotwire it to start it up. To my surprise, I saw the key fob in the center cup holder. I tossed my backpack into the passenger seat and climbed in. It roared to life as I pushed the button to start it. I threw it in drive, spinning the tires down the drive. All I needed was to get to Nonna's coffee shop. Then I could leave the car there and the fob with her.

I turned on the music, scanning my surroundings as I drove to the city. Nonna greeted me as I entered her shop.

"When Matteo comes, can you give him this?" I asked, handing her the fob.

Her brows furrowed. "Who is with you now?"

"No one, it's just me."

She swallowed, and said, "I see my grandson stuck his foot in his mouth."

I offered her a small smile. "No, there are just some things I have to do alone. Thank you for everything you've done for me. I really do appreciate you coming to check on me."

With a nod, I turned to walk away. I moved along the back alleys around the city. My mind tried to form a plan. Where would I go? *Somewhere they won't be expecting you.* They are going to look in all the places I wouldn't normally go, thinking I'd be in hiding. *We could hide in plain sight, girl.* They wouldn't expect me to be at any of the places I used to go. The coffee shop and apartment were a no go. Escaping from the confines of those locations would be hard. Especially with a minimal amount of people. The parkour park had a ton of people. I could blend there. My feet changed their course, heading straight there.

"M?" someone called as I walked over.

I looked up to see Enzo jogging toward me. He wrapped me up in a hug. It caught me off guard for a moment but he didn't seem to notice. His smile was full when he pulled back, resting his hands on my shoulders.

"Where have you been? I was worried about you after the state you were in the last time we saw one another."

"Oh, I got busy with work," I lied. "You really helped that day. Thank you."

"Want to join me on a run?" he motioned toward the course.

"No, I'm just here to hang out actually." I grabbed ahold of my backpack straps tightly, "I'll come watch, though."

"I have a better idea. Let's go grab a coffee from that stand in the parking lot and come back. I'll keep you company."

It seemed innocent enough and I would stay out in the open. It also gave me the perfect opportunity to blend in. There were a ton of people out and about together. Being alone might draw attention to myself. I nodded, letting him lead the way.

"You didn't have to buy," I said as he handed the guy at the stand cash.

"I wanted to. Come on." He pulled his phone from his pocket, looking down at it, "Oh shit. Hold on." He typed one-handed ferociously before looking back to me. "Sorry."

I shrugged, scanning the area again. "No worries."

We sat on a bench together in front of the start of the course. I was greeted by the other guys who we normally ran with. We watched them complete their runs, adding difficulty with each turn. Enzo put his arm on the back of the bench after a while.

"So, in the time we've run together I've not heard you mention anything about family. Does your family live around here?"

"I-uh-don't have any family. It's just me."

"Do you ever go out and let loose?"

"This is my way of letting loose." I motioned at the course with my hand. "I've even taken my runs to rooftops in the night."

"No shit! That's impressive. Maybe you'll take me on a night run? It would be the best adrenaline rush I've ever experienced."

"Maybe."

"What's with the backpack?"

"I came straight from work. I've had some late nights there and didn't want today to be another one. My coworkers can get... annoying."

He chuckled, "Can't most? You've told me before you work at The Core. What do you do there?"

"I'm a part of a security team."

"What do you guard?"

I smiled. "Nothing major. I mainly just find information for people. I'm not in the action scene of it at all."

"Oh, so you dig around on the computer for intel?"

I thought of Elliot sitting behind his screens. *That's it, he can help track down Igor.* I took my phone out of my backpack, turning it on.

"Exactly like that," I lied again. "Hold on, I have to make a call."

I slung my backpack over my shoulder. I moved a few feet away from Enzo so I would have some privacy for my call.

"Rogue?" Elliot answered.

"I need a secure line."

I hung up, waiting for him to call me back. It rang in my hand only seconds later.

"Hey," I answered.

"What do you need? I'll do anything, just tell me."

"Actually, can we meet somewhere you have access to computers? I need you to look into something for me."

"I will send you the address over a secure message."

"Thanks Elliot."

"Be safe, Mia."

I walked back over to Enzo.

"Unfortunately, I have to head out."

"Already?"

"Yeah. Duty calls. Thanks for the coffee Enzo, I'll see you later."

"See you, beautiful!" he said with a smirk.

I rolled my eyes. "I like M better!"

He laughed. "As you wish, night M."

With a wave I made my way to the address Elliot sent me, keeping my eyes peeled for any suspicious characters, Russian or Italian, who might be tailing me.

START A REVOLUTION

I APPROACHED HIS APARTMENT DOOR, seeing a tiny camera attached to the doorframe. I knocked, hearing the door unlock itself.

Well, that's either really wicked or terrifying. Why did he need that? Although being Elliot, he probably wanted it and then invented it. I stepped inside, hearing the door lock behind me.

"I'm in the kitchen," he called.

He was pouring two steaming mugs of tea when I walked in.

"I made you some tea."

"Thanks."

He slid one of the mugs across the counter, leaning on his elbows. I brought it to my lips, feeling it warm me inside out. He watched me for a minute before walking around the counter. Without saying another word, he gently took the mug back from me, setting it down. I wasn't sure what was going on until he wrapped his arms around me tightly in a hug. *What's with all the hugging lately?* My body tensed, but then returned the gesture.

"I'm glad you are safe, Mia." He pulled away, resting his hands on my shoulders. "Now, let's get to work."

He led the way into a room that was all him—in furniture form. From the computer screens to the table of tech pieces he was operating on, it was him. I sat down in the computer chair next to his. He laced his fingers together, cracking them as if to warm them up.

"What are we looking for?"

"I need all the information you can get me on a man by the name of Igor Petrov."

His fingers went to work, furiously typing away. Screens of information began popping up on his monitors.

"He's Russian, which I assume you already knew. He moved a lot when he was a child. Was in and out of different schools but has lived here for a few years."

He followed you when you were younger. You can use him to get information about you.

"Wait, where did he live when he was younger? How far can you trace him back?"

"I can use his school history to trace him back to the age of five. Before that, if we assume he lived with his father, I can trace him back to birth."

"Where did he live just before I turned eight, so...thirteen years ago?"

"Florida, in a town called—"

"La Belle," I finished for him. "Where did he live before that?"

"How did you know that?"

"That's where I lived when my family gave me up to the system. I have no information from before that. I don't remember but what I do know is that he has followed me my entire life. We can use him to track down my own identity."

"He stalked you when you were little too?" he asked. "Does he know you're not with the extraction team at the safe house?"

It then hit me. *He could hurt Elliot. Girl, what were you thinking?* How could I have forgotten? I stood up.

"You're right, I don't know if he knows. I'm sorry for taking a chance with your life. Just text me if you find anything. I'm sorry Elliot, I didn't mean to put you in danger."

"That's not what I meant." He shook his head. "You don't have to leave."

"I do, if he sends his goons here, you could get hurt."

Dammit. It's time to go, get out of this city to somewhere you know no one. Where you won't have leverage in the form of people you care about everywhere you look. I grabbed my backpack, throwing it over my shoulder as my heart pounded in my chest. An alarm started to ding as I turned to leave.

"What does that mean? Are they already here?" I asked.

"He's making a call. Do you want to listen to it?"

I stepped closer to him, nodding my head.

"They can't hear us, by the way."

"Who is he calling?"

Elliot paused before meeting my gaze. "Matteo." Then he pressed the space bar.

"What do you want?" Matteo answered, his tone already annoyed.

"I heard you lost that beautiful gem, Mia. Is that true?"

"No, it's not, she's perfectly safe and sound."

Igor's evil snicker echoed through the phone. "Is she? So you just let her out to play then? I got a message she was fraternizing with your enemy. You are both idiots, being so clueless as to who she is."

"Since you are so wise, why don't you enlighten me?" Matteo spat.

"Why would I do that? Please, if I start sharing her identity now, she'd have every damn Italian mafia swarming your city after her. I'm just trying to keep her safe from you Italian assholes. She's mine, Sartori, and she's going to come to me willingly. Especially when she finds out what a monster you are. Don't worry we'll name our first born after you." His laugh brought back those memories, causing bile to rise in my throat.

"You're not going to lay a finger on her, Petrov, or I will kill you with my bare hands."

"Why do you care so much?" he laughed. "Don't tell me you like her. She's out of your league, just like precious Giovanni was. You are both weak and pathetic excuses for men."

"Come say that to my face," Matteo snapped. "Oh wait, last time you said something to my face you ended up tied to a chair for three fucking days. How are you recovering?"

Igor let out an animalistic growl. "Stay away from her, she's mine!"

With that, he ended the call. Even though the call was over, I stared at the screen. The words echoing in my mind; every Italian Mafia head would be after me. *What the hell did you do girl?* I hadn't done anything that I could remember.

"Mia?" Elliot's voice was calm. "Sit down, we can dig some more. He won't find you here, you are safe."

It was then Matteo's words hit me; she's perfectly safe and sound. My eyes darted to Elliot.

"Did you tell any of the extraction team I was coming here?"

He didn't have to answer, the look in his eyes told me so.

"I just want you safe. When Dante texted me that you'd left, he also asked me to try to track you. I was surprised when you called, but glad you came. I made sure Dante promised not to come to get you. You're free just like Matteo said you were, but you are also welcome to stay here. My apartment is like a giant panic room. The Russians can't get inside."

How does he know so much? In fact, this whole time he hasn't asked many questions, almost like he knew the entire situation. My eyes narrowed at him, taking a step closer. Is he the rat?

"How do you know so much about the situation?" I asked. "You were texting Dante? Who are you to them?"

"Don't be mad at me." He swallowed, "My name is Elliot Luciano."

Where have you heard that last name before?

"I'm Dante's little brother," he added.

I flinched at his words like he had physically hit me. Then the emotions came at me all at once. Annoyance. Anger. Betrayal.

"I trusted you," I snapped "What else have you told them about me?"

"Nothing." He stood up, reaching for me to calm me down. "I haven't told them anything about you, Mia. All the research we've done has stayed between you and me. Just like all of this will. I told them not to bother you here. We can figure out who you are, just stay."

"You told them nothing about what we are doing?" I squinted at him.

"No. Nothing, call and ask them if you want. I made a deal with you to keep everything we've discovered quiet and I wouldn't break your trust, Mia. How distrusting you are of others didn't go unnoticed. I knew the night you approached me to help you it was hard for you to open up about yourself. I would never betray you like that. We're friends, whether you like it or not."

The sincerity in his voice told me he wasn't lying. My eyes flickered to his screens. *He's got a good lead and you know he's the best. What could it hurt to stay a few more hours?* No, he couldn't be a target.

"I need Igor's number," I demanded.

"Why?"

"To make contact with him."

"You can't go by yourself, Mia; he's got men with him. You'd be walking into your death."

"I'll be fine. Get me his number."

"No," he said firmly. "Not unless you take someone with you."

I growled in frustration. "I don't need to take anyone. I can face him myself. Either you give me his number or I will let his men lead me to him."

He didn't say anything, only typed on his computer for a moment. Then my phone pinged with the new information.

"Mia, let me help you."

"You can, by continuing to dig into his life. Text me with any new information. I'll be in touch soon."

Without another word, I left him standing there. I made my way outside, heading away from his building. I was hoping that if they were watching me I'd lead them as far away as possible. Once I was at a safe distance, I dialed his number.

"Hello?" he answered.

"Igor Petrov, I believe we have some unfinished business to attend to."

"Ah, my beautiful Mia. Are you ready to come home?"

A humorless laugh escaped me. "The only home I've ever had, you destroyed. Stop with the bullshit. I'm going to send you a location. I'd tell you to come alone but I know you're not a man of honor."

"And your Sartori boy is?"

"He's not mine," I spat through gritted teeth. "I have no one because of you."

"So, you won't mind if I kill him?"

My stomach tightened. *It's a trick to see if you care about him.* I had to convince him I didn't care. I transferred my emotions to feel that of the utmost confidence. I'd successfully gotten to him just like I'd wanted. My gaze scanned my surroundings as I kept walking down the sidewalk.

"Go ahead, what would that matter to me? I've learned my lesson, Petrov, I don't have friends this time around. You have no leverage against me."

"You don't care for him? You saved him from my sniper, tell me why then if he means nothing to you."

"I needed him alive for information. He was a means to an end."

"You kissed him in the mall. My men were there," he growled. "You know you've been extremely hard to track. Your rogue skills have only blossomed as you've gotten older. I've had someone on the inside working to keep an eye on you since you came to work with that disgraceful family. He's given me frequent updates."

There it is. The piece of information that I didn't know, but now do. The rat was a man. That left Spencer and Luke. *Unless it was one of the four at the safe house.* But Elliot cleared them.

I scoffed, "Right...well if you are done being insecure—"

He growled into the phone, "I am not being insecure. I'm making sure you don't have feelings for that Italian bastard. You are mine; we are supposed to be together. My dad was supposed to have you waiting for me but that damn Giovanni had to ruin everything. We are to start a revolution Mia, together."

The information he'd just given me didn't make sense. I couldn't connect it to anything Giovanni had ever said. Revolution? *Last time he called it destiny.* What did it all mean?

"I need you to do something for me first. Just to prove you don't have friends for me to leverage against you," he said, interrupting my thoughts.

"What?"

"Go back and kill your little tech pet you just paid a visit to."

I swallowed. "I don't have time for your games, Petrov."

"Fine, I'll just have my men pick him up and bring him to the location you send me. He can join us on our little reunion."

I let out a frustrated sigh. "Whatever, I'll go kill him now then if it means that much to you."

"How sweet of you love. Keep me on the phone, I want to hear everything."

"Stop with the pet names, asshole." I sneered, wrinkling my nose at his term of endearment. "The only thing I'm going to love about you is the torture that will lead to your slow and painful death."

I did as he asked, making my way back to Elliot's apartment. It didn't take him long to unlock the door. I walked in just as I had the first time. Assuming he was still in his tech room, I walked back there. When I opened the door he stood up. His hands were up in surrender. The step back he took was shaky as his body trembled.

"Mia please, don't do this," he whispered, his lower lip quivering.

Good, he was listening to the call. My fingers reached back behind me, curling around the handle of my gun. He backed into his wall, shaking his head. The ring of his phone sounded. I glanced at it, seeing Dante's name. He probably wanted an update on me, nosy asshole.

"I thought we were friends?" he mumbled.

"I don't have friends, sorry Hacker."

I kept my voice calm and even. A complete contrast to what my heart was doing. It was better this way. At least I wouldn't have to worry about him being captured and tortured. Instead, he'd avoid feeling that long-term pain of what the Russians were capable of inflicting. My mind would be at complete peace knowing Igor wouldn't have any more leverage over me. I raised my gun as he started to protest. Meeting his gaze, I pulled the trigger. The shot echoed through the room with a loud bang. Elliot fell forward onto the floor. His body collapsed onto itself with a thud.

"It's done," I stated.

"Send me a picture of his body along with the location. See you soon, beautiful."

He hung up. I glanced at Elliot on the floor, his body slumped before me. There was a moment of silence that filled the room. It was thick and heavy. I stared at him for a couple of minutes, gathering my thoughts on how to proceed. Finally, I squatted down to him.

"Hey," I tapped his shoulder with the butt of my gun, "dramatic much?"

With a smirk, he glanced up at me. "I had to make it believable."

I rolled my eyes. "He wasn't watching, he was listening."

"Did you hear the thud though? Sounded real, didn't it? He believed it, too. Take a picture of me on the floor like this. I can edit blood into the picture and encrypt the image so he can't tell it's been tampered with."

"All right, put your head back down how you were."

After taking a picture, he did just as he said he would. I sent it to Petrov along with the location of a parking garage and a time to meet. I could then ambush him there. If I killed the men he'd surely have with him then I could force him to take us to the woods just outside the city. There were secluded cabins out there that I could use to torture him.

"Also, I found something of particular interest as I was researching his locations as a child compared to yours," he stated. "Stay a minute, it might help when you confront him."

"What is it?"

"I was looking into families that acquired a child with minimal adoption papers from the city before La Belle. I found nothing with adoption papers but I did find a family that all of the sudden had a little girl. Documents say that the little girl was their niece from another state they were taking care of." He pulled up a picture of them. "That little girl looks a lot like you, Mia. You didn't start your life in foster care."

He brought up a picture of them on the screen. I swallowed, their faces reminding me of something so faint I closed my eyes.

"I remember them, not completely, but they feel familiar. Are they related to me or was that all a hoax? Or can we call them, maybe they can tell us where I came from?"

"I'm sorry Mia, they were murdered just after they gave you up to the system."

There was a ball of fire building inside me. My fists clenched so tight it made my knuckles white. *I bet you Nicholai Petrov killed them.* As my jaw ticked with the anger, I stared at the image of myself as a young girl on his screen.

Elliot's phone pinged and the mechanical noise of his front door opening sounded. We got up, walking down the hallway to see whoever came in. When I came around the corner Dante punched me in the face. His knuckles connecting with my cheek. I fell to the floor, trying to shake the blurriness out of my eyes.

"What the fuck, Dante?" I snapped.

I flung myself at him, tackling him to the ground. The target was his face as I swung on him. There were voices yelling at us to stop, but I wasn't going to stop defending myself. He didn't so much as flinch, taking my hands and rolling us over to pin me against the floor. His eyes were wide with rage as he straddled my body. He bared his teeth at me, like an animal, pressing his gun against my temple.

"He was my brother, you psycho!" he growled. "Now it's your turn to die!"

"Dante stop!" Matteo grabbed onto his shirt, pulling him off me. The pressure of the cold barrel on my temple faded as Matteo slammed him into the wall. "He's standing right here!"

"I'm fine," Elliot reassured him. "Mia would never hurt me."

Dante wrapped his arms around his brother in a tight hug, the tense muscles in his shoulders relaxing. I laid there, catching my breath from the adrenaline of it all. *Wow, he really thought you killed Elliot.* The tension that was overwhelming the room began to fade away. Dante turned, holding his hand out to me. I thought he was going to help me up, but when I took his hand, he yanked me into his arms.

"I'm sorry Mia," he blubbered, his voice sloppy with emotion. "I thought you killed him."

My arms were frozen at my sides before I gave him a pat on the back.

"I get it, he's your family," I said, pulling away. "Wait, how did you know what was going on the entire time?"

His eyes flickered to Elliot. My shoulders fell.

"Dammit, Elliot," I complained.

"What? It helps if we're all on the same page. As you can see, if Dante would have known it was an act, he wouldn't have punched you in the face."

"I should have just shot you," I grumbled.

"When did you figure out she wouldn't?" Sal asked him. "The call did sound very convincing."

"I knew she wouldn't hurt me." He held up a finger. "I will say, though, a small part of me thought she might when I saw the look in her eyes. All dark and angry, dominant. Almost as scary as when Matteo succumbs to his anger. Then she raised her gun and it was pointed at the wall." He offered me a smile. "Come on, there's more."

As we began our walk back to the tech room, I felt the guys behind me. *You're just going to leave after this. Not like they won't dig for information once you are gone.* I took my seat, seeing an alert pop up on his screen.

"What's that mean."

"I've found the first family to have you after your parents gave you up."

"Tell me everything."

The taps of his keys were the only sound in the room, until he brought up another picture. Our heads snapped to one another.

"Holy shit," I said, as my eyes darted around his desk for the photograph. "Where is it?"

He walked around me to open a blue folder on his desk. Retrieving the photo, he held it up to the screen with the photo of my first family. They were identical.

"Where did you get that picture?" Dante asked.

"It was in the manilla envelope on the last mission. There were three pictures in it. This one, one of Igor and I in kindergarten that you saw, and another one."

"What's the other one?" Matteo asked.

"Giovanni and me walking in the park when we were older," I stated, looking back at the screen.

"That baby is you, Mia." Elliot sat back down, typing some more. "They were your first family. They were the Bianchi family. The woman's name was Rose and her husband was Andrew. They were the first ones to raise you. They have pictures with you up until you turned four when you went to the other family."

The screen flashed with more pictures of me growing up with them. I seemed happy, and so did they. Almost like they actually loved me as their own. There were birthday pictures, holiday pictures, and family pictures which appeared to take place twice a year. Then one of a handwritten letter. *Why would they have a picture of a letter?* I leaned forward in my chair to read it on the screen in front of me.

He will come for her if he finds her. Protect her with your lives. Raise her to be prepared for her future. She must be the one to accept her path. You may not give her any information about her past except what was given to you. Most importantly, you may not tell her who she is. If you cannot keep her safe send her to the Russo family. Contact information for them will follow. They will be waiting. If you fail and she is harmed, you will pay with your lives. -Imperatore

Imperatore was Italian for emperor. *Do they have those in the mafia hierarchy?* I wasn't sure, but I did know one thing for sure. That same signature was on my application to The Core. I shot up from my seat, meeting the blue eyes of Matteo.

"Who is the emperor?" I ordered.

His brows furrowed. "How would I know?"

"Stop bullshitting and tell me who he is," I demanded grabbing two fistfuls of his shirt.

"Mia, I don't know anyone that goes by that name. I don't know why you think I'm involved."

"That name was on my application to The Core."

He grimaced. "It was on your application to The Core?"

"Yeah. I was at the safe house Giovanni's family set up for me. There was an envelope left on the doorstep when I went to leave. Inside was a plane ticket, an address to my apartment I'd lived in until shit hit the fan, a note, and an application to The Core." I released his shirt, my hands falling to my sides.

"What did the note say?" Dante asked.

"It said I would be safe here and he would see me when the time was right."

"He who?"

"*Imperatore*. That's who signed the note," I explained. "So tell me your involvement, Matteo, because if you had anything to do with Giovanni's death I will—"

"I didn't." He cut me off, putting one hand on my cheek. His eyes stared deep into mine, locking me into place in front of him. "I swear on my own life. I had no idea who you were until I started to take over for my father at The Core."

"Maybe your first family can tell us," Sal offered, looking to Elliot.

As if on cue, his fingers moved elegantly across the keys once more. I back out of Matteo's embrace, his simple touch making me feel like my skin was on fire with need. *You can't be around him much longer. He's going to try to convince you to stay.* I rejoined Elliot, watching the screens pop up so fast I couldn't read anything. When his face twisted my heart fell into my stomach. I swallowed the new lump in my throat.

"They were killed too, weren't they?"

His eyes were watery. "I'm sorry Mia."

"Look up every set of foster families I've had."

"Why?"

"Just do it, Elliot," I growled.

As he typed away, I paced behind him. The guys took a step back to give me space. My skin felt hot, but this time it was due to the rage that pumped through my veins. After a few minutes, he spun in his chair to face me.

"Tell me which ones are still alive," I ordered.

He stood to cut me off, making me meet his gaze.

"How many?" I asked.

"Mia…" his voice trailed off.

"That's what I thought."

Every family? They've killed every set of parents I've had! I snatched my backpack from its place on the floor. *Time to face him.* I was surprised when they let me walk out the door.

A TASTE OF REVENGE

IT WAS A FEW MINUTES early when I arrived but Igor was already there. He was leaning against his car, a man on either side of him.

"Mia, my beautiful girl, I'm so glad to see you." He smiled as I walked into view.

"You only brought two?" I asked.

"Well, I assumed you were coming alone, so why would I need more?"

With his verification, however true that was, I pulled my gun. I fired two shots, one in each of their chests. They didn't have enough time to react before sliding down the side of the car. His body went rigid, his jaw parting in shock. *He didn't expect you to kill them.* I aimed my gun at Petrov. *Time to prove I'm not that weak little girl anymore.*

"Time to take a ride, you're driving. Get in," I ordered.

We climbed in, me sitting behind him in the back seat. I made sure to buckle, knowing he could try something to offset my balance.

"You follow my directions to the location and you don't get shot in the car. Got it?"

"If you wanted me alone all you had to do was ask, love."

I pressed the barrel of my gun against the back of his head.

"Enough with the pet names," I snarled. "Leave the garage and take a right."

Guiding him to the edge of the woods, I made him park on the side of the road. When we got out, I guided him to an empty cabin through the cover of the trees. Flicking on the light, I pressed my gun into his back. It made him walk forward to the kitchen area. I had packed zip-ties in my backpack for this exact moment. I tied his hands behind him pulling just tight enough to make it uncomfortable on his wrists. Then shoved him in a chair and zip-tied each of his legs to that of the chairs.

"What do we do now, love?" He leaned back, his cocky attitude pissing me off even more.

"Why was I promised to your father?"

"I am unable to say."

"I hear you speaking just fine. Maybe I should cut your tongue out so you won't be a liar," I threatened. "Answer my questions."

"Not until you know who you are."

"Then tell me that first."

"I will. In due time, love."

We can figure that out later. Right now, let's just enjoy this torture, for Giovanni.

I bent down, clutching the handle of the knife I kept in my boot. It's a long blade so sharp it could cut a piece of paper in one slice. The light reflected off the metal. I admired it for a moment, seeing my reflection in its surface. Igor didn't seem fazed by the sight of it.

"That's fine, I'll figure it out when we are done having fun." I cocked my head to the side. "Tell me, where was the first stab wound you gave G?"

He snorted, "I give you credit my love, I didn't expect you to shoot my men. Now this act can stop. I know you are just a rogue. Being trained by one who couldn't stomach the sight of blood. I think you can put that away now. It's time for us to go."

I turned away from him, transferring my emotions to rage with a touch of calm. The calm was what kept me from making brash decisions out of rage alone. I spun on my heel to him, leaning in so our faces were only a few inches apart. He leaned back, his eyes bulging out.

"What happened to you?" he breathed. "You're different."

His breaths were quick and raspy now. He was afraid and it brought a wicked smile to my face. *This was going to be fun.* I brought the blade of the knife up against his cheek.

"You happened, *Iggs*. And now I have the chance to properly thank you. After seeing you tear apart the only family I had, it did something to me. It broke me. From that moment on, I became a person who you will wish you'd never met."

There was only a little bit of pressure needed to slice his cheek open. He let out a yelp in pain, wincing. I watched the blood drip slowly down his cheek.

"Mia, stop!" he ordered. "I don't want to have to punish you for this later."

"Aww, you think you're getting out of here alive?" I started to slowly circle him, letting my fingers trickle across his chest. Dragging them along his shoulder as I moved behind him. "Let me remind you, Giovanni never made it out alive. That means," I paused, and leaned into his ear from behind, lowering my voice to a whisper. "You won't either."

I shoved the knife into the top of his shoulder. Another scream ripped through the air. The metallic smell of blood started to form in a cloud around him. His chest was rising and falling as he panted to try to calm his heart rate. I was sure it was up with the adrenaline and invasion I was causing his body. His plain t-shirt stuck to his shoulder, wet with the blood his body was leaking.

"He didn't deserve you. He was worthless," he spat. "I deserve you."

I punched him in the face. His lip burst open, blood filled his mouth. I could tell by the way his teeth were now stained pink instead of white. He spit a mouthful of blood on the floor.

"You need to stop before you do something you'll regret."

"The only thing I regret is not coming for you sooner."

I punched him again as hard as I could. I leaned my body weight into it. His head bounced backward, then fell. He squeezed his eyes shut, shaking his head as if to get rid of the sting of the punch.

"That's enough!" he ordered.

The sound of the back door being smashed in ripped through the cabin. A man that had similar facial features to Igor walked in. Although he seemed much younger in the face, the full suit and dress shoes gave him a superior aura to that of Igor. Two goons stood behind him. I shot one, then the other, like I had in the parking garage.

"Who are you?" I asked moving my gun to the last one.

He glared at me. "That wasn't nice, Miss Mia, I liked them." He walked closer, but not to me, instead toward Igor. "I see you and your love are getting along great, brother."

"Fuck you, Alexei." He snapped, wincing as he tried to wiggle his wrists in the ties. "Cut me out of these. What took you so long?"

"The Italians were close behind us. I left a few men to fight them but the one is proving to be quite the challenge. He becomes quite feral when he is upset."

Brother? Oh shit, you are outnumbered now.

"That's Sartori," Igor grumbled to his brother. "Bastard is always in my business."

My brain started to think of an escape plan. I took a step away only for a minute before a man ran in. He leaned into Alexei's ear, whispering something before he gave him a nod. He then approached me. I pointed my gun at him, pulling the trigger only for it to do nothing. My eyes flew to it. Dammit, I didn't remember the last time I reloaded it. He grabbed ahold of my arms tightly at my biceps. The gun fell out of my hand as I tried to wriggle out of his grasp. When I kneed him, he let me go, then another few Russians came in. I swung my knife, trying to fight them off. But with three of them coming at once, I ended up being pinned against the wall.

Alexei bent to cut Igor free. He rubbed his wrists where the tie had been before cutting his own legs free.

Alexei walked over to me, tilting his head to the side like he was inspecting a creature he'd never seen before. His hands were tucked casually into his pockets. He carried himself differently than his brother. With more grace, and, although he was in charge of the men in the room, I could tell they listened because they respected him instead of fearing him..

"You are strong, I give you that, but can't take on an army alone, *printsessa*. I do admire your determination," he stated. "Too bad your future was determined by my father and this first-born asshat. We would have made a better team."

"Fuck off!" Igor scowled. "Stop talking, she doesn't know who she is yet."

His brother's eyebrows rose. "Oh, he hasn't told you?" he asked me.

"No," I answered.

"Come with me willingly and I'll tell you everything." He held out his hand to me, and giving his men a look, they released me. They didn't move from around me, but they no longer had their hands on me.

"No! You can't!" Igor lunged at his brother.

One of the men standing near me cut him off, knocking him to the ground. Alexei didn't even have to give him an order to do so, it was automatic. It gave me an opening to run, but my feet stayed cemented in place. *He would tell you everything. But he's also the brother of your enemy.* I watched the situation unfold as Alexei turned to his brother on the floor. The way he peered down at him, his lips pressed together. After a heavy sigh, he shook his head.

"Do not try to interfere brother. We both know father is expecting you to fail. That's all you've done since you killed her love and she escaped you."

"I almost had her!" he growled coming to stand. "Giovanni was a bastard!"

"Shut the fuck up, Igor, or I'll give your other cheek a matching gash!" I threatened.

Igor fumed, "You will *not* speak to me that way!"

"Fuck you!" I spat.

The tension was broken by a throaty laugh. I looked to Alexei, seeing his head tilt back as he let it out.

"She's perfect." He laughed. "I like her spunk."

"She's mine! Her escape won't happen again. Besides, she wouldn't have escaped if you'd not been a distraction to father with your training."

"That is where you went wrong, Iggs. She should have never escaped because she shouldn't have been locked up. You tortured the one person who was supposed to feel love from you. You didn't treat her with respect or dignity. Now I have to clean up your mess, like I have been doing for years." He turned to me. "Miss Mia, please, we must go."

He held his hand back out to me. I stared at it, contemplating whether I should go with them. *He was different than his brother.* This could also be a ploy. I had to take precautions.

"I'm not going with you."

I had completely expected him to put up a fight. The tension in my muscles readied me to begin swinging. There was a crash outside the cabin but no one dared look away from each other.

"Very well." He gave me curt nod. "We will see you when you know who you are." He turned, walking to the back door where he'd come from. "Igor, let's go."

"She's coming with."

"She is not, she doesn't want to. Let's go," he ordered. "Father is waiting."

"You don't get to make the decisions. I am the head of this family! We are taking her with us by force!" he screamed.

Alexei shook his head, "Very well, deal with the angry Sartori on your own then."

"I'll be out of here before he can get to her."

"Think again," a voice growled from the doorway.

My eyes flew to him as his posture demanded the attention of the room. It was like his rage had consumed him. His muscles strained against his shirt as he took angry deep breaths. The aura he carried exuded dominance, causing one of the Russians to step away from me in fear. There was blood all over his swollen knuckles and hands. His shirt was spattered with droplets yet he appeared uninjured. Manic would be the best way to describe him as he stalked over, throwing one punch to the side of the Russian's head that was standing in front of me. He fell straight to the floor, knocked out cold by just the one hit. I hadn't expected him to move as fast as he did for his size. The other two then tried take on Matteo together.

"We'll see you again, Miss Mia!" Alexei called from the back door.

I saw Igor start to back away, trailing behind his brother.

"No!" I yelled.

It was like the cement my feet had been stuck in evaporated. He couldn't get away, not this time. I bolted forward to chase after him. I didn't know what I was going to do once I got to him, but I knew I didn't want him to walk away from this alive. I promised myself—hell, I promised G. But two arms wrapped around my waist before I could get to the door.

"Mia, we have to go."

Dante. Always in the fucking way. I thrashed against him, trying to get loose. That was when Matteo turned his attention to us. Arturo and Sal cut him off.

"It's Dante, he's not hurting her." They yelled.

With his eyes locked on me, Matteo shoved Sal. There was so much force behind it he flew into the chair, crushing it under him. I froze, watching him then toss Arturo like he weighed nothing into the wall. Dante released me from his arms.

"Shit." He started backing up.

Matteo's eyes never left Dante. They were swarming with rage. The veins in his neck pressing hard through his skin. It was like he was possessed by his anger. He was hurting his own people now.

"Mia, run!" Arturo ordered, scrambling to his feet. "Go with Sal."

"You put your hands on her," Matteo's voice was low, threatening to Dante.

My eyes darted from Matteo to Sal. He had his hand out, waiting on me. When Matteo swung at Dante, my feet moved without hesitation. I ran right in between them.

"Don't!" Dante shouted, as Matteo reared back again to swing.

"Matteo stop!" I yelled, placing my palms on his chest.

He froze, his eyes coming to meet mine. Lowering his fist he blinked a few times, taking in his surroundings. The place was silent. He looked back at Dante, swallowing hard, suddenly avoiding my eyes.

"I'll meet you at home," he stated before stalking out.

I turned to look at Dante, baffled as to what to do. Part of me wanted to chase after him, the other part worried about what I'd find.

"Is he all right?" I asked.

Dante nodded. "Mia, come back with us, please."

I grabbed my bag from the kitchen. With a nod, I followed them to the car. They were silent the entire ride there, we all were. I stared out the window, wondering about Matteo. *Where did he go?* I brought my things into my room at the safe house. I took a shower, wanting to wash the events from the day off me.

There was too much information learned that night. Too many unanswered questions about what was going on. Yet every question led back to me finding out who I was. It all evolved around my identity. I wanted to watch the videos Giovanni gave me. I *had* to watch them. It was time to figure out who I was. In need of a laptop, I walked out of my room and down the hallway. Before I raised my hand to knock on the door I heard their hushed whispers.

"She snapped you right out of it, boss," Arturo stated.

"How?" Sal asked. "No one could ever do that before."

"I don't know," Matteo said, his voice calm now.

"You do know, you just won't admit it. You like her, Matteo, that's why she can do that."

"I like you three and you don't snap me out of it," he countered.

"You know what I mean, don't be an ass about it," Dante spat back. "She's different because you want her to be yours. No matter how bad you are trying to honor what she wants and leave her alone, you can't help it."

"Yeah, I mean we all know you have a crush on her," Arturo stated.

There was a thump.

"Ow. You didn't have to punch me. That wasn't kind, boss," Arturo complained.

I covered my mouth with my hand as if to silence my smile, bringing my other hand up to knock on the door. The room fell silent for a moment. I composed myself before Dante opened the door.

"Can I borrow the laptop again?" I asked.

"Sure."

Matteo was walking over with it, his eyes locking on mine.

"Thanks." I took it and headed back to my room.

Taking a deep breath, I laid down on the bed. There was a new determination inside as I started the videos. The determination that dwindled the moment I hit the spot I always stopped at. I rolled over onto my back, covering my face. *Why can't you watch them through?* As my eyes stung with tears, I found myself wanting to talk to Dante again. I cracked my door, making sure the coast was clear. I scurried down to his room, knocking on his door loud enough for him to hear yet quiet enough to not draw too much attention if someone were coming up the stairs.

"Want to talk?" he asked, taking in my watery eyes.

"Same place." I nodded.

I shut the door behind us, following him to his balcony just as I had the time before. We took a moment to take in the dark sky around us. The tears trickled down my cheeks silently as I tried to blink them away.

"Mia, what's wrong?"

"I want to talk to you about Giovanni," I admitted. "Is that... all right?"

"Yeah, of course."

I took a deep breath. "Giovanni knew everything. Who I really am, my 'destiny,' that the Russians were after me, and why they wanted me so badly. He knew he was going to die before it all happened."

"How do you know all that?" Dante asked.

"He's the one that sent me that zip drive. There's another folder on it with five videos he put together. Then a day before everything happened, he mailed it to the safe house his family set up for me."

"Do any of the videos have your real identity on it?" he asked.

I looked down at my hands. "The first three and a half don't."

"You haven't watched them all?"

"I can't make it through them all. The last video—he titled it 'goodbye amore mio' and I can't bring myself to watch it."

"What if you skip to that one first?" he suggested.

"His request in the first video is that I watch them in order."

"Would it help if I watched them with you? Or all four of us? Then we would be there for you through it."

Would it? It was hard enough to watch it on my own. I chewed on my lower lip for a moment.

"I don't know. That would expose my entire past to all of you. I don't know that I'm ready for that."

"Are you ready to find out who you are?"

"Yeah, I want to know my real identity and who my family is. Even though they gave me up I still want to know where I came from. The only reason I know I'm Italian is because I looked in the file my caseworker had. It said my ethnicity was Italian-American. Elliot also found the name Bianchi—my first family's name." I shook my head, looking at my hands, "I was so close to getting revenge. The satisfaction was intoxicating. Then everything went to shit."

"If we worked together, we could have had him for you on a silver platter." He reached out, putting one hand on my shoulder. "But I think there's another reason why you don't want to make it to the end of those videos. One that you're not ready to confront."

I felt the tears sting my eyes once more. *What is going on with the tears, girl?* When I opened my mouth to speak, I finally admitted aloud why I was so reluctant.

"I don't want to say goodbye to him yet."

Dante nodded, knowingly. "It won't be a goodbye; it will be a new start for you. He will always be with you in your heart. Letting go of that sorrow that comes with losing someone can make you even stronger, you just have to be ready to accept it." He leaned his elbows on his knees. "Think about it, it's late. You don't have to decide tonight."

I gave him a nod, wiping my cheeks.

"Why did you come to me and not Matteo?"

I shrugged. "I feel like you have outside, unbiased advice. You're neutral and I appreciate that because your loyalty should reside with Matteo."

"It does, I just know what's good for him," he chuckled. "I also know what's good for you and that's opening up. Even taking Petrov out of the picture, life will be a million times easier if we all work together to figure out who you are. To do that you have to give us some leeway when asking questions about your personal life and past."

"Yeah, I'll think about it," I mumbled.

"Can I tell the guys about the videos?"

"As long as you tell them not to ask additional questions."

He got up, walking with me back through his room. Matteo was standing in the mid-motion of a knock when Dante opened the door for me. His eyes glanced from my puffy ones to Dante and back.

"Oh good, my next client is right on time," Dante teased in a professional tone. "Please come in good sir, my last appointment was just leaving."

I smiled, punching him in the arm.

"Shut up, you're not a damn therapist."

"I am for the two of you. I'm about to start charging the both of you so you learn to talk to one another."

I rolled my eyes. "I'm going to bed."

"Good night." They called to me.

"Night."

PRETTY GIRL

THE NEXT DAY I WAS pacing in my room. They should all be having their morning coffee right now at the kitchen island like they did every morning. The first cup was together while they ate breakfast. The second, they dispersed to do whatever was next on their agendas. I'd thought about it all night, letting them watch the videos. I had to figure out who I was. I peered down at the picture of Giovanni in my hand.

"You know, you'd like them, G. They would fit in with us," I whispered. "Maybe it is time to share you, huh?"

I scooped up the laptop, bringing up the first video. I paused it, walking straight down the stairs. Every step I took, the bundle of nerves in my stomach tightened into a knot. Their laughter echoed through the kitchen. *You sure about this?* It's time, at least just the first video. I walked in, feeling their eyes on me. I sat the laptop down on the island to face them, my chest rising and falling rapidly as I scanned their faces. They were quietly watching me. I closed my eyes, transferring every ounce of myself to determination. When I was ready, I reached around the laptop and pressed the spacebar.

His voice came to life before them:

"Hey la mia vita, I know you are going to be sad when you get this in the mail, so watch them as you can. My only request is that you watch them in order. I put them in an order for a specific reason. It's okay if you can't make it through them all right away. I'll be gone if you are watching them, but I hope you will have someone that loves you as much as I do to watch them with. Shit, some of these videos may help him understand your crazy ass," he laughed. *"So get ready because you are about to watch the story of us."*

They were silent for a few minutes.

"So, he knew you were crazy, as well," Arturo stated.

Matteo punched his arm, causing him to wince.

"Again? That's the same arm, boss," he complained, rubbing his bicep.

A giggle escaped me. I had no idea where it came from. Their heads snapped to mine. *Okay, it wasn't that bad. Maybe try the next one?* I turned the laptop, bringing up the next one. When Matteo got up, I froze. So did everyone else.

"Sit back down, Matteo," Sal whispered not taking his eyes off me. "We want to see the next one."

I thought he was leaving, instead, he walked around the counter. He reached into the cabinet and pulled down a mug. He filled it with coffee, two spoons of sugar, and a dash of cream just how I like it. Without saying a word, he handed it to me. I took it with both my hands. That's when he put his hands on my shoulders, guiding me around to sit in his seat. I felt my body want to melt under his touch. He pulled the laptop closer and the guys moved in. The only thing he didn't do was press the spacebar to start the video. He leaned into my ear, whispering to me.

"Whenever you are ready, *cattivella*."

His breath tickled my skin, making the hairs on the back of my neck stand up. I peered down at my coffee. *He pays attention, Mia, he cares. No matter how much that terrifies you, let it be your strength right now. You must figure out who you are.* I took a small sip, taking a deep breath. Didn't I transfer my emotions to determination? What happened? *His hands on your shoulders, his breath on your skin.* That can't be. I reached out using my pointer finger to press play.

When it flashed to me jumping roofs, the guys leaned in.

"Oh shit! I thought you fell." Sal smiled. "My stomach fell right out of me."

I smiled to myself, turning my attention back to the screen to watch Giovanni look into the camera as I was wrapped in his arms. "*She's a damn badass.*"

"He was proud of you," Dante noted.

"How far was that gap?" Sal asked.

"Eight feet."

"Holy shit!" Arturo's brows rose, shaking his head to himself.

"*What are we working on today Mia?*" he asked me. "*Sharpening the senses of hearing and touch,*" I smiled. "*I get to shoot G with a paintball gun today, basically."* He laughed. *"Don't sound so excited about it, cattivella."*

I saw Matteo's jaw drop in the reflection of the screen, but I didn't dare look at him. Then his head hung for a second, almost like he was upset. I wondered if I should pause it but he looked back at the screen before I had a chance to. My eyes were then glued to the screen as I saw myself kiss G's cheek with a giggle before he set the camera up to view the entire room. They watched on in silence as it played me shooting at G with a paintball gun.

"Well out of ten times, you got me seven." He smiled, taking the gun. *"That means I get seven shots on you, better start running."* As I ran around the room giggling, I dodged his shots.

The next part of the clip where I raced his father on opening locks was intriguing to the guys. I felt them lean forward in awe to watch the race unfold.

"Damn, Mia," Arturo whispered near the end of the race.

His comment brought a small smile to my face. One that disappeared as the final part of the clip started. I was cuddled up against Giovanni. As I sat there, I wished I could feel his arms around me once more. I'd give my own life to get lost in his arms again.

"Look at this girl right now, she loves to cuddle. Don't let her badass persona fool you she's a sucker for being snuggled." He turned to the camera again, like I had memorized from all the other times I'd watched this. *"I'll tell you what,"* he whispered to not wake me up, *"if someone other than me watches this video*

with her, you better enjoy this shit, you never know how long you have on Earth. Never take her for granted."

I could feel them smiling around me. Especially when I woke up groggily suspicious at what he was doing.

"G, what are you filming now?" He laughed. *"Uh...nothing."* I was squinting at him suspiciously. *"Put it away, snuggle with me."* He flipped the camera back to him, giving it an I-told-you-so look. *"I'll snuggle you to the end of time, cattivella."* You could hear me giggle before the clip ended.

I took a deep breath as it came to an end. The second one was harder to watch. Mostly because it was more intimate and it brought on feelings I could only dream about. A tear escaped down my cheek.

"Mia, why don't we stop?" Matteo asked. "We watched two already."

"I want to watch them all, I just—I know he sent me these for more than memories. He always had a well-thought-out reason for everything." I wiped my cheek. "He was smart and calculated."

"Then let's take a break. We can watch the rest of them later tonight," Dante offered.

My head hung at their pressure to wait, worried I'd lose the nerve. Matteo spun me in my chair, lifting my chin with his fingers to meet his intense pools of blue.

"It's not that we don't want to see them. It's that your mind needs a break. If you keep your emotions bottled up it's going to break you when you watch them. So, let's do something to get out what you are feeling." His voice was calm and soothing,

"I think I just want to go back to sleep for a bit," I admitted.

He stepped aside, letting me head upstairs. I took my coffee with me. The giant comforter swallowed me as I lay down. The tears that had come with the memories started to wet my pillow. I rubbed my thumb across Giovanni's face in our picture. My heart hurt again, a pain that I wasn't sure could ever be healed. A knock sounded at my door. I sniffled, wiping my cheeks frantically, as if it would erase all evidence of me crying.

"Come in."

I didn't look to see who it was. He came around, sitting on the edge of the bed. He ran a hand through his hair, pausing to rub the back of his neck. I sat up, setting the picture on the nightstand. For a minute, we stared at one another. The gold ring in his eye seemed to glisten with the light hitting it through the window.

"I don't want to lie to you," he started. "I've seen the first video."

"I put three on there."

"I know, but after watching the first one I thought that you should be the one to share them with me when you were ready. Watching them would have felt like I was betraying your trust."

"Thank you for telling me."

The silence fell between us once more.

"I didn't mean to push you to stop sharing him with us. I just, I want you to be able to express yourself and I know you keep things bottled up inside to handle them when you are alone," he explained.

"I can transfer my emotions, Matteo." I finally verified his suspicion. "It's not that I'm keeping them bottled up. I mean, I am in a way, but I do let myself shed those emotions that I push away in the moment."

"You can transfer all of them?"

I nodded. "Except lately I've been struggling to do so. I used to be so good at it."

"You might be overwhelmed." He stood up to leave. "Get some rest. If you need anything just yell. Nonna has informed me that she is coming to make dinner tonight. Maybe after that we can watch the other videos if you feel up to it."

"Thank you."

He started to move away, then stopped.

"I'm sorry, Mia, for yelling at you. For refusing to hear you out when you tried to come talk to me. I do get it, and I'm trying to give you space. I'm trying to not get attached. If I'm being honest with you, though, I think I already am."

A foreign warmth spread from my toes to my head, making my cheeks hot. *Did he just make you blush? What the hell?* I immediately took interest in my lap, lowering my head to hide the new color of my cheeks.

"After yesterday and all the shit that went down, I need to find out who I am. If that means I have to open up to you guys and let you in, then I will. I guess what I'm trying to say is...I'm all right forgetting that conversation if you are."

I peered up at him, seeing the way his smile reached all the way to his eyes. It gave them a different kind of sparkle. One that wasn't from the light but from his emotions.

"I would like that." He took a step back. "I'll see you later, get some rest."

Nonna and I were in the kitchen cooking up something together when I heard laughter coming from the backyard. I moved to glance out the kitchen window. They had a wooden box in the middle of a grassy area. Taking turns, they were running and jumping over it. *Were they trying to do parkour?* I chuckled to myself, causing Nonna to lean over. She clicked her tongue three times.

"Well, *piccola*, I must say you picked the right bunch to open up to. Look at them out there, *bambini adulti* (adult children) is all they are."

"Yeah, you have that right."

"I'm glad my grandson removed the foot from his mouth." She noted, "he has a different look to him when you are around. Even if he tries to hide it, I've seen it." She stirred the ingredients she had in a bowl on the counter, "Are you happy, *piccola*?"

The question brought my attention back to her.

"I—" I swallowed, dropping my gaze to my hands as my fingers played with one another, "at times I am. There's still a lot to process in all this."

She stopped, reaching out to me. Her wrinkly skin was soft as she took my hands with hers.

"You are strong, I believe you will get through this and much more."

The genuine tone she used along with the warmth in her eyes was overwhelming. It pushed me to find somewhere else to place my sights. Ending up on the guys outside again, I heard her chuckle.

"Go, I'll make dinner." She motioned outside with her head. "Show them how it's done."

She didn't have to tell me twice. I scurried outside, walking up next to them.

"What are you all doing?" I asked, a cheeky smile on my face.

"Trying to do shit like you. Teach me your ways!" Arturo begged with his hands clasped together.

I spent the evening teaching them a few things before dinner was ready. I was quiet as I listened to them converse around me. Their laughter and rowdiness echoed through the dining room. What was even more entertaining was that Nonna sassed them right back anytime they began poking fun at one another. They even teased her a bit. After dinner she made them all cappuccinos for dessert.

She didn't stay much later. I began cleaning up the kitchen, and not long after, Matteo came in with his empty coffee mug.

"Mia, I would have helped you if I'd known you were in here cleaning."

"I can do it, it's not a big deal."

"No, we all help around here."

He let out a loud whistle. The three of them came in moments later, joining right away in the process of cleaning. It wasn't until everything was put away that I turned to them.

"I want to watch the videos now," I stated.

"Come on, we have a surprise for you." Dante smiled.

My brows furrowed. "I don't like surprises. Just tell me."

I followed him, nonetheless. The rest of them around me with smiles they were doing a poor job of hiding on their lips.

"You'll like this one," Sal assured me.

We came to a door. It was a little wider than the rest of the doors in the house. It also had a sideways handle instead of a knob to open it. Dante swung the door open, moving so I could step inside. The dim lights flicked on when I entered, scanning the room. It was set up like a movie theatre. It had two different platforms; a lower one and one that was one step up. They were carpeted with fuzzy dark tan carpet. Each had a huge couch in the center with a reclining chair on either side of it. The giant white screen against the wall was complete with surround sound speakers hanging from the walls.

The screen was frozen on Giovanni's face. They'd hooked up the laptop so that we could watch the videos on the big screen. I took a few steps inside, my eyes peering up at the screen. My feet carried me to the bottom level, standing to stare at his face.

"We thought it would make it feel like he's surrounding you." Arturo stated. "Like a hug from him...but from only his voice."

My lower lip started to quiver. I covered my face with both my hands, crouching down. They'd done all this for me. I turned around to face them.

"Thank you," I mumbled.

They took their seats as I looked back to the screen. The way they went straight to their spots told me that it was always the same each time they'd come into the room. The front recliners were claimed by Arturo and Sal. Dante and Matteo had sat on either side of the couch. That left the middle open for me. Arturo threw me a blanket and Sal reached across Matteo with a bottle of water. My heart could have exploded at their kindness. They didn't have to do any of this.

"Ready?" Matteo asked.

With a nod, he pressed the spacebar on the laptop to start the third video. Giovanni's voice came through the room. Arturo had been right; it was like a hug from him. One that I would now be forever grateful for. I would never forget the grin Giovanni had when he filmed himself creeping up on me.

The video of fun facts played before us. My singing earned a glance from Dante who offered me a smile. Sal gasped when he saw my wrist casts, then couldn't contain his laughter as I explained that a dog was the cause of it. When it came time for the hair-dying dilemma G had faced, Arturo scoffed.

"You would look weird with pink hair. It doesn't scream badass like the purple does." He commented.

"Then what does it scream?" Sal asked him.

"Barbie? Or better yet, valley girl," he admitted.

I could feel Matteo's eyes scan the exposed part of my tattoo as the last bit of the video played out. Then he intensely inspected the close-up of Giovanni's when it zoomed in on the screen. After it ended there was a beat of silence before Sal spoke up.

"I have questions."

"Okay, what are they?"

"How tall was the dog?" he asked, trying his best to hide his grin.

"Tiny, maybe a foot tall," I admitted. "But when I fell forwards, I didn't want to take a step because I was afraid I'd step on him and crush him. So I just let myself fall, thinking I'd catch myself. Which I did...just not like I planned."

"If he got pink hair dye how mad would you have been?" Arturo smiled.

His question made me crack a small smile.

"Pissed, for at least a week. After he got this color, I haven't changed it. I really do like it." I explained.

"What does the 'C' stand for in his tattoo?" Matteo asked.

"What 'C'?" I asked, my brows furrowing.

He found the section of the video where Giovanni showed a close-up, and paused it. Sure enough, there was an 'MC' hidden in his tattoo just like my 'G.'

"Do you think those are my real initials?" I asked.

"Are you sure Clark isn't your real last name?" Dante asked.

"Positive, an 'ego' created Mia Clark for me. There's no way I chose my real name with an ego. That would be one hell of a coincidence."

"What last name did you have when you were with Giovanni?" Matteo asked.

"Davis. So why would he get MC?" I thought out loud.

"It has to be a clue. He was trying to tell you," Sal stated.

"Play the next video," I stated, moving to sit on the edge of the couch wrapped up in the blanket like a burrito.

"Mia I titled this video la mia anima. I know you are working on your Italian so let me explain what that saying really means. La

mia anima translates to my soul. I choose to name this video that because..." He paused. "*you breathe life into my soul, I love you with my entire being. You are everything I've ever asked for and I found you at just thirteen years old. I mean we are sixteen now but damn, I still can't believe it. I know I'm not going to be around to grow old with you, someone else will have to do that. I just hope we can have many more years to come before you have to watch this. But never forget in that giant heart of yours how much I love you, cattivella.*"

The video was then filled with random clips of us. Laughing without a care in the world, doing parkour, hanging out in the pool. Watching movies or staring up at the stars from their rooftop.

"Pause it," I ordered.

They all looked at me for an explanation.

"I haven't watched past this point yet," I sighed. "Maybe you should watch it without me."

"No," Matteo said firmly. "We will wait for you. If he tells you anything else you should be here. Mia, he gave this to you for a reason, like you said. He wants you to watch them to help you figure it all out. He's trying to tell you who you are."

I leaned back, hugging my knees to my chest. They let me sit in silence to gather my thoughts, resting my head on my knees. I marinated in the words Matteo had said. He was right, Giovanni was trying to tell me something and it was time to face it.

"Play it, I'm ready."

I watched the screen as the rest of the video played out before me.

We were at the park and he was filming us as we walked when he snapped his head backward to look at something. "*Who is that guy?*" I asked him. "*No one, just some asshole. Let's go home.*" He put his arm around my shoulders as we walked. The camera flashed to me reading on my bed. He sat the camera down and I suddenly remembered that night. He pulled me to my feet. That was when I noticed he was upset. "*What's wrong, G?*" I asked, alarmed. He hugged me to him, "*Hug me cattivella.*" When I did, he leaned into me, and said, "*There's not enough time in the world for us.*" He pulled back, kissing me once. "*I love you principessa.*" I kissed him again, and said, "*I love you too, but what does that word mean?*" He hugged me again, turning us so he was looking straight at the camera, "*It means pretty girl, come on, you are sleeping in my room tonight.*"

That's when it ended. I was on the verge of crying now.

"Go back to the park, see if you can get a part where the guy he saw is in camera," I ordered not tearing my eyes from the screen.

Matteo did as I asked, even though we all knew who it was Giovanni saw that day. It explained how the third picture from the envelope of us was taken. Igor himself had taken it that day. Matteo fiddled with the play/pause button until we finally got the evidence we needed. I began pacing as I ran through everything in my mind.

"He knew Petrov found me that day. *Principessa* doesn't mean pretty girl, it means princess. Why wouldn't he tell me that then?" My eyes widened. "Alexei called me *printsessa* at the cabin too." I was holding back tears with all my willpower. "He knew it all, he had a heads up, why didn't he run? Why did he knowingly stay with me? We could have run away together, instead he—"

"You three, some space." Matteo stated, knowing I was about to break.

They stood up. "Got it boss."

He didn't wait for them to leave before coming to me.

"He loved you, Mia, that's why. He wanted to make sure you got out alive. He already knew he had a limited amount of time with you. With each video he's giving you another clue. We will figure it out, but we are done for the night."

He held me against him as I cried into his chest. Scooping me up, he carried me to my room. Sitting me on the bed he brushed my hair out of my face. In that moment, I didn't want to be alone. I wanted him there with me, holding me against him.

"Don't go," I cried.

He put his hand on my cheek. "Get your pajamas on, I'll be right back, okay?"

He waited for me to give him the okay to leave. I did as he said, changing through tears that had forced their way out no matter how hard I tried to reel them in. I fell into bed and waited for him to come back. When I felt him crawl next to me, I turned around to face him.

"We will figure it out," he whispered. "There's a reason for everything that's happened."

He let me cry against him, as all my barriers completely shattered at his touch. His hand rubbed my back in smooth, gentle movements, before pulling me closer to him. Not a single part of me panicked, I felt so comforted in his arms. My sobs turned to soft breaths as my sleep took me.

CREATE YOUR OWN DESTINY

I WOKE UP THE NEXT morning with my head on Matteo's chest, my body tucked under his arm. His hand was resting on my side. I felt his fingers brushing back and forth against my skin as my shirt rode up in my sleep. My heart rate quickened at the realization he'd been there all night. I looked up to see him smiling at me. My cheeks blushed, which then made him laugh. Hearing his laugh calmed me. I buried my face back into his chest so he wouldn't see anymore.

"Thank you," I finally said, "for staying with me."

"It was mutually beneficial," he teased, "I'll do it again tonight."

I looked back up, squinting at him.

"Don't push it," I threatened as he chuckled.

He fell quiet as his hand played with my hair.

"Mia?" he said, his voice gentle, I looked up toward him. "Does it bother you that I call you *cattivella*?"

At that moment, his reaction to hearing G call me *cattivella* in the video made sense. He was worried that it hurt when I heard it again from someone other than Giovanni.

"No. I mean, maybe it would have if you'd started calling me it after you watched the videos. But you started before you knew about any of it."

"I'm not trying to replace him, no one could ever do that. You will never lose the love you have for him. Opening up to me doesn't mean you love him any less or are trying to forget him. I know you are terrified that everything will repeat itself, but it won't."

"How do you know?" I said, my voice cracking. "What if it happens all over again and I can't save you either? Or Dante? Or any of the rest of the guys?"

He pulled back to look at me better, turning on his side to bring me closer. Resting his hand on my cheek, he looked so deep into my eyes I was sure he could see clear to my heart.

"We are going to figure out who you are and take care of Petrov, together, as a team. That's what's different. We will all be on the same page, no one will be left in the dark."

That would be different, Mia. I had no idea what was going on last time. They left me out of it to protect me. But Matteo was willing to include me this time, and I him, so we all knew what was going on. Still, there was that nagging question I've lived with my entire life. Who was I? The answer had to be in the last video. I laid against him, thinking through all the new information I'd gathered the night before.

"I have a suspicion about who you are, Mia," he stated.

"Tell me?"

He shook his head. "I'd like more information first. I was hoping it'd be in the last video."

"Okay." I started to get up. "I'm ready."

"Why don't you eat breakfast first? Then we can watch it."

"Yeah, all right, fine...breakfast then video. Let the guys know."

We separated, meeting downstairs where Al was making pancakes. I had beaten the guys down there, making my plate as I thought about what the last video could have on it. I heard them coming down the stairs. After that, it wasn't long before we were in the theatre. I took a deep breath, wrapping myself up in the blanket as Matteo pressed play.

It started with Giovanni's parents on their couch.

"Mia it was an honor to protect you," his dad started. *"I hope that everything we've taught you these past couple of years will help keep you safe until you find your true self. Thank you for loving Giovanni the way you did."* He looked at his wife who now looked at the camera teary-eyed. *"You are already such an amazing young woman. Thank you for allowing us to care for you. I'm so proud of who you've become and I'm sad it was such a short time. You are going to be a great leader one day. But don't let our deaths prevent you from living your best life. I know you will feel like it's your fault, but it isn't. We chose this path to help you reach your destiny. We*

knew this time would come. So, don't carry that guilt. I wish we could tell you who you are but that's for you to figure out on your own. We love you, Mia, and I want you to know that given the chance, we wouldn't change a thing."

Now it was Giovanni, alone, on camera in his room.

"Cattivella, they are coming for you the day after tomorrow. So this will be the last video from me. I have to tell you," He paused, then smiled. *"I still cannot believe that you were such a huge part of my life and that you loved the shit out of me. I'm sure my parents told you in their clip that we've known who you were since I introduced you to them. You carry the mark so they figured it out almost instantly. Know that the moment my parents told me who you were and what would happen if I chose to invite you to stay with us, I didn't look back. I knew I was going to die for you to live. I also know that it's going to hurt you...so I want you to do some things for me. I know they might not make sense or seem crazy, but just do them for me, cattivella."*

He paused and I see him take a breath before continuing.

"First, I want you to always remember the fun times we had. The laughter and snuggles you loved so much. Just don't forget me and know I'll be watching you from above after I'm gone.

Second, and I mean this, Mia Davis," he said, his voice was playfully stern, like he was pretending to lecture me. *"Don't you dare close yourself off. I know when something upsets you that you stop letting people in. Don't do that. I want you to feel love again after all this. It might take you a while, but do it for me. Find your principe.*

Third, and I mean this too because I know it's going to happen. Do NOT go after Igor Petrov alone. Make sure you take your team with you.

Last thing, I want you to know that I don't regret a damn moment. I love you, cattivella, and I always will." He held up the picture of us that he'd given me. *"I'm giving you this tomorrow and remember this?"* He held up an ink pen with invisible ink. *"I'm writing you a message on the back. I hope you kept this picture; it might help you figure out who you are one day."* He looked at the camera and winked, *"I'll be watching over you from above Mia, never forget that."* He blew the camera a kiss before the clip ended.

I sat there momentarily gathering myself as the tears free-flowed down my cheeks. Since when did I cry so much? *Curse Matteo, making you feel comfortable enough to cry that first time, now they come all the time.* They were staring at me, waiting for me to say something.

"A great leader? I carry the mark? Find my prince? Take my team?" I repeated, looking to Matteo. "Do you understand what any of that meant?"

"Do you have that picture?" he asked, ignoring my questions.

The picture! I wonder what he wrote. I bolted from my spot, still crying in a full-on sprint up the stairs to find it. My hands were shaking as I pushed the door open. I took the picture down to the guys who were waiting for me at the bottom of the stairs now.

"Please tell me you have a blacklight," I begged.

"No, but there's one at headquarters," Dante responded.

Matteo nodded. "Go get the car." He looked at me, wiping my cheeks with his thumbs, and asked, "Are you okay?"

"I still don't understand it all. But if G wanted me to live my life and do all that stuff he said then I'm going to honor it—or at least try to." I paused, looking into his gorgeous blue eyes. "Ready to be a team and take down Igor?"

"More than you know, *cattivella*," he said, smiling.

Dante pulled into the garage, passing the door. I watched as we went underground to a secure entrance I'd never seen before. They circled me as we made our way up to the fifth floor. When I saw the S-Rank team hanging out on the couches, I hesitated. Elliot wasn't with them.

They ran to me and I stepped out from the circle of men. Luke got to me first, scooping me up into a hug. He had a goofy smile on his face, kissing my cheek. Then Scarlet. Spencer waited, giving me an extra tight hug. I noticed the guys had moved and were silently waiting on me by the door to the secure conference room.

"Are you back for good?" Luke asked hugging me again.

"Not yet, just here to work on something. I'll be back soon, though." I smiled taking a step toward the guys.

"S chetyr'mya takimi krasivymi muzhchinami ya by davno ne vernulsya," Scarlet said as she smiled back at the guys. "Kto zash-chishchayet tebya v posteli noch'yu, Mia?" (With four handsome men like that I wouldn't be back for a long time. Which one protects you in bed at night Mia?)

I laughed, and responded, "Oni vse odinoki, chto ya znayu o Scarlet, prosto sprosite odnogo." (They are all single that I know of Scarlet, just ask one out.)

"I'll have to decide which one first."

Shaking my head with a smile, I walked into the secure conference room with the guys. When the door shut, they circled me once more.

"What did Scarlet say?" Arturo asked.

"Where's Elliot?" I asked them.

"In his office. He's supposed to be dead and there's a rat. He's pretending to be dead, remember?" Matteo explained. "We know it's either Luke or Spencer since we heard the phone call. He's still working on it."

"Now tell me what Scarlet said," Arturo demanded. "Us, I mean tell *us* what Scarlet said."

I rolled my eyes. "She said you four are handsome and if she were me, she wouldn't be back for a while. Then she asked, which one of you protects me in bed at night."

"Who'd you say, Matteo?" he laughed.

Without warning, Matteo punched his arm.

"What, boss, it's not a lie?" he complained, rubbing his arm.

Matteo went to punch him a second time, but he stepped out of reach. I giggled, seeing the corners of Matteo's mouth twitch up in the slightest smile.

"All right, sorry, boss."

"I said I thought you were all single to just ask one of you out."

"Did she say who she was interested in?" Arturo smiled.

"No, that's when she said she'd have to decide which one of you to ask first."

Dante got the blacklight out as Arturo started to debate on what to do. He decided to wait as we stood around the table. I sat the picture down on the screen. Taking a deep breath, we all leaned in. *Create your own destiny, Mia Costello. Love, G.*

"Mia Costello," I whispered to myself, a smile creeping across my lips.

I finally had found it, my identity. The happiness engulfed me. I glanced up only to notice Dante, Sal, and Arturo were all staring wide-eyed at me.

"What now?"

"I thought so," Matteo said to himself. "Mia, you should sit down." He waited until we all sat down to continue. "The mark Giovanni was talking about is your birthmark. Every Costello-born baby has their initials branded onto their skin shortly after birth. It's a way to tell a direct Costello from an indirect Costello."

"A what from a what?" I asked.

"A direct Costello is a person whose last name has been Costello since birth. An indirect Costello is one that was married into the family and consequently had their last name changed to Costello. Only a direct Costello can take over as head of the family. You are a direct blood relative of Dario Costello."

"Wait, back up." My brows furrowed. "Let's start over. Who is Dario Costello?"

"Only one of the top Italian mafia bosses of all time," Dante explained.

"So, my father is a mafia...celebrity?" I asked

"No, your grandfather is Dario Costello. Celebrity isn't the right word. He's more like the most powerful boss over all the other families. Like a CEO," Dante further clarified.

"A ruthless, all-business, terrifyingly serious CEO," Salvatore added.

"What about my father? Who is he?"

Arturo shrugged. "I don't know. Your grandfather was the one that's made such an impact on our community."

"You are the next one in line to take over for your family. Mia, you are the one who will bring the Costello Mafia into power with another family," Matteo explained. "We got a call from Petrov while you were—"

"I heard it. Elliot and I were going through Petrov's phone when he made the call," I informed them.

"Then you heard what he said about every Italian mafia searching for you. If legend is true, he is right. But they don't want to hurt you, they want to merge families with you," he explained.

"How do they do that?"

"Through marriage." He stated.

I started laughing, clutching my belly as my abs began to hurt. Coming to my feet I patted him on the shoulder.

"That was funny. No more joking, though. We should probably make a plan of attack on Petrov now that I know my name."

"Mia." His voice was serious. "It wasn't a joke."

My smile faded, "I'm not getting married."

"The first-born Italian mafia sons are going to come to court you," he stated. "That's what was decided when you were born."

My eyebrows flew up. "I'm sorry, they are going to come to *what* me?"

"They are going to try to woo you," Dante explained, "to win your heart so you will marry them to merge families."

I pinched the bridge of my nose with my thumb and pointer finger, letting out a sigh.

"Let me get this straight. I was born and a group of men decided that when I grew up, it would be a great idea to throw first-born assholes at me who only want to marry me to merge families?" I restated with a huff, "What's so special about my family aside from the fact that my grandfather is some famous mafia boss."

"Your family is the most powerful. To merge families with you means even more power would be brought upon the Costello name. They are legends. Their bloodline is the most sought after in our world." Arturo noted.

"Aside from the wooing and marriage situation, why does Petrov think I'm owed to his father?"

"I don't know that. All I know is that you are going to be the one in charge of your family's mafia. You are the sole heir to it. My father will know what to do," Matteo stated. "And probably answer your questions better than I can. Let's head back, I can have him come over."

They stood up, ready to go figure this out. But my mind was reeling. The moment this gets out I'm going to have to put up with trying to let more men in. I didn't want a husband; I didn't want to be wooed. Why couldn't I just live?

"Wait," I ordered. "I feel like it's just going to get crazier from here. Can I just...have one night to keep this a secret? To be Mia Costello and nothing else that comes with it?"

Their hard, determined eyes now held a gentle sparkle in them as they glance back at me. Matteo moved, stopping a few inches in front of me.

"Is one night all you want, *cattivella?*"

"We can keep this a secret for as long as you want." They agreed.

My eyes were starting to water. *Oh no you don't, Mia. NO. MORE!* I hardened myself, holding them back.

"I'm just overwhelmed."

"Then how about three days?" Matteo offered.

Agreeing, they took me back home. I went straight up to my room, tossing myself onto my bed. I put the picture on the night-stand. *I will do everything you asked, G, I just need some time.*

Matteo came in around dinner time. He didn't knock but left the light off.

"Hey," he whispered, sitting on the edge of the bed. "Want to come eat?"

"No," I sighed. I looked up at him and he smiled, then started to get up. But I touched his hand for a moment, not wanting him to leave yet. Not when I have so many questions still. "Hey, what's with the references to me being a princess?"

"The legend nicknamed you as the Costello Princess. Why don't you come eat something, then we can come back up here and talk about all the stuff on your mind?" he asked. "Or I can bring the food up here and we can talk while we eat?"

His soft side was out, I could see it in those beautiful pools of blue, the gold ring in his left one attracting my attention to its shimmer. I could get lost in them and be at peace with it.

"Will you bring it up here?"

It didn't take him long to come back to me with two plates of food. I sat up, turning on the lights and taking my plate from him. He joined me on my bed, waiting for me to say something.

"If I'm Mia Costello," I began. "Who is running my family's mafia now?"

"Probably your father. It's handed down to the sons normally."

"If I don't want it, he can just keep running it then?"

"Unfortunately, no; you are a direct bloodline of Dario Costello. It's yours, and the only way to relinquish control is by merging families to have your husband run it. Even then you will have a huge part in how it's run."

"Matteo...I don't know how to run a mafia. What do you do? Like what's your job?"

He shook his head, "Each family plays a part in their own type of work. For us it's The Core. That's our legal company that hides our other...business ventures. But for some families, they may own a restaurant or hotel chain, something that is legitimate."

"What does my family own?"

"No one knows. That's been one of the best-kept secrets."

I chewed a bit of food while I thought about it.

"I *have* to get married?" I asked.

He nodded. "I'm almost positive that's what happens with a princess."

I glared at him, using my fork to point at him.

"Refer to me as a princess again, and I'll stab you," I threatened.

He chuckled, "Why are you against it?"

"Because of the incoming princes that are going to attempt to 'woo' me," I groaned.

"Are you against marriage?"

"No, I never thought about it. Just in case you didn't notice, I have a hard time letting people in." I paused. "And I'm only twenty-one, I'd rather not have to report to someone for permission to do things."

His brows furrowed. "Well, if you marry someone who truly cares for you, you won't need permission to do anything." He laughed to himself, before continuing, "You've met Nonna. Do you think she asks for permission to do things?"

"Nonna is a badass, though." I smiled.

"So are you, *cattivella*," he informed me. "You don't take anyone's shit and you don't back down from a challenge. Are some...suitors going to have a hard time with that, you bet your ass they will. But if they are right for you, they will admire and embrace it."

I let out a sigh. "I have too many questions. Does this mean my parents didn't really sell me for drug money? Who promised me to Petrov?"

"I don't know, I don't know the entire legend, growing up we never thought it was real, to be honest. It was just a story we were told because it dealt with our generation." He sat his empty plate down on my bedside table. "You don't have to investigate or worry about anything for a few days, *cattivella*. Just hang out. Process all this later or a little at a time, whatever you want to do."

"I'm kind of bummed about it all, honestly."

I handed him my plate to stack on top of his.

"Why are you bummed?"

"I've been searching my whole life for my name. I thought that if I could have that, then I'd know who I truly am. That it would bring me a sense of...identity. I'd be able to have roots and know where I came from. I'd stop being this nomad. But now I feel more lost than before."

"Mia, the only thing that changed is your name. Who you are isn't found in that, it's found from inside you." He smiled a little, and said, "I like to think of home as where you are happy, not a shelter or a physical place."

"You have a valid point." I nodded. "Mia Costello, sounds all right, I guess."

He laughed. "I have a feeling you are going to get through this just fine."

"Why do you say that?" I smiled a little at his optimism.

"Because..." He gave me a sly smile. "You're you."

I tried to punch his arm playfully. His hand grabbed my fist with a laugh.

"What's that supposed to mean?"

"You'll see, *cattivella*." He leaned in and left a faint kiss on my hand before he let go. Without another word, he stood, collected our plates, and left the room.

Elliot called me later that night.

"Hey Hacker," I answered.

"I heard you found your name."

"Yeah, I did. Mia Costello. That's who I am."

"How are you feeling now that you know who you are?"

"Honestly, I'm filled with even more questions. Like, how did I get into foster care and who promised me to the Russians?"

"Want me to dig for some answers?"

"If you want, but Elliot, be careful. Please. I don't want them knowing you are alive."

"I will be sneaky like Ninja." He chuckled.

"All right." I smiled. "Thank you."

"I'll swing by if I find anything. Take care until then."

"You too."

I dropped my phone next to me on the bed with a sigh. I laid down but I was wide awake in bed, thinking of everything all over again. It was like my mind wouldn't shut down. I let out a huff, looking over at the clock; 2:18 am.

Come on Mia, think of something that calms you...Matteo. Wait... what? No, why did he just pop into my mind? I said something that calms you...sleeping in Matteo's arms. Well, hell.

I got up, sneaking to his room. It was locked. Me being the rogue I am, picked it in only a few seconds.

He was sleeping, his back to the door. *Holy shit, he was shirt-*

less. The outline of the muscles in his back were bathed in the light from the hallway for the moments the door was open. *This is a bad idea, Mia, go back to your room.* I took a quiet step toward him. *This is not the way to your room, girl.* I gently climbed into the empty spot next to him. There was a half second of peace before he had quickly rolled over. One hand on my throat and the other reeling back to punch who he thought was an intruder. I reached out with my hands to catch his wrist, which stopped when he realized it was me.

I giggled, "Are you always this jumpy at night?"

"You scared the shit out of me!" he said, and then smiled to himself. "Did you pick my lock?"

"Maybe."

My eyes scanned his bare, chiseled upper body. His right pec muscle had a tattoo on it that fed into his sleeve. My heart started to race as my tongue swiped out across my lips to wet them. *What you wouldn't give to run your hands up that. He was damn sexy. Uh-oh, you just thought that.* He rolled to my side, facing me with a smile that told me he just caught me checking him out.

"To what do I owe this surprise, *cattivella?*"

His voice was low, almost a growl in desire. It flooded me with tingles as my body responded to it. A sudden need came over me. I needed to feel his arms around me.

"I can't sleep," I admitted. "Will you—"

He pulled me against him with one arm wrapped around my back. He leaned into my ear, his beard tickling my cheek.

"You don't even have to ask."

I reached an arm around him, trailing my fingers up the bare skin of his back. His skin was soft and smooth. I noticed he got goosebumps where my fingers had just been. Smiling to myself, I pressed my cheek against his chest, feeling his warm skin. Just as I thought, it was easy to fall asleep in his arms.

THE RAT

THE SPOT NEXT TO ME was empty when I woke up. Stretching where I was, I looked around. He wasn't here. Heading to my room, I got cleaned up. Al poured me a coffee once I walked into the kitchen. Thinking through all the things I knew, I tried to figure out where to start.

"Morning," a smooth voice whispered into my ear.

Instinctively, I threw back my elbow for it only to be blocked.

"Matteo, you're an ass," I groaned.

He joined me at the island, and Al poured him a coffee.

"What's the plan today?" he asked, peering at me as he took a sip of his coffee.

As I opened my mouth to speak, someone called my name from the foyer. I turned as the voice got closer. Elliot walked around the corner, followed by Dante. Elliot was wearing a giant backpack.

"I think I found something, but I need your help."

"Let's see it."

"I have to set everything up. Come with me."

I got up, following him to the dining room. He put his back-pack on a chair, unzipping it to reveal two laptops inside. He sat them on the table, along with two skinny Bluetooth keyboards. I thought he was done until he dug around the side pocket and placed two identical mice on the table.

"Got anything else in there?" I snorted.

He wiggled his eyebrows at me. "Wouldn't you like to know."

"Wait, before you get all this set up, let me show you something," Dante interrupted.

We silently followed him upstairs to the third floor. He led us into an empty bedroom, then stopped at a door on the back wall. He turned toward Elliot, opening the door. Inside was a tech room identical to what he had at home.

"Why have I never seen this room before?" he exclaimed, sitting down in the computer chair like it was a throne.

He ran his fingers across the chair arms before trickling them across the desk. It was like he was a kid who just got the best gift ever.

"After Petrov mentioned you, Matteo thought it might be best to move you in here for the time being. This is your room and your tech cave, if you'd like it," Dante explained.

I turned back to look at Matteo. He winked at me before extending his hand to me. It had my coffee mug in it. I took it, taking a sip to hide my smile. Because, while everything Dante said made sense, I wondered if Matteo did this because he knew Elliot was my friend.

"Hell yeah, I would love to stay here!" he beamed, pulling the second computer chair out and patting the seat. "Come on Mia, we have work to do."

I joined him, setting my coffee at the end of the desk. Elliot woke up the computers, bringing their screens to life before us. After waiting for him to bring up what he wanted, he moved it to my screen.

"Each person on S-Rank has a file that The Core keeps on them. I found this in his file and I'm not sure what to make of it."

"Why do you think I'd know what it is?"

"Because it's also in your file."

My brows furrowed, turning my attention to the screen. It was a picture of a scanned birth certificate. To the average eye, it seemed like any other birth certificate. Until you looked down in the corner. Elliot pointed at it.

"What's that squiggle? It's on your birth certificate, as well."

"Rotate the image to the left."

He did, leaning over to inspect it again.

"It looks like the outline of a face," Dante said over my shoulder.

"It is. Because this birth certificate was made by an 'ego'," I stated. "He's the rat."

"How do we find this specific 'ego' to figure out his real name?" Matteo asked.

"'Egos' like to keep similar names to those that you had so the information transfer is seamless. Look for anyone with a version of his name that stopped doing things around the time he started at The Core," I advised.

As Elliot got started and the computer did its thing, Dante and Matteo sat down on the couch behind us. We spun in our chairs, letting the silence fall between us.

"This doesn't make sense," I started. "I've been on S-Rank for four years. If he's always had eyes on me, why didn't he make a move sooner? The S-Rank team has gotten together outside of work, trained together, gone out on missions together, everything, and not a move was made. Why now?"

"Maybe he saw Dante take interest in you. That could have given him the impression that the Sartori mafia had figured out who you were," Elliot guessed. "We all know he doesn't want you with anyone Italian."

"He could just be there for intel," Dante mentioned.

"How do we draw him out?" Elliot asked. "He's not just going to admit it if he's the rat."

"I have an idea, but it's going to take a lot of trust."

Matteo nodded, and said, "Tell us."

After a game plan was determined, we made our way back down to find Arturo and Sal. They were in the kitchen, eating the last pieces of that chocolate cake. After explaining the plan to them we sat at the kitchen island.

"Wait!" Arturo shouted leaning in to look at us better. "If all of S-Rank is coming over that means Scarlet is coming, too, doesn't it?"

"Yes, she is coming."

He shot up from his seat and started sprinting away without another word.

"Arturo," Matteo called after him.

He came back around the corner, panting.

"Boss, come on, you have to give me the day off. I have to prepare. I've got to work out, figure out what to wear, shower, pace around thinking of things to say to her, please," he explained, desperately as he listed off more things he would have to do.

Matteo laughed. "I was going to say take the day off."

Arturo's desperate look disappeared into a smile. Then he took back off.

"Good looking out boss," he yelled from the next room.

I giggled, looking back to my refill of coffee.

"Do you want me to have Al pick up any specific alcohol for you to drink? I know we aren't getting drunk, but something to take the edge off if you need it?" Matteo offered. "All we have here is whiskey and the hard stuff."

I leaned onto my elbow to face them, a cheeky grin on my lips.

"What do you think I drink?"

They were quiet for a minute, looking to one another for any suggestion of an answer. Elliot tried to contain his giggle through his hand that cupped over his mouth.

"I feel like this is a loaded question," Dante finally admitted.

"Luke brings the drinks normally, but there are more of us. I don't know how much whiskey you have but you might want to grab a few more bottles," I smiled. "Scarlet drinks wine though, red. Don't ask me the name, I have no idea."

"You drink whiskey?" Sal asked.

"Neat." I winked.

They laughed at me before getting back to their coffees and

phones. It was an hour later when we were in the basement. Dante and I were sparing against one another. Matteo and Elliot were watching as they spoke outside the ring. Arturo was working out like his life depended on it. I could tell it was because he was nervous about Scarlet coming over, which made his workout even more special.

"Who taught you how to disarm someone?" Matteo asked after we stopped for a drink, "What you did at the church was... impressive."

"Luke. He taught me how to fight properly too. We would train five days a week. I knew most of the rogue and parkour stuff before coming to The Core. Ironically, we were working on getting out of pins before I went on that last mission."

"We could teach you." He offered.

"I would appreciate that."

We spent another hour working on getting out of pins, using Dante as the pretend attacker. Matteo walked me through the steps while Elliot hung out. It made the day go by faster as my excitement grew inside at seeing the team again. *You mean the ones who aren't the rat.* It wasn't until after a much-needed shower that I rummaged through my clothes, realizing that if I was staying here, I'd need a wardrobe. I set out to find Matteo in the library, his laptop on his lap. *He's cute when he's in work mode.* I moved to sit beside him, causing him to look up.

"Hey so weird question, since I'm not running anymore, is there a way to get more clothes?"

"You can order them."

"I don't have a card on me. I left mine at the apartment above Nonna's store taped under the nightstand for future emergencies," I admitted. "any other ideas?"

"You can use my card. Just let me know when you need it and I'll give you the information." He handed me his laptop.

"That will work, thanks." I smiled.

He got out a book, reading while I shopped online. I basically ordered an entire wardrobe. But then I added up my carts and wondered if there was a limit.

"Ready?" he smiled.

"Well...what's my spending limit here? I mean I have cash to give you to cover it but—"

"Don't worry about it," he said with a laugh.

"But my total is a lot. I bought a whole new closet of clothes and stuff." I informed him.

I had also bought shoes and sexy bra and panty pairs, but he didn't need to know that. Now that I wasn't running, I wanted to wear my normal style. *The sexy stuff was just because I liked them... sue me.*

"Okay you want a number?" He smirked. "A million dollars. And don't worry about giving me your cash."

"Why does it sound like you are serious?"

He dug his wallet out of his back pocket, fishing out a sleek black bank card. He held it out for me to take.

"Because I am being serious."

I opened my mouth to protest, but he stopped me.

"Don't argue. I want to, I know I don't have to, and I know you can pay me back. But I want to do this. So take the card, buy your clothes...and stuff, and don't worry about it."

So, he knew what the "and stuff" things were. I could tell by the mischievous glint in his eyes. I took the card, hiding my blushing cheeks behind my hair as I checked out. I began to plot a way to slip him the cash. He even insisted on choosing the fastest shipping. That brought my total to $2,827.61 with tax. At least I'd have everything now. Workout clothes, tops, bottoms, shoes, undergarments, pjs, work clothes for when I went back, a couple of bathing suits, everything I could think of. The closet in my room was large enough anyway. I could probably buy more just to fill it if I wanted. Handing over his card, I closed out everything on the laptop.

"MIA!" Arturo screamed frantically. "MIA! I need help!"

I shot out of my seat, running to the bottom of the stairs. Panicking, my heart raced as Arturo ran down to me. Matteo had also run behind me. Dante and Sal came running in from out back. Arturo put his hands on my shoulders. Matteo apparently didn't like this as he shot a glare at him.

He dropped his hands. "Sorry boss." Then he turned to me. "Mia, you have to help me."

"What's wrong?"

"I need you to help me figure out what to wear. What does Scarlet like? Tell me everything."

I punched his arm. "I thought something was seriously wrong. You just gave me a heart attack. Wear clothes, Arturo."

"Please?" He rubbed his arm where I'd punched him, "*Please.*" He drew out the 'e' as he begged.

He stuck out his lower lip and gave me big puppy dog eyes. I stood there for a minute before letting out a small laugh.

"Fine, but just this once. After that, you're on your own."

I walked next to him up to the third floor. He showed me his room and closet. His closet was huge and I'd never known a man to have so many clothes. Then again, I'd never been in a man's closet before. I just assumed they had fewer clothes than women. Reaching up, I pulled down a pair of worn blue jeans I knew Scarlet liked since she's commented on the way they looked on guys before. The top was different. *Hmmm, what would Scarlet like better, something stylish or something that showed off his muscular body? Oooo, or both!* I picked out a t-shirt and flannel. After he changed, he walked out to show me my handiwork.

"Feel better now?" I smiled. "You look nice."

"Yeah, now I just have to figure out what to say."

I laughed. "Just be yourself. She likes people who are genuine."

It was about time when I walked out of my room. Excited and not paying attention, I turned the corner of the stairs and smacked into Matteo who was coming up. He caught me by my waist, pressing me firmly against him to prevent me from falling backward.

"You okay?" he asked dropping his hands from my waist.

"Yeah, sorry."

"I was coming up to get you, they are here."

I smiled, and said, "Thank you for trusting me with this. I know it's your family's company, but I really appreciate it."

His smile was warm and his eyes were soft. "I'd do anything for you, *cattivella*. That includes trusting you to handle this with me."

My cheeks began to turn red, I could feel it. *We're in trouble. The blushing has become a problem.* I pointed at them.

"See what you did," I teased. "Better stop that, or else."

He took a step closer to me, his smile now full of mischief. "Or else what?"

"That's for me to know...and you to find out."

I walked around him with a devilish smile. Downstairs I greeted each of them with a hug. Al got the food started and Matteo introduced everyone formally. S-Rank only knew the extraction team by their titles. Elliot stayed hidden until the time was right, which was after dinner. I noticed as we ate that Scarlet and Arturo were getting along great. He seemed more relaxed around her now that she was here.

"These are for you." Luke smiled holding out two tubes of unmade cinnamon rolls.

"What are those for?" Salvatore asked.

"Every time Mia drinks, she asks for cinnamon rolls. We haven't gotten drunk together often, but of the rare few times we did, that's what she asked for," he explained.

"Thanks, Luke." I took them, putting them in the fridge.

S-Rank was under the impression that we were hanging out to play cards and drink. We walked into a room that was two doors down from the theatre. It had a stocked bar, a pool table, two giant L-shaped couches that formed a square when pushed together, and a giant square table that sat in the center of them. The far wall was the backside of the house and had a sliding door that led outside.

"This has been here the entire time?" I exclaimed.

Dante laughed. "Your first night here you weren't up for much of a tour, if I remember correctly."

"Touché," I stated, flipping him off.

Matteo and Sal started getting glasses out for all of us. We made our drinks. Arturo took Luke, Spencer, and Scarlet out back on the deck to see the complete view of the backyard. I heard them greet Elliot who was, as planned, standing on the deck above. He joined us downstairs after that.

We made it through a few rounds of cards and drinks. When Luke refilled my glass, I looked at how full it was.

"That's too much," I giggled. "You drink some first."

He smiled, taking a few sips before handing it back to me.

"Thanks. Anyone want some cinnamon rolls?" I smiled.

"Are you that far gone already?" Spencer laughed. "You've only had like two drinks."

"Hey!" I warned with a grin. "I haven't drank, or drunk, or dranken like this in a while, so this is long overdue. I'm going to prep them. I'll be right back."

Heading into the kitchen I pre-heated the oven. I'd gotten out the pan when I heard his voice behind me.

"Need some help?"

"Sure, thanks Spence. Grab the rolls out of the fridge for me."

He did as I asked.

"Spencer, why is it that you don't like me going in armed on the missions we have?" I asked him as we laid the rolls out on the pan.

He sighed, and said, "I thought you'd have enough on your

plate. Your tasks are more dangerous than ours as you are always going in after the source of the assignment. I guess I thought if you were armed, you'd be tempted to help Luke defend you instead of keeping focused on your part of the mission."

"I wouldn't have."

"Yeah, I know that now. I didn't realize how skilled you were. For future missions, I won't hesitate to let you go in armed." He patted my shoulder. "You really worried all of us that night, Mia. I'm glad you got out safely."

"Me too."

I slid the rolls into the oven. We made our way back to the others, who were playing cards. The only break we took was to enjoy the cinnamon rolls when they were warm. Scarlet and Arturo were sitting cozily on the couch next to one another. We called it a night around two in the morning.

"I think you all should stay here tonight," Matteo annouced. "It's late. You've been drinking."

They started to protest, but I insisted.

"I really think you should stay." I looked at each of them, then to Luke, who was sitting next to me. "Please?"

"You worried about us, Rogue?" Spencer teased.

"Don't flatter yourselves." I scoffed with an eye roll.

Luke laughed, bringing his arm around my shoulders.

"Show me to my room."

"Dante will have to do that. I'm going to take Scarlet to her room. Come on, Scar. Sweet dreams everyone."

She threw one last smile at Arturo before leaving with me. I led her up to my room where she collapsed onto the bed. Now all I had to do was wait. I sat down next to her.

"So, which one is it, Matteo or Dante?" she finally asked, giggling.

I played dumb. "Which one is what?"

She squinted at me, "Mia Clark, you admit it right now. You finally have feelings for a guy. I've known you for four years and you always push guys away. Hell, you push everyone away. So tell me which one."

"Fine, but don't make a big deal out of it. It's Matteo." I smiled at my admission, and then quickly shifted the focus to her, instead. "How do you feel about Arturo?"

Her eyes lit up in the moonlight. "He's adorable, right? And so funny. I think I might ask him out. Do you think he'll say yes if I do?"

I laughed as I explained the events that happened with him leading up to her arrival. It only made her swoon even more.

"It's decided, I'm going to ask him out tomorrow before I go, then." She wiggled into her spot before looking at me again. "I've missed you, Mia. I know it's only been like two weeks but putting up with those two without you isn't the same. Even Elliot hasn't been showing up for work."

There was a knock on the door. I yelled a quick "come in" before Arturo peeped his head inside as if to make sure we were decent. We stood, meeting him halfway.

"Matteo and Dante want you," he told me. "I'd also like to say good night to Scarlet."

I hugged her, a happy grin on my lips. "Good night, Scar."

The guys were waiting on me in the office on the second floor. Matteo rubbed the side of his jaw nervously, his short beard remaining unbothered by the motion.

"Ready?" he asked.

"Yeah, I'm going to head up now. Arturo and Salvatore are headed in for the night as well, right?"

Dante nodded. "We're the only ones left. Spencer is in the top right room; Luke is in the top left next to Elliot's."

"Let's hope this works then. I'll be in touch."

I turned, heading up to Elliot's room for our investigation. Once I was safely inside Elliot's tech cave we waited. I wanted to wait an hour so it would give time for him to think everyone was sleeping to make his move. We decided to pass the time by going through more of his life. Elliot was reading his past text messages as I was reading past emails.

"Oh shit," Elliot whispered. "Read this, it's from tonight when we were playing cards."

He pulled my chair closer to his. I leaned in reading the texts to myself. The conversation was in some sort of code. It was between him and his boss—who was Russian.

the bug is alive.

BOSS:
we need the reptile

the reptile is with courage

BOSS:
then it must be exterminated

what do I do with the crown?

BOSS:

steal it

"What the heck? Okay, the bug must be you since you are the only one that is supposed to be dead." I deduced.

"Right, but what does the rest mean?" he asked.

I stared at the words. Why would they call him the bug? *Maybe like a computer bug, his codename is Hacker.* If that was true then the reptile was—oh shit! *Chameleon.* He's going to go after Scarlet. I shot to my feet. The plan was no longer going to work.

"Call Matteo!" I ordered. "Scarlet is the target, not me."

There was no time to think about my next moves. Her safety was my first concern. I dashed down the stairs, barging into my room. I ran to the bed, seeing that it was empty. The sheets were pulled back like she'd been laying there and got up. I turned to check the bathroom. It was empty, the lights off. *Did he already get to her?* My heart was pounding in my chest, my breath quickening. Matteo ran in.

"She's gone. He took her."

"The house is locked up, no one's been in or out. I would have gotten an alert on my phone. He's still here and so is she."

I ran out, seeing Dante jog over to us. Matteo began to whisper, explaining everything. I closed my eyes, calming myself to keep a clear head.

"Split up, find her," I ordered.

THE CHAMELEON

DANTE HAD GONE UP TO the third floor, Matteo took this one, and I headed downstairs to cover the main floor. The kitchen, theatre, and living room were clear. I was making my way across the foyer to the other side of the house when Luke came running down the stairs.

"Mia, thank god, we have to leave. They are running around the house with guns. I don't know what's going on, but I don't think you're safe."

As he approached me, I swung back, punching him square in the jaw. He stumbled back in shock.

"Lukas Koslov," I growled—his real name. "Where is she?"

His eyes turned dark, and I watched as he transformed into someone I didn't even recognize. An evil smirk took over his lips and he slowly clapped his hands together three times as if congratulating me on finally figuring it out. Then he backed away slowly, squaring off like he was going to fight me. I got into my stance.

"You know, you shouldn't be around the Italians any longer. It makes the boss very perturbed to know you've been spreading your legs for these degenerates once again," he taunted.

I growled, launching myself at him. We exchanged a few swings before his knuckles met with my chest. It knocked the wind out of me. I fell onto my hands and knees, gasping for air. He didn't hesitate to kick me in the side of my ribs. I heard a snap. A sharp pain jolted through me. *That feels like a broken rib.* He took out a knife from the waistline of his jeans, kneeling to me, muttering, "Time to go."

"Mia!" Matteo yelled from the top of the stairs.

He ran down, Dante close behind. Luke didn't hesitate to swing at Matteo as he charged him. Dante ran to me, helping me to stand. *Shut your pain off until this is over.* I took a few deep breaths, feeling the pain drift out of my body.

Luke was wielding that knife like I knew he could. Matteo blocked each attempt flawlessly, knocking the knife out of his hand and punching him so hard in the face that he stumbled backward. Taking two fistfuls of Luke's shirt, he pinned him against the wall. Blood was pouring from a gash on Luke's eyebrow. He was dazed and the light that was flooding into the room from the front porch shined across their faces. Matteo's eyes were dark. It was like he had two sides of him, his soft, caring side, and this dark side that I swear could be the devil himself.

"Welcome to hell," he growled at Luke as Salvatore came down the stairs. "Take him downstairs," he ordered, tossing Luke to Sal.

Arturo was behind him. He was protecting a very terrified Scarlet. She had a hold of the back of his shirt. Luke tried to jump at her when Salvatore led him by. Arturo shoved his gun under Luke's chin.

"If you ever touch her, you will die," he threatened through gritted teeth.

Salvatore yanked him away, Luke's arm twisted behind his back for leverage, as he protested. Elliot came down the stairs as we formed a circle in the foyer.

"What the hell is going on?" Scarlet asked.

"Where were you, Scar?" I asked.

"She was with me," Arturo answered.

She wrapped her arm around his, leaning against the side of his body as he tucked her sweetly under his arm. It was then she held onto his waist.

"Where's Spencer?" I asked.

"He sleeps with earplugs. Probably not his best choice in life, but he's still sleeping. I checked before I came down." Elliot noted.

"Let's go sit in the office, we need to fill everyone in so we are on the same page," Matteo ordered, leading the way.

"Elliot and I were going through his texts and emails when we noticed a conversation from tonight in his texts. It was in code," I explained as we all sat down.

"I can bring it up on the screen," he said, taking his phone from his pocket. "Mia and I can translate it for you."

"First Luke says the bug is alive, meaning Elliot is alive. Then his boss says 'we need the reptile' meaning Scarlet as her code-name in S-Rank is Chameleon. Luke responded with 'the reptile is with courage.' I'm not sure what that means."

"It means Arturo," Elliot explained. "That's the meaning of his name; courage. He told his boss that you two were getting closer."

"To which, his boss responds for Luke to kill her by saying she needs to be exterminated."

"When Luke asks about the crown, meaning Mia because she's a princess, his boss says for him to steal her."

"Wait." Scarlet's eyes widened. "You're a *princess*?"

I glared at Elliot. "Thanks for that."

"Wait, and they want to kill me?" she continued, looking to Arturo. "Who wants to kill me? Why would Luke be talking to whoever this guy is?"

"His real name is Lukas Kozlov. He was sent to apply to The Core the day after Mia under his alias. He is working for Petrov, so we can assume he was sent to keep tabs on Mia for him."

"Who is Petrov?" Scarlet asked.

"Wait," Matteo ordered. "Don't say anything more. Arturo, come with me."

They disappeared through the door. I knew they were most likely discussing how much Scarlet should be involved. With Arturo taking to her, Matteo was trying to make sure he was included in the decision. She reached out, taking a hold of my hand, refusing to let it go until they reappeared from the hallway. Arturo scratched the back of his head nervously as they stood in front of us. She stood to face him. He gave Matteo one quick glance before his shoulders fell.

"Scarlet," he started, "you have a couple of options going from this point forward. I want you to pick the one you are most comfortable with."

"All right," she said, her voice weary.

"The first option is that you rest here and then leave. You won't be put in any more danger but you won't see any of us again. You will be marked as a retired agent from The Core and given your full retirement package to get away and start over." He paused, letting her have a moment to comprehend what the option entailed.

"Or?" she finally asked.

"Or, you stay here to live. We train you and you keep your job at The Core. But you will have a giant target on your back. It will be dangerous for you. If you choose to stay then there's no going back."

She looked at me, speaking in Russian.

"Is this a cult?" she asked. "And do I really have a choice?"

"No." I smiled. "And yes."

She was quiet for a minute before looking at Arturo.

"How much danger am I in if I stay? Livable danger or the kind of danger where I'm going to die in a month?"

"I can't answer that," Arturo admitted. "I'd like to say livable so you stay, but that's me being a selfish bastard. With what we do, the next day is never a guarantee." He took a step toward her, his eyes locked on hers. "The only thing I can promise is that I will protect you with my life if you choose to stay with us."

"You'd protect me?"

"Every day." He nodded.

A slow flirtatious smile crept across her lips. She motioned for him to come closer with her index finger.

"And what about at night?" she asked, one of her eyebrows raised.

He slid his hands onto her hips, pulling her against him.

"Oh, I'm sure we could work something out." He smirked, saying, "How's my bed sound?"

She wrapped her arms around his neck.

"Comfortable," she giggled. "I want to stay, Arturo."

My heart was warm watching the two of them. They wrapped one another up in a hug. After that, he sat down, tugging her next to him. He put his arm around her, cuddling her against him. I took a deep breath, feeling the hesitation in my lungs. *Time to turn the pain back on, we need to know the amount of damage done to our ribs.* I took another deep breath, letting my pain come back to me. It hit me so hard that I let out a yelp in pain, clutching my side. All eyes flew to me.

"Are you all right?" Matteo's eyes softened as he looked at me.

"I think he broke a rib or two," I admitted.

I lifted my shirt just enough to see that my side was already swollen and red.

"I'll go get some ice," Dante offered, standing up.

"I'll call the doc." Arturo pulled his phone from his pocket.

When he returned, I pressed the ice against my side.

"Back to my questions." Scarlet gave a pointed look to Matteo. "Who is he?"

Elliot shot an image of Igor onto the TV in there for us to see. She would need to know who he was before understanding Luke's involvement. Besides, Igor wanted her dead. She needed to know who she was up against. Elliot opened his mouth to speak but Scarlet gasped.

"Hey, I know that guy!" she exclaimed.

We were all silent as we waited for her to explain how she knew him.

"I was at the library," she thought back, "three or four weeks ago. It was the day I came into work late. He offered me a job. He wanted me to work for him. I told him I had one already and to buzz off. But then he said, 'a woman of my talents would be better used for his company.'" She sighed. "He followed me out, gave me a business card, and left."

"I bet they knew about her because of Luke," I mentioned.

That's when Elliot nodded. He started to explain what he had found.

"The Russians want Scarlet as their personal chameleon. When word got around she turned them down, they had Luke start keeping an eye on her too. When he said she was coming to our side, they had no other choice but to get rid of her so we can't have her."

"That son of a bitch!" she exclaimed. "He was going to kill me?"

"I want a few minutes boss," Arturo noted.

Matteo gave him a silent nod.

"It also explains why he never tried to take Mia. He was watching both of them." Elliot noted.

"Why would he be watching Mia?" Scar's brows furrowed, creating a wrinkle between them. "And back to the princess part. What the hell?"

Arturo rubbed her thigh. "It's a lot to process Scar. Maybe tomorrow or when Mia feels comfortable, she can tell you her story."

"Tomorrow, Scarlet." I nodded. "Just take in what you now know tonight."

"The doctor is here," Dante stated, looking at his phone.

"Come on, Mia, let's get you looked at." Matteo stood up.

We made our way back down to the room that replicated a hospital area.

"Mr. Sartori, what can I do for you this early in the morning?" the doc teased.

"She needs an x-ray of her ribs, one or a couple might be broken." He stated.

The doctor nodded, motioning for me to follow him into the next room over. There was a table in there and against the wall was a machine on wheels. He had me stand on a blue 'x' on the floor before wheeling the machine over. Lining it up with my ribs he grabbed a little remote.

"What can I call you?" he asked.

"Mia." I smiled a little.

"All right, Mia, when I say go, I want you to take a big breath in and hold it as long as you can."

I waited for him to give me the signal. It hurt like hell and I held it for as long as I could like he asked. My side pinching more as I exhaled.

"FUCK!" I said, holding my side. "I'm going to punch him."

I let out a sigh, if I turned my pain back off then I wouldn't know how it was healing. I can handle it. Waiting with an icepack against it I sat on the edge of the table. Matteo was now standing in front of me.

"Can I ask you something?" he said.

"What?"

"Why didn't you feel that pain until way after it happened?"

I chewed on my lower lip. I knew now I could trust him.

"I need your word you won't tell a soul. Not yet."

He stepped closer, cupping my cheek with one hand.

"Then you have it."

"I can turn my pain on and off. I don't know how I learned how to do it. It kind of came while I was being tortured by the Russians when they had me in that freezer. I was trying to transfer my emotions to become focused but all I could feel was the pain. Then it slowly disappeared and I felt nothing. It was one of the main reasons I escaped them. I could no longer feel how much pain I was in," I admitted, my voice small.

"Why didn't you do that when you got grazed by the bullet?"

"It's dangerous. If I don't feel the pain I don't know how bad the wound is or how it's healing. The only time I really do it is mid-fight, especially if feel like I might be in danger of losing. Sometimes I do it as a precautionary measure if a fight is a possibility, but even that's rare. The downfall is when I turn it back on, it hits me all at once. Almost like the pain is paused, then it comes back with all the hurt I was supposed to feel while it was off. I've learned to control it better but it took me harming myself which I knew wasn't healthy, so I stopped. That's when I asked Luke to train me. I figured I could practice it more in a real fight."

He wrapped me in his arms, and said, "I wish I could take your pain, Mia."

My head rested against his chest, melting into him. *This is nice.* Shit. It was. The doc called us over to the other room with my x-ray results.

"Mia you have just a bruised rib, your lowest one. It's not broken but will still take some time to heal. Ice it, rest, and make sure you take a couple of deep breaths every hour to prevent pneumonia. Tylenol will help the pain. If you want something stronger just give me a call."

We rejoined the rest of them in the downstairs office, except for Sal who I assumed was still watching Luke.

"Ready?" Matteo asked Arturo.

"Fuck yeah, I am."

Dante stood as well. Scarlet and I started to walk behind him. A chuckle escaped him as he turned to stop us. He put his hands up before we could make it through the doorway.

"Where are you two going?" he asked.

"If he speaks in Russian, what are you going to do?" I stated. "I want to be down there."

Dante looked back at Matteo.

"I'm going because I was the target and I want to slap him before you two..." Scarlet paused, waving a hand in the air, "have at him."

The three guys traded glances before Matteo began to speak.

"Scarlet, you have one minute, no longer, then you leave. Mia, you can be there while I question him, then you leave too. Arturo can talk to him after that." He looked at me. "That's my only deal and it's non-negotiable."

Agreeing, we left Elliot who was already buried back into the laptop that was at the desk, oblivious to what was going on around him. We followed behind them downstairs into a room I'd not been in yet. Stepping into the door to see it was an observation room. Sal was leaning against the wall, watching Luke through the large one-way glass window.

"What did I miss?" he said, seeing Scarlet there.

While Arturo accompanied Scarlet to where Luke was, Matteo filled him in. Luke was fastened to a chair by his ankles and wrists so he couldn't have control of his limbs. Scarlet slapped him so hard it echoed through the room. Arturo followed her back out with a laugh.

He smiled and said, "Damn *gattina*, you slapped the shit out of him."

Gattina, kitten. How adorably accurate that was. Scarlet was beautiful yet could have claws of wrath when need be. I could tell by Arturo's smile that he was impressed with her. She turned, pushing him against the door lightly by his chest. She leaned in closer to him.

"I'd do it again! He was going to kill me!"

Arturo took her hand, leading her back up the stairs. Matteo glanced at me.

"Ready, *cattivella?*"

I nodded. "More than ready."

When I stepped into the next room behind him, I saw a tray

of tools to my left. It had knives, a hammer, a taser, a gun, and everything that could be used to torture someone. A baseball bat leaned against it. Luke laughed when he saw me.

"Are you going to slap me too?"

"Don't tempt me," I threatened.

"What does Igor want with Mia?" Matteo asked.

"His father owns her, she was promised to Igor."

"By whom," Matteo asked.

"Why are you here?" he snapped. "This conversation should be between Mia and me."

I could tell Matteo was holding back because I was in there. It seemed like he wouldn't allow anyone he was interrogating to speak to him in such a tone. His jaw tensed as Luke looked at me, speaking in Russian now.

"Petrov will get you one way or another. Just turn yourself over to him."

"Who promised me to him?" I asked in Russian.

"He doesn't give details, he gives orders."

"Who gave you the order? Igor or Nicholai?"

"Igor is the head of the family now."

"Are you sure? When I spoke with Alexei it seemed as though he might be the one to take control?"

"Alexei," Luke hissed. "Is no one compared to Igor. Stay away from him."

I snickered. "I'm not going near any of them."

"You are owed to Nicholai Petrov."

"He doesn't know anything," I told Matteo.

On my way toward the door, Luke yelled at me in Russian.

"Come on Mia, you are better off with Igor. The Italians are dangerous, they could hurt you. I know you, we're friends."

My anger bubbled with his words. He was no friend of mine. He didn't know me at all.

"Besides, you weren't the target; Scarlet was. Help me out here. I know you might be scared but Igor can help. Just like he helped you before with that other Italian kid."

Everything flashed red. I grabbed the knife from the tray squeezing the handle so tight my knuckles were white. My rage caused my hand to shake as I stalked over to him. Matteo didn't stop me as I shoved the blade as hard as I could into Luke's shoulder.

"That's for targeting Scarlet!" I twisted the knife inside his shoulder as he yelled out in pain. "That's for saying we are friends." I pulled the knife out of his shoulder and thrashed it into his stomach, "and that...was just because."

I pulled the knife back as his head fell forward in pain. Placing the tip of the knife under his chin, I tilted his head up so he could face me, leaning in closer to meet his eyes.

"You have no idea who I am or what I am capable of," I said in Russian.

Dropping the bloody knife back on the tray, I used the towel hanging off it to wipe my hands, having gotten blood on them. My adrenaline was going ninety miles an hour as I walked to the door, turning back to Matteo.

"Sorry I broke our deal," I stated, before stepping out.

Seeing the guys standing there was when it occurred to me that they had just observed the entire thing. They'd not seen what I'd done to Igor, this was the first time they'd seen me that angry. Although they didn't seem fazed by it. I had forgotten they were even there.

"You okay, Mia?" Dante asked.

"Yeah," I said, confused. "I'm going to shower."

I glanced down at my bloodstained hands. I walked straight upstairs to my room. I scrubbed my body clean of all the blood residue I had on me.

When I was done with my shower, I went to find Scarlet. She was in the main floor office with Elliot. We sat in a comfortable silence, my arm wrapped around her gently. My head rested on her shoulder. After a while she laid back, pulling me with her. I leaned my back against the back of the couch as I stretched out. Her arm around me as I hugged her waist.

"I won't let anyone hurt you, Scar," I said in Russian.

"I love you too, Mia." She smiled, knowing that was my way of telling her I loved her.

I fell asleep holding her against me to make sure no one else could get to her. Until I felt someone gently lifting my arm from around her. I immediately shoved them away, looking to see who it was.

"It's just me," Arturo whispered, "she's safe, Mia."

"Sorry," I mumbled, my voice groggy from sleep.

I let him pick her up. She curled into his embrace, burying her face in his neck as he moved to bring her up to his room. Matteo squatted down in front of me as I laid back down across the couch. His hair was wet from a shower. A loose couple of strands fell onto his forehead. His eyes were filled with worry.

"Are you okay, *cattivella?*"

"My side is sore," I admitted.

"I meant emotionally."

"Oh, yeah." I bit my lip. "I mean I'm upset about Scar being the target but I'm also just relieved she's alive."

"And about Luke?"

"What about him? I figured you would kill him after everything." I paused. "Did I...cross a line with your interrogation?"

"Do you feel like you crossed a line?"

"No, he was going to kill, Scar."

"I know." He put his hand on my cheek. "As long as you are all right."

"I'm fine...but the way you're looking at me right now, though... is there something wrong with me?"

"Why do you ask?"

"Because I kind of tortured him and I don't feel any remorse about it," I admitted. "That's not normal. Now that I think about it, I didn't feel any regret when I did the same to Igor either."

"Mia, there's not a single person in this world who wouldn't do what you did to protect their family. It's just your family looks different than a traditional one. You did what you did to protect

Scarlet. There's nothing wrong with that." He paused. "Can I ask what he said to you?"

I repeated the conversation to him verbatim. When I finished, he held his hand out to help me up. I winced in pain as I stood. *Are you sure you don't want to turn your pain off?* But it wasn't that bad. He had me follow him to get more Tylenol before walking up with me. As we approached my door, he laced his fingers through mine. My heart skipped a beat at the gesture. I leaned closer to him. Bringing me to his room he locked the door behind us. He reached for me, his hand gently sliding to my hip, giving my body a rush of warmth. I smiled at the reaction, scooting closer to him. The sun was coming up as we fell asleep.

I'M A ROGUE

THIS TIME HE WAS THERE when I woke up. His hand running through my hair felt so soothing to wake up to. I smiled wide, reaching out across his waist to pull him closer. That's when my side reminded me about my injury. I sat upright, having to take a deep breath, slowly letting it out to make the sharp stab of pain go away.

"Want some more Tylenol?" he asked, sitting up in alarm, his hand resting gently on my back.

"Yeah, please."

Matteo appeared beside me with a glass of water and pain meds only minutes later. "Here."

"Thanks." I took them before sitting the glass down on the bedside table.

I laid back down, wanting to absorb all the time I could in bed before having to get up and face yet another shit situation life had handed me. Matteo crawled back beside me, tucking my hair behind my ear before letting his hand rest on my hip. I closed my eyes, reaching out to feel his skin. It was then I realized it was-in fact-bare skin. My eyes flicked open to make sure my brain was right.

"Are you shirtless?"

"I slept shirtless," he admitted.

"Hmm, your torso must not have been very memorable if I am only just now realizing it."

His laugh came out unfiltered. The genuineness in it brought my own smile to my lips.

"My ego is bruised," he claimed with a lopsided smile. "That one hurt."

"Wish I could say I'm sorry but I'm not. Your ego seems like it could be taken down a notch or two," I teased, closing my eyes again.

"You just woke up and chose violence today, didn't you?" His voice was playful.

"Maybe."

He rubbed my cheek with his thumb for a moment, letting the light mood settle around us. A quiet sigh escaped him before he pressed his forehead against mine.

"I'm glad you are all right, *cattivella.*"

"It'll take more than a bruised rib to take me down, Matteo."

"I know—I just—I saw you on the ground and wanted to kill him right there in the foyer. The only reason I didn't was because I didn't think he had hurt you like he did. If I'd known, he wouldn't have made it downstairs." He took a deep breath before continuing, "Listen, I know that Igor is yours to take down, but I want five minutes with him."

My eyes snapped to his, pulling my head back to get a good look at him. "Why?"

"Because he hurt you."

"You didn't even know I existed back then."

"I know, but I know you now and just the thought of what he did to you makes me want to unleash every ounce of rage I have on him." He took another deep breath as if he was thinking of those images I knew he saw in the video of my "*cleanse.*"

I put my hand on his cheek, and said, "Five minutes only if you promise not to kill him before I get my revenge."

"Deal."

His eyes were dark storms. This time it wasn't the kind that I saw when he was angry. It was the same darkness that I saw at The Core while he was trying to help me clean my lip. My heart started to beat faster and his gaze dropped to my lips. *He's going to do it.* Anticipation pumped through me. He swallowed, peering back into my eyes. It was like he was searching for something, and when he found it, he didn't waste another second.

He dipped his head, pressing his lips to mine. Every thought I had in my head became scrambled as I leaned into him. Those soft full lips taking control over me, causing me to melt right into the mattress. The hand that was in my hair moved torturously slow down my back to rest on my hip. It left behind a trail of goosebumps. When I felt him squeeze my hip, a bomb of heat exploded inside me. My arm snaked around to his back, pulling him even closer so that he was pressed against me. *You should stop this before it goes too far.* I pulled back before a moan could escape me, resting my forehead against his. He moved, tucking me under his arm. A whisper of a smile decorated my lips as I lightly traced the tattoo on his chest with my finger.

"Matteo?" I asked, my voice quiet.

"Hmm?"

"How many are there?"

"How many what?"

"Firstborn assholes coming to woo me."

"Oh, five." He started trickling his fingertips up and down my bare arm. "Why?"

I let out a heavy sigh. "Just wondering. Five sounds like a lot."

"It's better than all the smaller mafia families sending their sons. Then it would be more like fifteen of them."

"When you say that, five doesn't sound so terrible," I admitted. "Do you want to get married?"

He paused. "When I was younger, I couldn't wait to get married. My parents showed me how much fun a marriage could be. Don't get me wrong they had their fights, but at the end of the day they were still insanely in love with one another." He took a deep breath. "But life throws you for loops and after a couple of shitty years, it's not so much a priority anymore."

"Are you sure we can't skip the finding a husband part?"

"I'm sure, well almost sure. That would be a question for my father." He explained, "It could be fun, you know."

He's trying to make you feel better.

"Would you feel that way if it were you in my position?" I raised one eyebrow.

"I'd probably be as upset about it as you, but I'd make the best of it...like I know you will."

I narrowed my eyes at him, and asked, "What's that supposed to mean?"

A lopsided grin appeared on his lips. "Oh nothing, I just know a certain son is going to irritate the shit out of you. It's going to be highly entertaining to see the ways you're going to make sure he knows he's not the hot shit he thinks he is."

"He sounds like prince-charming," I scoffed.

"Oh? Maybe he's fit for the Costello princess then," he teased.

"Doubt it." I poked his side. "Is your father going to spread the news right away?"

"It will take a couple of days for the five families to meet after we talk to him. We would also have to let whoever oversees your family's mafia know that you were found."

"Like I was lost," I said, my voice laced with sarcasm. "Oh shit, that means I'd have to meet my parents."

My hands became clammy at the thought. I sat up, running my hands through my hair. How would I react to seeing them? Would I be angry or happy? Could they tell me the real reason they gave me up? An entirely new list of questions exploded within my mind. He sat up, his free hand coming to rest on my back. *Are they going to make more choices for you? Do they already have your life planned out to benefit them and your family name? The control we've clung to is being ripped from our hands, Mia.*

"Hey," he said, his voice was soft, almost a whisper. "What's wrong?"

"I finally get my name and it comes with no freedom. I am losing my control, my choices. I'm about to lose who I really am." I sighed, getting out of bed to head to my room, "I'm going to shower so I can accept my fate."

"Accept your fate?" he repeated, brows pulled together. "Mia, wait." He threw the covers back, rushing to come between me and the door. He put one hand on my cheek. "You know who you are, *cattivella*. That's deep within you and doesn't change because of your name. Don't push her down to be the person you think Mia Costello is." He pulled me against him, taking care to not aggravate my side. "Come here."

I wrapped my arms around his torso, tucking my face into his neck. His hands moved up and down my back to soothe me. After a minute of silence between us, he pulled back, his eyes peering so deep into mine it was like he was searching my soul.

"You are a highly skilled, stubborn as hell, badass. You don't need to change because your name has. Be the Mia you know you are."

"Yeah." I attempted to smile. "I'll try."

I pulled away, trudging down the hall to get cleaned up. The hot water brought me some comfort, yet the more I thought about what Matteo said the more determined I became. He was right. I know who I am, I'm a Rogue. I wasn't about to allow anyone to take away my control. *That's right girl, this is our life, we control it! We should figure out how to run our family's business without a husband. One way or another we'll do it.* I nodded to myself. The business was mine for the taking, no one else's.

I threw on clothes and marched downstairs. Everyone was out back on the porch. I flung the door open, causing them to all turn my way. Matteo stood up, his brow wrinkling with worry.

I took a deep breath and announced, "I'm going to take over as head of my family without a husband. I will play the politics of the process but at the end of it all, I will run my family's business alone. I don't give a shit what anyone says or the hell I will have to endure to get there, but it's mine and I'm taking it. I don't need a man by my side to do so. I am a strong, independent Rogue that is capable of handling herself."

I met each of their eyes, waiting for their reaction to my declaration. However, it wasn't until I met Matteo's blues that I saw the pride gleaming in them. He moved straight to me, engulfing me in a hug.

"Hallelujah!" Dante cheered. "The real Mia is back!"

"I'll be there every step of the way," Matteo said into my hair, kissing the top of my head before pulling away.

"When do we start this process?" Sal asked.

"I'm ready now. Let's get started."